# THE WHALE CALLER

# THE
# WHALE CALLER

*Zakes Mda*

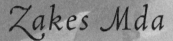

FARRAR, STRAUS AND GIROUX

NEW YORK

Farrar, Straus and Giroux
19 Union Square West, New York 10003

Printed in the United States of America
Originally published in 2005 by Penguin Books, Great Britain
Published in the United States by Farrar, Straus and Giroux
First American edition, 2005

Library of Congress Cataloging-in-Publication Data
Mda, Zakes.
    The whale caller / Zakes Mda.— 1st American ed.
        p.   cm.
    ISBN-13: 978-0-374-28785-6 (alk. paper)
    ISBN-10: 0-374-28785-6 (alk. paper)
    1. South Africa—Fiction.   I. Title.

PR9369.3.M4W47 2005
823'.914—dc22

                                              2005014196

Designed by Cassandra J. Pappas

www.fsgbooks.com

1   3   5   7   9   10   8   6   4   2

*I sing the breathless moments of this love story to Gugu Nkosi,*

*who is herself a love child*

# ACKNOWLEDGEMENTS

The people who introduced me to whales are Mike Bruton of the Two Oceans Aquarium in Cape Town (*The Essential Guide to Whales in South Africa*), Vic Cockcroft and Peter Joyce (MTN Whale Watch). I am grateful to them. I am also thankful to two lovely women: Julie Wark of Barcelona, Spain, who tirelessly read and corrected and inspired; and Debe Morris of Toronto, Canada, whose gifts of toy whales started me on a collection.

The National Arts Council of South Africa funded the research. I thank them too.

And now the blessings:

If Wilson Salukazana (the real-life whale crier of Hermanus) really did call the whales to himself; if one special person in my life, Gugu Nomcebo Nkosi, was not dead scared of the dark; if young Lunga Tubu had not sung arias in his unbroken voice, bringing tears to my eyes; and if my then four-year-old daughter Zenzi had not invented the names Saluni, Sharisha and Mr. Yodd, there would be no story to tell.

# THE WHALE CALLER

# ONE

**T**HE SEA IS BLEEDING from the wounds of Sharisha.
But that is later. Now the tide returns in slight gentle
movements. Half-moon is the time of small tides. The
Whale Caller stands on one of the rugged cliffs that form an arena
above the bay. He has spent the better part of the day standing
there, blowing his horn. Blowing Sharisha's special song. Blowing
louder and louder as the tide responds by receding in time to the
staccato of his call. Yet she is nowhere to be seen. His eyes have
become strained from looking into the distant waters, hoping to
see Sharisha lobtailing in the glare of the setting sun. It is September and the southern rights have returned from the southern
seas. But Sharisha is not among them.

Night is beginning to fall. Slowly the Whale Caller makes his
way down the cliffs to pour out his pain to Mr. Yodd. He selects
the longer but safer route that traverses the concrete slipway on
which blue, green, yellow and red boats are displayed. They used
to belong to fishermen of a century ago. He makes certain that he
does not stumble against any of them for they are brittle. If he
were to trip and fall on one of them it would surely disintegrate.
Experts from Cape Town spend months trying to restore them to

their former glory, so that present and future generations, brought up in these days of engine-powered trawlers, can see how fishermen of old endured the stormy seas in small open boats powered by their own muscles.

When the Whale Caller is in a happy mood he can see the weather-beaten fishermen shrouded in the mists of time, taking to sea in their fleet of small boats. Some are rowing back with their catch, while others are gutting the fish or drying it on the rocks. He can see even deeper in the mists, before there were boats and fishermen and whalers, the Khoikhoi of old dancing around a beached whale. Dancing their thanks to Tsiqua, He Who Tells His Stories in Heaven, for the bountiful food he occasionally provides for his children by allowing whales to strand themselves. But when there are mass strandings the dance freezes and the laughter in the eyes of the dancers melts into tears that leave stains on the white sands. The weepers harvest the blubber for the oil to fry meat and light lamps. They will ultimately use the rib bones to construct the skeletons of their huts, and will roof the houses with the baleen. Ear bones will be used as water carrying vessels. Other bones will become furniture. Or even pillows and beds. Nights are slept fervidly inside variable whales that speckle the landscape.

But first the weepers will eat the meat until their stomachs run. They will dry some of it in the sun. They cannot finish it though. Most of it will putrefy and fill the shores with a stench. Hence they weep for the waste. Tsiqua, He Who Tells His Stories in Heaven, should learn to strand only one whale at a time. One whale after seasons of migrations to the southern seas and back, and the bodies of the weepers explode into laughter once again. Once more the Men of Men—which is what the name Khoikhoi means—thank He Who Tells His Stories in Heaven for the bountiful provision.

Today the Whale Caller is not in the mood to amble in the

mists of the past. He is racked by the sadness of the present. His whole body is pining for Sharisha.

He treads carefully down the crag until he reaches the grotto that Mr. Yodd shares with the rock rabbits that have become so tame that they don't run away from people. In daytime they can be seen scavenging in dustbins when there are no tourists to feed them. The grotto is just above the water made brown by seaweed that looks like dirty oil. He squats on a rock and looks into the grotto. A rock rabbit appears, looks at him closely and languidly walks back to its hole to resume its disturbed rest.

❦

HOY, MR. YODD! She has not come. Like yesterday. Like the day before. I waited and waited and waited. She stood me up. They sail back, she does not. She lingers in the southern seas, and she thinks I care. I've got news for her, Mr. Yodd. I don't give a damn. If she wants to play that sort of game, she will find that two can play it just as well. She will find me ready and willing. Or she won't find me at all. There are plenty of fish in these seas. The leviathan with a whore's heart. There are plenty of fish in these seas, Mr. Yodd. And I bought a new tuxedo. Hire purchase. Not rental this time, but hire purchase. Six monthly instalments and I own it. Pay-as-you-wear. I bought it specially to welcome Sharisha back. No more hired tuxedos for me. I needed something permanent. Something that will absorb the odours of my soul and become part of what Sharisha associates with me. In any case, in the long run it's expensive to hire a tuxedo. It is cost-effective to own your own. Variety is nice, but stability is more important. It has never happened like this, Mr. Yodd. I fear something might have befallen her. I worry. I am a worrier when it comes to Sharisha. She may yet come, you say? I cannot help but entertain the unthinkable. What if whalers have harpooned her, and as we speak she is being cut into pieces for Japanese palates? I think the worst. I cannot help it. She has never done this before, Mr. Yodd. Southern rights appear on this coast as early as June. But I am never unduly worried when I don't see her in June because that is not her month. She waits for the winter rains to have their run and the warmth of spring to return. She is always punctual. In the middle of August she returns in all her breaching glory from the southern seas. Now September is about to end. Yet she is nowhere to be seen. Ya! Ya! I know that they are still coming back; that for the whole of September and October groups of them will be coming back. It is unlike Sharisha to be a straggler. If she comes in October, it means I will only have a month or two with her before she voyages back to the southern seas. She cannot give me the thrill of her massive splashes into the new year because by January the southern rights are almost all gone. A month or two with Sharisha is not enough. No, Mr. Yodd, I think you are just trying to twist the knife that she has already planted in my back. You seem to rejoice in my pain. Three years, you say! But Sharisha . . . Sharisha comes every year. Not on a three-year cycle as other southern rights may do. Sharisha cannot live for three years without me, Mr. Yodd. She comes every year.

❦

HE STANDS UP and attempts to walk up the crag. He has plodded only a few steps when he slips and falls on his knees. He is too tired to stand up again. Or perhaps too despondent. His confession to Mr. Yodd has failed to perform its intended function of lifting his spirits. He touches his left knee. His fingers are wet with warm blood. He hopes the lacerations are not too deep. In the sunshine of the day these rocks are beautiful in their bright yellow, grey, metallic brown and white. But they are sharp and at night, in the emaciated light of the half-moon, they can easily be deadly. He thanks his stars that he was not wearing his new tuxedo today. It would have been torn at the knees like the blue dungarees he is wearing. He is pleased with himself that he does not feel any pain. But he is even happier that he was able to save his horn. His options were clear: to fall on his hands and save the rest of his body, or to fall on his knees and save the horn. In the first option the horn would surely have broken into pieces since he was holding it. He sacrificed his knees for his horn. He chuckles at the silliness of it all. He can always get a new horn by making it. He cannot get new knees. But perhaps it is not silly at all. He has a sentimental attachment to this horn among all others that he owns. He has used this particular horn for the last three years. It has a special timbre that strikes a tingling chord for Sharisha. No two horns can sound exactly the same.

He decides to spend the night in the company of the stars. He holds his horn close to his heart. He dare not press it too hard against his chest, lest it break. He remembers how he created it out of the fronds of the kelp that grows among the rocks of the sea. Storms brought it to the shoreline. He took the wet fronds from the water and placed them on the roof of his house in the crooked and twisted shapes suited to producing the deep and hollow sounds of the whales. The seaweed dried up to become pipes. He has fashioned a number of horns this way.

The little waves break with a monotonous rhythm on the rocks, bringing with them more kelp. He remembers his first kelp horn.

It was forty years ago. He was a strapping young man in his early twenties. He loved the Church—as it was officially known—and looked forward to the Sundays when he and the other congregants would be dancing to the beat of the drums and the music of the harps and tambourines. For him the most heavenly part of the service, besides the snow white robes of the worshippers, was the kelp horn that an old man blew to accompany the hymns. He was so fascinated by the deep and hollow sounds of the horn that he asked the old man to teach him how to play it. He became so adept at it that His Eminence the Bishop made him official horn player after age had stolen the old man's breath. He inherited the old man's horn. That was his very first kelp horn. And he played it so celestially that His Eminence decided to do away with harps and tambourines, for they seemed to dilute the innocence of the horn. This caused an argument whose proportions had never been seen before at the Church. The Elders of the Church said that harps were by nature heavenly. Angels sang to harps and tambourines. To do away with them was playing into the hands of the Prince of Darkness. But His Eminence stood his ground. A kelp horn, he said, was a natural musical instrument that took the congregation back to its roots. It was an instrument that celebrated the essence of creation. God would lend a sharper ear to the prayers of those who praised Him to the accompaniment of an instrument that was shaped by His own hand through the agency of the seas. This led to a schism in the Church. The Elders appointed a new bishop among themselves, and His Eminence led his followers to a new church that would worship God in its own creative way. It became known as the Church of the Sacred Kelp Horn, and the Whale Caller—who had not learnt to call whales then—was anointed Chief Horn Player.

The Church of the Sacred Kelp Horn met every Sunday at Hoy's Koppie, a conical hill in the middle of the village. The flock and its shepherd sang and danced for the Lord among the fynbos that grew in front of the Klipgat Cave, which used to be the home, variously, of the Khoikhoi and the San peoples long before the village came into being. In their white robes—with blue sashes to distinguish themselves from the members of the

Church—the worshippers waltzed and tangoed among the trees. When the winter rains came the service was conducted in the cave, which was too small for ballroom dance. The congregants itched for the foxtrots and rumbas of sunny Sundays.

Like His Eminence, the Chief Horn Player felt that the new church brought the worshippers closer to nature, and in greater communion with the spirits of the forebears that were hovering above the tall cliffs and in the cave. He blew the horn, sometimes to accompany the hymns, or just to arouse the spirits and to stir the members of the congregation into a climactic frenzy until they spoke in tongues.

The most exciting times for the Chief Horn Player were the Sundays when the sea became a baptistery. The worshippers stood on the white sands and sang their praises to the Lord. His Eminence led those who were to be christened further into the sea. The Chief Horn Player followed, blowing the sacred sounds of baptism. His Eminence then immersed each one into the water and out again three times, in the name of the Father, the Son and the Holy Ghost. The Chief Horn Player accompanied each immersion with bellows that caused tremors on the land under the water. It was on one such occasion that a whale surfaced about a hundred metres from the baptism. It swam closer to take a curious look. It seemed to be attracted by the sound of the horn. The whale stole the attention of the congregation from the baptism. The Chief Horn Player himself was fascinated by this big creature of the sea, which he had never seen at such close quarters. It might have been a humpback or even a killer whale. In those days he did not know the difference. A whale was a whale was a whale. What intrigued him most was the notion that it was his horn that had drawn it to the baptism.

It submerged and waved its tail above the water. It began to lobtail—slapping the water repeatedly with its tail. The congregation cheered. The Chief Horn Player blew the horn to the rhythm of the splashing water. His Eminence was struck by a brilliant idea for an instant sermon on Jonah and the whale.

"We are being sent to Nineveh, my children," he boomed above the din. "Like Jonah of the Bible, God is sending us to Nineveh."

He asked for a Bible from those who were standing on the beach. A saved woman waded in the water, raising her robe above the knees with one hand, and lifting the Bible to the sky with the other hand. She gave it to His Eminence and waded back. He turned the pages to the Book of Jonah. He raised his hand, demanding silence. And there was silence. Even the whale stopped lobtailing. He read from the Book of Books: " 'Arise, go to Nineveh, that great city, and cry against it; for their wickedness is come up before me.' God is speaking through this whale, my children, sending us to cry for Nineveh! Are we going to heed the call or are we going to flee to Tarshish?"

"But where is Nineveh, Your Eminence?" asked one of the worshippers.

"Out there in the sinful world," responded His Eminence. "In this very village. Wickedness is everywhere and God demands that we cry against it."

The congregation broke into moans and wails and screams, crying against Nineveh's wickedness. The whale began to sail away.

"I think Nineveh is in Cape Town," suggested the Chief Horn Player, remembering the trip to Cape Town that the congregation had been planning and postponing for the past three years. When the Church of the Sacred Kelp Horn broke away from the Church, the carrot His Eminence dangled to attract more followers—in addition to the introduction of ballroom dance as an integral part of the rites of worship—was a bus trip to Cape Town, to evangelise the multitudes that gathered on the beaches indulging in worldly joys and that wasted the summer nights away in night-clubs and strip joints.

"If we flee to Tarshish," continued His Eminence, "God will send His whales to swallow us, for it is written, 'Now the Lord had prepared a great fish to swallow up Jonah. And Jonah was in the belly of the fish three days and three nights.' Of course today we know what the writers of the Bible did not know; that a whale is not a fish. After all those days and nights living inside a whale, it vomited him out on dry land, and he ran straight to Nineveh to preach to the glory of the Lord! We must not be like Jonah; whales must not first swallow us before we can work for God. The sceptics among you will ask, how is it possible to survive in the stomach of a whale without being digested? But I ask you, my children, if Jesus himself believed in the story of Jonah and the whale, who are we to question it? In Matthew 12 verse 40 Jesus says, 'For as Jonah was three days and three nights in the whale's belly, so shall the Son of man be three days and three nights in the heart of the earth.' What more proof do we need that the story of Jonah is true?"

It was obvious to all that the spirit of Jonah had taken over the baptism. The whale had hijacked the whole ceremony, even though the creature's tail could now be seen sailing a distance away.

"It is sailing away!" screeched the Chief Horn Player.

He blew his horn with great vigour and the whale stopped. Once more it lobtailed. He was convinced that through his kelp horn he had the power to communicate with it. This discovery excited him no end, and he remained at the beach blowing his horn long after the rest of the congregation had gone home.

He gradually drifted from the Church of the Sacred Kelp Horn and spent most of his days at the beach, holding conversations with the whales through his horn. He was determined to refine his skill, and spent many years walking westwards along the coast of the Indian Ocean, until he reached the point where the two oceans met, and then proceeded northwards along the Atlantic Ocean coast right up to Walvis Bay in South West Africa, as Namibia was then called. He survived on fish, some of which he bartered to non-fishing folks for grain and other necessities. He stopped for months at a time in fishermen's villages that dotted the coastline. In hamlets where women were buxom and welcoming he stopped for a few years. Sometimes he hired himself out as a hand to the trawlers that caught pilchards off the west coast of southern Africa. But he spent every second when he was not sleeping or eking out a living talking to the whales. He was listening to the songs of the southern right, the humpback and the Bryde's whales, and learning to reproduce them with his horn. He also learnt to fashion different kinds of kelp horns: big horns with deep and rounded tone colours and small horns that sounded like muted trumpets.

After thirty-five years he returned to his home village of Hermanus and with his meagre pension rented a two-roomed Wendy house in the backyard of a kindly widower. The village had grown into a beautiful holiday resort. But it had not lost the soul of the village of his youth. Many landmarks were as he remembered them—such as the Hoy's Koppie of his devout days. The village still nestled comfortably between the Kleinriver Mountains and the sea. The mountains still wore their crown of mist on special days. Many things had changed though. Along the coastline there were more houses, mostly white cottages and bungalows, roofed with black or red tiles while others were thatched with grass that had blackened with age, and there were some double- and triple-storey buildings. Many of these, he heard, belonged to rich people from as far away as Johannesburg, who spent part of the year enjoying the spoils of their wealth in the laid-back ambience of the village. Other houses belonged to retired millionaires who had decided to live here permanently. It had now become impossible for an ordinary person to buy property at his childhood paradise.

Another change was that the village had become popular with tourists. A new fashion had developed, that of watching whales. They seemed to have multiplied tenfold since the days of his youth. September and October were peak whale months, and thousands of tourists from many countries of the world gathered on the cliffs and the beaches every day to watch whales frolicking in the water and performing their antics to the cheers of the spectators. On a good day there would be as many as twenty whales leaping out of the water and falling back in resounding splashes.

He saw all these things and felt like an intruder both in the lives of the whale watchers and of the local citizens. No one knew him anymore. People wondered who the tall and brawny stranger in blue dungarees was. They marvelled at his big bald head and craggy face, half of which hid in a rich silvery beard. They looked at him curiously as he stood on the cliffs, blowing his horn for the whales, sometimes fully donned in black tie. He did not seem to be friendly towards human beings, so they kept their distance from him. They were strangers to him. Almost all the people he used to know had either left this world altogether or had left the village in search of a better life in the cities of South Africa. Even His Eminence the Bishop of the Church of the Sacred Kelp Horn had long departed Nineveh for celestial shores.

He saw the official whale crier, who was employed by the tourist office. A gracious gentleman from Zwelihle Township a few kilometres away, he was dubbed the world's only whale crier. The Whale Caller did not begrudge the whale crier his world title. The Whale Caller was not in competition with the whale crier. The Whale Caller was not a whale crier but a whale caller!

He saw how popular the whale crier was, both with the tourists and the locals. He watched the whale crier, resplendent in his beautiful black and white costume and strange hat, blowing his kelp horn to alert whale watchers to the presence and location of the whales. Sometimes whales surfaced at the Grotto or the Voelklip beaches. At other times they might surface at Kwaai-water or Siever's Punt. The whale crier blew his kelp horn in a particular code that was interpreted on the sandwich board that he wore, and whale watchers knew exactly where to go to see the whales, and how many there were. Sometimes the whale crier acted like a tourist guide, showing the visitors sites of interest in the village.

Although at first the Whale Caller envied the attention and the fame that the world's only whale crier received, he soon re-alised that his mission in life was quite different from the whale crier's. The whale crier alerted people to the whereabouts of whales, whereas the Whale Caller called whales to himself, much like the shark callers of New Ireland.

The comparison with the shark callers had once been made by a sailor who had watched him call whales. The sailor told him that the shark callers of New Ireland—a province of Papua New Guinea—use their voices and rattles of coconut shells under wa-ter to attract sharks. The sharks swim to the boat where they can be speared or netted. Sometimes the rattling noise attracts the shark through a noose. A rope attached to the noose is connected to a wooden propeller that is spun around to tighten the noose while pulling in the rope. The shark is then unable to move.

When the Whale Caller first heard of the shark callers he hated the comparison. He did not call whales in order to kill them. Eat-ing them would be tantamount to cannibalism. He called them because they gave him joy and he gave them as much in return. And if he could help it, he preferred to call them when he was alone, so as to have intimate moments with them. He was not a showman, but a lover. Since returning to Hermanus he has hardly any privacy because the place is always teeming with tourists during the whale season. He has, however, been able to continue with his conversations and singalongs with the whales unobstructed by the activities of the village and its whale-watching culture. And has managed to stay out of the way of the official whale crier.

He has owned hundreds of kelp horns since his first. But this one that he holds so lovingly against his chest is the best of them all, for it is the horn that first introduced him to Sharisha. He closes his eyes and is sucked by a whirlpool into a dreamless sleep.

When he wakes up the next morning there is already a trickling of whale watchers on the cliffs above him. They are watching the horizon with their binoculars. He is slightly embarrassed that he became hysterical in his confession to Mr. Yodd last night. What will Mr. Yodd think of him? He promises himself that despite the feeling of wounded rejection and his fears for Sharisha he will maintain his calm dignity at all times. He will swallow whatever pride he might have and go back to Mr. Yodd to apologise. He stands up. His muscles are stiff. He takes the few uneasy steps back to Mr. Yodd's grotto.

HOY, MR. YODD! It was a joke . . . last night. You thought I was being serious, did you? You thought I meant it. Last night. All the hysteria about the Japanese eating Sharisha. And all the insecurities about her deserting me. I must have sounded pathetic. I admit I was a bit rash last night, Mr. Yodd. Accusing you of things you are not capable of . . . such as twisting the knife in my back! I am sorry. Fortunately you do not hold a grudge. That is what is beautiful about you. A grudge can take its toll on your health. It is like a parasite that feeds on you. At first it gives you a feeling of warmth. The thought that you will get even gives you comfort. Then the ungrateful guest begins to eat your insides. It gets fatter while you are gradually reduced to a bag of bones. It destroys you. That's what a grudge does to one, Mr. Yodd. You thought I had lost control of myself, hey Mr. Yodd? It was the kind of night that brought hallucinations to the sanest of minds. To the soberest. It must have been the fumes of death that permeated the air. Decay. Death. I could smell it from the sea. The wind brings it from the western coast. Yes, you told me many times before, Mr. Yodd. These are not today's smells. They have lingered for more than two hundred years. A two-hundred-year-old stench from the slaughter of the southern rights by French, American and British whalers at St. Helena Bay in 1785. Five hundred southern rights in one season! They harpooned the calves in order to get their mothers who would come to the rescue of their little ones. Seasons of mass killings! The smell still haunts these shores. Yes, they are protected now, Mr. Yodd. But only since 1935. The whales have come back since then but I cannot presume that Sharisha will be safe on her voyage from the southern seas. There are pirates and poachers! What if . . . There I go again with what you refer to as hysteria. I apologise, Mr. Yodd. It was not me talking last night. All right, Mr. Yodd. Go ahead and laugh. I don't mind at all. Laugh at me as much as you like.

HE IS MORTIFIED as he walks on the pavement near the parking lot. And it shows in his gait. The crowds have already gathered. They are the usual tourists with floral shirts and funereal faces. As if someone forced them to come here. Binoculars and cameras weighing down their necks. Sandals flip-flopping like soft coronach drumbeats as the feet trudge in different directions. Fat Americans, timid as individuals, but boisterous and arrogant in groups. Puny Japanese, excitable and fascinated by the most mundane of things. Inland South Africans who look apologetic and seem to be more out of place than the Americans and Japanese. All clicking away at the slightest provocation. Following everything that moves on land and sea with camcorders.

They are in greater numbers today, the whale-watching invaders. The town is celebrating its annual Kalfiefees—the whale calf festival. The locals, who don't usually care much for whale watching, are also out in throngs. Some are out to flog their wares. The parking lot has been taken over by stalls and tables displaying Cape Malay delights, candyfloss machines, ostrich biltong, citrus preserves and whalebone jewellery and toys. Spicy and sweet aromas intermingle with the compound smell of salt and dead kelp that is brought by the heat from the sea.

Many have come just to watch the spectacular street performances of jugglers, mimes, banjo-strumming buskers and dancers in grotesque whale costumes. Or to hold their collective breath as adrenalin junkies bungee-jump down awesome cliffs only to be pulled back seconds before their bodies hit the rocky shallows of the sea. Pallid boys from Zwelihle Township perform the haka, the ceremonial Maori war chants accompanying a fearsome dance learnt from the New Zealand rugby team. Others sing *Shosholoza*, the work song that has been adopted by the South African rugby team as its anthem, while performing an out-of-step gumboot dance. Processions of tourists go through the ritual of dropping coins into enamel bowls or cold drink cans without paying much attention to the performances of the boys. There are those who prefer to make offerings of fruit and sweets, ever suspicious that the boys may use the cash for such narcotics as glue, benzine or even mandrax pills.

The Whale Caller negotiates his way among the rainbow people. People of what is fashionably referred to as the new South Africa, even though it is ten years old. Ten years is a second in the life of a nation. Rainbow people sport rainbow hairstyles. Heads looking like frosted birthday cakes. Black hair with silver stripes. Orange and blue hair with golden stripes. Peroxide blondes with black polka dots. Leggy model-types and stout granny-types. Broad-shouldered bare-chested men in wet Bermuda shorts, wearing green, blue, black, purple and yellow serpent or dragon tattoos on golden brown tans.

Hair. It is a blight they must carry on their heads, exposing the position each head occupied in the statutory hierarchies of the past. The troubles of humanity are locked in the hair. Yet the people have managed to disguise their shame by painting it in the colours that designate them all a people of the rainbow. Without exception. Without a past. Without rancour. Without hierarchies. Only their eyes betray the big lie. In these eyes you can see a people living in a daze. Rainbow people walking in a precarious dream that may explode into a nightmare without much warning.

He looks at the colourful hair of his compatriots and he is thankful that he was liberated from his quite early on in life—in his mid-thirties—long before there was any notion of a rainbow people, when his hair fell out, at first gradually as he brushed it, then furiously even as he slept. He was still a wanderer from one fishing hamlet to the next on the west coast when the rude Cape-of-Storms storms blew strands of it away. Until his pate was smooth and shiny. He compensated with a rich crop of beard and a bushy chest. Silvery grey.

The whales do not disappoint. It is as if they know that the citizens of Hermanuspietersfontein—as the town was originally known—and their visitors from all over the world are out celebrating their return from the southern seas. Incidentally, the lazy tongues that have reduced his town to Hermanus irritate the Whale Caller. He resolves that from now on he will call it nothing but Hermanuspietersfontein. Even when its name is changed, as it is bound to in keeping with the demands of the new South Africa, he will continue to call it Hermanuspietersfontein. The southern rights don't bother with the politics of naming. Two thousand of them will migrate annually from the sub-Antarctic to the warmth of South African waters whether the whale-watching town is called Hermanus, Hermanuspietersfontein or something new South African. Five hundred of them will converge along the south coast, and some of these will be seen from the shores of this town, as they are seen on this day of the Kalfiefees. They congregate here in greater numbers than anywhere else because this is a sheltered place. They stay for long periods here because the sea is quiet. There is not much activity of ski boats or even whale-watching boats. Almost all whale watching is done from the land. The boerewors-roll-chomping tourists, mustard and ketchup dripping from their fingers and chins, train their binoculars in the direction of a group of southern rights—mothers and calves languidly sailing in the grey distance. The Whale Caller does not need binoculars to know that none of them is Sharisha.

He dreads the crowds and would like to take the shortest route possible to his Wendy house. But the mobs are blocking his path. Something is happening here. Placards and an Afrikaans hymn tell him that it is a protest march of sorts. Pastor Pietie le Roux leads a small crowd of dour yet angry Christians. The Whale Caller recognises him—one of the few people he remembers from the old days when he used to play the kelp horn at the Church. Pietie was one of the young people who had remained with the Church while the Whale Caller and others followed His Eminence, the late and lamented Bishop, to form the Church of the Sacred Kelp Horn. Pietie is now a grey-head pastor of the Holy Light Ministries and is punching the air with his angry fist.

The Whale Caller tries to slink off.

"You can skulk away all you want, but you cannot hide from the Lord," says Pastor Pietie le Roux, looking directly into the eyes of the Whale Caller.

"I don't need to hide from you, Pietie le Roux," protests the Whale Caller.

"You turned your back on the Lord," shouts the pastor. "Do you now want to turn your back on your responsibility as a member of this community?"

His followers punctuate this crucial question with a few amens and hallelujahs. On the side of the road dissenters heckle the holy man to the chagrin of his followers. But the holy man will not be deterred. Among the hecklers the Whale Caller sees a woman who has a tendency to pop up everywhere the Whale Caller is. On occasion he has practically run away from her, but like a bad penny she will pop up again somewhere in his vicinity before that day is over. It could be at a supermarket where he buys provisions for the week, mainly his staple of macaroni and cheese; it could be at the beach where he blows his kelp horn for the whales; it could even be outside the gate of the Wendy house where he lives. Whenever the Whale Caller sees her, he changes direction. She never seems to mind him. She usually just stands there, looking at him intently until he disappears. Then she pops up again somewhere else later that day when he is busy minding his own business. Thankfully she has never popped up at his confessions to Mr. Yodd. That would be embarrassing. What would Mr. Yodd think of him? To pre-empt her appearance at Mr. Yodd's shrine he has mentioned her to him once, by way of seeking advice on how to deal with the pest of a woman who seems to be stalking him. As usual Mr. Yodd had laughed at him. He had left mortified, as often happens after his confessions to Mr. Yodd. He realised only when he reached the top of the cliffs that he had received no counsel from his confessor on how to deal with the stalker.

The woman never says anything. He has never heard her voice. She just stands there and looks at him with questioning eyes. He always averts his eyes. She enjoys this game, for she skips girlishly to the new spot where his eyes are fixed. His best defence is to

walk away. Almost running, looking back from time to time to see
if she is following. She never follows. She just stands there, arms
akimbo, intently staring after him.

On one occasion at the beach he mustered enough courage to
glare back at her. She did not flinch. He stood his ground for a
while, and occupied his mind with studying her face. It was ravaged by alcohol. Yet he couldn't help concluding that she was one
of those people who continued to be beautiful long after the
nights were gone. He studied her red matted hair, restrained from
running in all wild directions by a fine black net. She broke into a
smile, while still looking him straight in the eye. Four of her upper front teeth were missing, the result of the yesteryear teeth-
extracting fashion of the Western Cape that many of its followers
regret today. They try to hide the folly of their youth with false
teeth. The woman's teeth that were not missing were brown, perhaps from snuff or even too much alcohol.

He couldn't bear it any longer. He turned and walked away.
Quite briskly. Once more she had won.

Although the woman is with those who are heckling the pastor, she herself is not a heckler. She is staring at the hapless Whale
Caller, who is being harangued by the pastor. Fifteen pastors begin to surround the Whale Caller, raising their placards high. Bold
letters screaming: *Clean Out the Filth from Our Town, Hermanus Is
Not Sodom and Gomorrah, Away with Moffies and Their Plays* . . .

The Whale Caller remembers reading in the *Hermanus Times*
that fifteen pastors from various denominations are protesting
about the staging of a play titled *Have You Heard the Seagull Scream?*
as part of the Kalfiefees. Apparently what is galling the men of
God is that the play features full frontal nudity and explicit gay
sex scenes.

"Hey, the play has nothing to do with me, Pietie le Roux," says
the Whale Caller.

"It has everything to do with all decent people of this town," the pastor says. "It is an affront to all God-fearing townsfolk, and you cannot stand aside in your godless whale-hugging existence and do nothing about it. You must join us in this protest."

The theatre where the play is to be staged is just across the street and the Whale Caller cannot help noticing that the lines of those who want to buy tickets are getting longer. Those who have not seen the festival programme think they can get more information about the play from Pastor Pietie le Roux.

"Hey, Pastor le Roux, what is this dirty play about?" one of them shouts from the crowd.

"They say it is about fuckin' moffies," another one responds.

"Hey, I am asking Pastor le Roux, not you!"

This gives Pietie le Roux the opportunity to sermonise about the play. "We, the pastors of Hermanus, have been placed here by the Lord to look after the morality of this town. The people who attend the play will be affected by it. Plays like these are the cause of all our problems in this town—problems like abalone poaching and drug abuse."

"What is this play about, pastor, which causes people to steal perlemoen from our seas?" asks another smart-aleck.

"It is about a sailor who is secretly in love with his captain," says Pietie le Roux.

"Skande! Skande!" shout his followers.

"You don't think the captain could be a woman?" asks a spoil-sport.

"Ja," agrees another one, "in this new South Africa women are captains."

"Not in this play," says the pastor indignantly. "The sailor is a man and the captain is a man."

"So the pastor has seen this play yet he doesn't want us to see it so we can make up our own minds about it?" asks the woman. For the first time the Whale Caller hears her voice. It has a husky tinge to it, as if it was made for singing the blues.

"Who is this woman who blasphemes against the messenger of the Word?" asks the holy man.

"She is Saluni the village drunk," answers a member of the fold helpfully.

"How does the pastor know what the play is about if he has not seen it?" insists Saluni. "How does he know it is bad for the morality of this town?"

"God have mercy on you, my child," says the pastor, raising his open hand over her head as if to bless her. "I read in the festival programme what the play is about. I have not seen it because these eyes that read the Holy Book for the congregation of the children of God every Sunday cannot feast on such filth. None of us believers have seen this play. None of us will see it. And I would advise the village drunk, who is nevertheless still loved by the Lord, not to see it either."

"So what if the sailor falls in love with his captain?" asks Saluni, who is fast establishing herself as the unofficial spokesperson of the sinful theatrical production. "After all, the constitution of the new South Africa protects gays. It is against the law to discriminate against anyone just because they are fuckin' moffies. This is not the old South Africa where somebody else thought for us."

"So our village drunk is also a lawyer and a politician?" asks Pastor Pietie le Roux to the derisive laughter of his followers. "Before you run to complain to your Human Rights Commission let me tell you that it is not because of homosexuality that we are against the play, though indeed no moffie will enter the Kingdom of Heaven. It is because of explicit description and full frontal nudity! This is the last resort we are taking here. We did try to negotiate with the festival organiser. And you know what he told us? That Jesus is for everyone, including moffies. How dare he speak the name of Jesus upon his lips?"

Since the focus of Pastor Pietie le Roux is now on the impertinent Saluni, the Whale Caller manages to work his way out of the circle of pastors to the side of the hecklers. The only opening through which he may escape is next to Saluni. And he has no choice but to brush against her. She looks at him and grins triumphantly. Fumes of methylated spirits assail him. He cringes away and manages to stand on the fringes of the crowd. It is already dispersing, with most people rushing to join the line at the box office window of the theatre.

"We have not finished cleaning this town," says another one of the fifteen pastors, addressing the faithful. "There is yet another scandalous play called *Broekbrein*. And this one is about a middle-aged man who falls for a younger woman. This isn't going to do the morals of this town any good. We must think of our daughters, flowers of Hermanus, who may be misled by such drivel. And as usual we spoke to the writer, who is also the actor in this one-man play. We phoned him, warning him to stay away from Hermanus. Unfortunately he did not heed our warning."

Then he breaks into a hymn in his baritone. The fold takes it up and the march continues on its path of redemption. The Whale Caller walks slowly to his Wendy house. He is disgusted that he has touched the village drunk. It suddenly strikes him that when he brushed against her an image of his long-departed mother flashed before his eyes. He wonders why Saluni reminds him of a woman who died decades ago, when he was still a boy, before he even became an apprentice horn player at the Church. Saluni looks nothing like his mother. She obviously was not yet born when his mother sailed for celestial shores. He reckons there is a fifteen-year gap between Saluni and him, though it is hard to tell with people whose faces have been ravaged by spirits and the elements. Saluni is a village drunk and looks it; his mother was a strict Christian woman who walked a mile from any den of iniquity. Saluni is petite. His mother was a robust woman in corpulent dresses. But something in Saluni does remind him of his mother, and it bothers him no end that he can't put his finger on it.

SALUNI. Her life revolves around three rituals: spectating the Whale Caller, singing with the Bored Twins and gulping quantities of plonk from a flask she carries all the time in her sequinned but threadbare handbag. When times are hard the flask is filled with methylated spirits mixed with water. The third ritual usually accompanies the first two. She takes a ceremonial swig as she watches the Whale Caller or between songs with the Bored Twins.

Saluni was first attracted to the Bored Twins by their beautiful voices two years ago. It was not long after her arrival in the district from inland provinces, an exile from darkness. She was wandering from homestead to office building to farmstead, looking for employment. She was exhausted from traversing the postcard landscape and was chafed by constant rejection. Her toes in her pencil-heel shoes were sore. On the outskirts of town, from a patch of sparse reeds growing in a small swamp, she heard voices singing in two-part harmony. It was a children's song, the version of which she remembered very well from her jewellery music box, where it was played by what sounded like a harpsichord. The voices from the reeds gave the song new energy that evoked a feeling of nostalgia for a world Saluni had never known. Perhaps a world she had experienced in another life. Her body suddenly felt a surge of something akin to vibrational healing. The pain in her feet was dissipating fast. The tiredness in her body was gone. The voices seemed to connect her to an angelic realm.

She walked closer to the reeds, eager to satisfy her curiosity about the source of such ethereal sounds. She saw them for the first time, wading in the mud; their matching white dresses smudged all over. The girls were identical, though one was slightly bigger. She was later to dub them the Bored Twins. They were about seven years old and were very beautiful. Not only did they sing like angels, they looked as though they would sprout wings and fly to the clouds. She stood there and watched them for some time. She wondered what children of that age were doing playing all alone in a swamp so far away from any houses.

She tried to attract their attention by coughing. They looked at her. They didn't seem to be startled at all. She called them to come out of the mud and asked them where they came from. "I'll take you to your home," she said. "You shouldn't be playing so far away from people. I am sure your parents must be worried by now."

The Bored Twins merely giggled. It sounded like little pealing bells.

"You can laugh all you want," said Saluni. "You are too young to understand the dangers that lurk in isolated places. Even little girls of your age get raped these days."

The Bored Twins did not seem to take her seriously. She asked them to direct her to their home, as she wanted to talk to their parents. They said they would do so only when they had finished their game, and then jumped back into the mud. Soon it would be dark and she dared not allow darkness to catch her in the wild. She walked into the swamp and tried to grab their arms. They slipped through her hands like eels. They ran around in circles, shrieking and laughing while she chased them. They were having too much fun at her expense to care that she was becoming infuriated. One of her pencil-heel shoes got stuck in the mud. She muttered a few expletives as she pulled it out, cleaned it on the grass and put it back on her foot. She then sat on the grass, hid her head between her knees and sobbed. The remorseful girls came to comfort her, each one crying: "I am sorry, auntie . . . I am sorry, auntie!"

She saw her chance, and pounced on them like a wild cat, grabbing each one by the scruff of the neck, all the while cackling with laughter. For a moment the Bored Twins were astounded by her deceit, and then they screamed and kicked and scratched. But she was too strong for them.

Sulkily they led Saluni to their home almost three kilometres away—a derelict white Cape Dutch mansion that she had often seen on her wanderings in the district. She had never imagined anyone lived there. She knew of the story that was told in the taverns of Hermanus, that the mansion had been abandoned decades ago after a bankrupt ostrich baron had murdered his family and then committed suicide when the bottom fell out of the ostrich feather market. He was, in fact, taking his cue from a Dutch forebear who had killed himself after the tulip market crashed centuries before. It was during the Thirty Years War and Holland had gone crazy over tulips. Shysters abounded in the tulip trade. The forebear had been one of the speculators who had traded in bulbs that existed only on paper. When the government came up with legislation to curb that practice, he had tried to get out of the tulip market, but it was too late. The bottom had fallen right out. He had lost all his wealth and decided to hang himself. His surviving son, who had been his apprentice in the tulip trade, had sailed to the Cape of Good Hope to join the newly established settlement, then under the Dutch East India Company. His descendants had tried their hand at various trades until they found their niche, two centuries later, in ostrich farming. By the time the baron took over from his father the family had amassed untold riches from feathers that were in great demand by European and American fashion houses. He had built the mansion as a holiday home on the outskirts of the village of Hermanus. It was a replica of his other mansion in the Klein Karoo, where he had his ostrich farms. And then the tragedy happened, and the house remained unoccupied, until it became a ruin because it was reputed to be haunted by the ostrich baron's ghost and the vengeful spirits of his murdered family.

The girls' parents didn't seem unduly worried when Saluni brought them home.

"They like to wander around," said the father, as if talking of straying chickens.

"It can be dangerous out there," said Saluni.

"What can we do?" asked the mother. "These children get bored. We cannot look after them all the time because we are working people."

"We are casual vineyard workers," explained the father. "We took over this house a few months back when everyone was afraid of it. It is our base . . . our home. But we still have to travel to the vineyards in search of work."

"The twins know how to look after themselves," the mother assured Saluni. "Of course they do get bored sometimes."

They asked Saluni to stay for the night, since it had become too dark for her to walk home. The Bored Twins, excited at having a visitor, took her on a tour of the house. Each one was holding a candle. Saluni was amazed at the number of rooms. Yes, the mansion, though dilapidated, did look imposing from the outside. But she couldn't have imagined that inside it was such a maze. However, the Bored Twins knew their way around. They took her to all the bedrooms. Saluni counted eight of them, most with bathrooms en suite. But there was no water in the bathrooms, the girls told her. There was no running water anywhere in the house. The family drew their water from a communal tap almost a kilometre away. There were many other rooms whose original function Saluni could not determine. All devoid of furniture. All with rococo ceilings that used to be white. The ornate ceilings looked out of place in the simplicity of Cape Dutch elegance. Most of the rooms had spiders and other crawling creatures as permanent residents. It was obvious that the family only used three rooms: the kitchen, the parents' bedroom and the Bored Twins' bedroom. The rest of the rooms were full of dust and spiders' webs that ran from one wall to the other. The only other clean room was the wine cellar in the basement. Even the empty wine racks that lined its walls were dust-free. The Bored Twins told her that it was their secret room, which they used when they wanted to hide from their parents.

After a supper of snoek fish and rice, Saluni helped the mother clean the plates. Then it was time for bed. The girls became excited when Saluni offered to sleep in their room. Sponge mattresses were spread on the floor. The Bored Twins insisted on reading her their favourite bedtime story: *Dr. Seuss's Sleep Book*.

"But first we must put out the light," said the smaller girl.

"No, don't!" screamed Saluni. The Bored Twins were taken aback by her sudden anxiety. But she gave them a reassuring smile and asked, "How will you read me the story if it is dark?"

"We read it in the dark," said the bigger twin.

"We know the whole book by heart," explained the smaller twin.

"Please don't put out the light," pleaded Saluni.

"But Mother will be mad at us," said the bigger twin. "She says we must not waste candles."

Saluni took out a candle from her sequinned handbag. She lit it from the twins' candle before putting the twins' candle out.

"You carry a candle in your handbag?" asked the smaller twin.

"All the time," said Saluni. "Let's hear your story then."

"The news/Just came in/From the County of Keck/That a very small bug/By the name of Van Vleck/Is yawning so wide/You can look down his neck," began the smaller twin.

The bigger twin took over: "This may not seem/Very important, I know/But it *is*. So I'm bothering/Telling you so/A yawn is quite catching, you see. Like a cough/It just takes one yawn to start other yawns off." At this point the girls started yawning, so did Saluni. This tickled them no end. So it was true that yawning was infectious!

The story never came to an end though. The girls kept on adding their own silly details to Dr. Seuss's well-crafted story, which made it much longer than it really was, and left Saluni in stitches. By the time the girls reached the part with the sleepwalking creatures the story trailed off and soon both girls were snoring. Saluni couldn't help noting that even their snores sounded like distant pealing bells.

Before Saluni left the next morning, she promised the parents that she would occasionally come to check on the Bored Twins.

That was two years ago. To this day she continues to check on them, although sometimes she vows she will stop visiting their mansion as they have developed a new habit of playing silly pranks on her. She stays away for two or three days, and then finds that she misses them. She goes back to the mansion and indeed the Bored Twins have become sweet again. They sing for her. More than ever before they sing like angels. She sends them to the nearest tavern to buy her wine. After a few gulps she joins them in song. She has to be tipsy before she can open her mouth in song. Her husky voice blends well with the beatific voices. The parents are happy that an adult eye, however drunk it may often be, watches over their little angels. They reward Saluni with more bottles of cheap wine that they get from vineyard owners as part-payment for their labour.

THE SUN AND the moon pull in unison, and the tide rises.

The Whale Caller can hear the sounds of the sea from his Wendy house. His mind wanders to the events of the day as he prepares his late lunch of macaroni and cheese. He didn't have the best of days. What with his concerns for the safety of Sharisha! And the harassment by the pastors! Why did the pastors have to drag him into things about which he did not care? He had not even been aware of the plays that have caused so much upheaval in the town. He is of course aware of the festival, but it is not his business. He does not need a festival to celebrate the whales.

And the silent confrontation with Saluni! He still doesn't understand why the image of his mother flashed before his eyes. He does not remember ever thinking of his parents with any measure of nostalgia. He was quite young when his mother died, leaving him to fend for himself at the pilchard canning plants on the west coast. People said she had died from a broken heart. It was only a few months after her husband had disappeared. The Whale Caller has only vague memories of his father. A blurred picture of the sturdy fisherman who went to sea and never came back. After futile helicopter searches and a long wait, he was given up for dead. The rites for the dead were performed and the pastors declared that his soul was resting in peace in heaven.

In the early years, when he saw fathers play a crucial part in the lives of his friends, the Whale Caller used to have a searing longing for his own father. When he did odd jobs at the canning factories, and later when he blew the kelp horn at the Church, he would re-invent his father. He would imagine him taking one of the colourful brittle boats to sea, laughing and singing rude songs. The boat would disintegrate out there in the storms. For some time his father would be tossed by the waves while small piranha-like fish nibbled at him until they finished him. Thus he imagined his father's demise. Thus he killed him every time he thought of him. Until the sight of fish feasting on him lost its thrill. He had finally got tired of resurrecting him only to have him devoured by the fish again.

He is chewing on his macaroni and cheese with relish when he hears a song that has a familiar ring to it. Though the sound is quite distant and very low, he is able to isolate it from the festive noises that permeate the environment. He leaves the food on the table, takes his kelp horn and dashes out. At the gate he looks cautiously to the right and to the left, expecting to see Saluni. But she is not there. There is a tinge of disappointment in him that makes him angry with himself. Is he perhaps suffering from the syndrome of the victims of constant physical and psychological abuse who long for the abuser when the abuser is on vacation? He wades his way through the festive crowds and briskly walks to a high crag overlooking the ocean. On the horizon he sees a speck that he immediately identifies as a whale. It might be Sharisha. At a distance the whale's song sounds like Sharisha's. He curses himself for his failure to welcome her in style in his new tuxedo. There is no time to go back to the Wendy house to change.

He blows his horn and the whale responds. It is a haunting sound that is carried by the waves that race to the shoreline until they hit the rocks at the foot of the Whale Caller's crag, producing white surf. His ears are trained to hear these songs even at such a great distance. As the whale sails closer its outline takes shape. Patiently, he waits, occasionally blowing the horn in response to the whale's song. A crowd of curious tourists gathers behind him. Much as he strains his eyes he cannot see callosities on any part of the whale's body. Instead he sees very long flippers and a small dorsal fin that is positioned far back on the body. He begins to doubt the whale's identity. His doubts are soon confirmed by the whale's blow, almost three metres high and pear-shaped. That cannot be Sharisha. That, in fact, is not a southern right at all. It is a humpback. The dorsal fin is a further confirmation. It is a male humpback, and he guesses that it is almost fifteen metres long. As he walks down the crag he chides himself for being furious at the deceitful humpback. He should be furious with Sharisha instead. The humpback was singing its song, as humpback males are wont to do, though traditionally they sing at night, constantly composing new songs during the mating season. The deceitful humpback has started quite early in the day, perhaps practising for the nighttime mating rituals. But the deceitful humpback is not deceitful at all. Sharisha is the one who is an impostor in this case. After discovering that humpbacks were better singers than southern rights, the Whale Caller had taught Sharisha to sing like a humpback. The Whale Caller should rather be furious with himself, and not with the randy humpback. Not even with Sharisha. For the song, that is, not for Sharisha's standing him up.

He is too despondent to return to his Wendy house to finish his lunch. He slowly works his way along the cobbled path that winds down the bluff. He decides to sit on a green wooden bench that is placed near the meandering path for those who want to relax and admire the sea. He has lost sight of the humpback, which decided to sail in a different direction after it could no longer hear his alluring kelp horn. He watches a father with a fishing line leading his wife and a brood of children of varying ages. The mother gingerly holds a picnic basket. They walk precariously on the steep rocks to a hillock of boulders that juts into the sea. On this peninsula they sit down and begin to fish or just watch.

Although he regards this as his peninsula, he does not mind that the fishing and picnicking family have invaded it. He does not need it today. He usually likes to stand on it when he communes with the whales, especially when Sharisha is here. It separates him from the gawkers, be they curious locals or tourists, who'd otherwise crowd around him when he blows his horn. They never come close to him when he stands on the tip of the peninsula because they do not want to risk walking on the precarious boulders. The family obviously feels quite adventurous today.

The Whale Caller is startled by Saluni, who daintily walks down the path, holding a bunch of wilting flowers. She sits on a rock just below his bench and puts the flowers next to her. She does not give him a second look, and he decides that this time he will really stand his ground. She takes off her pencil-heel shoes and puts her feet in a pool of clear water that is separated from the rest of the ocean by a sandbank. She has given him her back and he notices her flaming locks that are tangled and are not restrained in a black net this time. He also notices that the roots are black with a few streaks of grey. He thinks she would look more dignified if she had not dyed her hair. As her dainty feet play in the water he stares at her stockings that have many runs. There are red spots in some places where Cutex nail polish was used to stop the runs. But this hasn't helped much as the runs always manage to find their way around nail polish. The stockings are obviously not pantyhose since they are tied with elastic bands just above the knees. The Whale Caller observes this when she crosses her legs and lights a cigarette in a long black holder. Her nails are manicured and painted red. She holds the cigarette holder quite elegantly; blowing delicate smoke rings in the direction of the Whale Caller. Her whole demeanour is delicate and elegant. Her clothes are clean but almost threadbare. She wears a fawn pure-wool coat over a green taffeta dress. She always has the coat on, even in the middle of summer.

After ignoring him for some time, she turns to look at him and her sun-drenched face cracks into a smile. Later the Whale Caller will learn that she is a creature of the day, hence the sun-drenched face. He averts his eyes. Once more she has triumphed. He is highly irritated by her cheek. He stands up to leave.

"May I follow you?" she asks.

"You always do . . . without asking me," he says.

"You always show anger in your eyes," says Saluni, "so I thought today I should be nice and ask."

She gives him the flowers. He is puzzled.

"What do I do with these?" he asks.

"It is a peace offering," she responds.

Now he knows why she evokes a memory of his mother. It is her smell. Not from her breath. Not the alcohol or methylated spirits. The mouldy yet sweet smell that his mother left in everything she touched. Saluni exudes the same whiff. And it overwhelms him with long-forgotten emotions. The smell has a force that seems to be stronger even than the force of energy generated by the rocks, the waves, the moon and the sun. He hates her even more for appropriating his mother's bodily odours, for reincarnating the grand old lady in the puny shape of a village drunk.

He breaks into a sweat and runs for dear life.

"I am a love child," shouts Saluni after him. "Don't do this to me, man, I am a love child!"

SALUNI She is a love child. This is what she tells everybody who cares to listen in the watering holes of Hermanus. It is a story she shares particularly with those who refuse to buy her a glass of wine. She is a love child, conceived on a windy day by a beautiful young woman who was involved in an illicit affair with an older married man. Much as the man professed his love for his young mistress, he would not leave his family for her. The pretty young thing pined for her lover for many years. She was consumed by her love until only her bones were left. For a long time she was a walking skeleton, and troubadours (yes, troubadours!) composed songs about her dire love. Then one day the bones just fell to the ground in a heap. After her mother's burial Saluni's aunts drummed it into her head that she was a love child and should be proud of it. Today she tells the habitués of the taverns that no one has the right to treat a love child shabbily. As a love child she must be handled with care and consideration.

Her mission for the day has been met with the usual failure. She is not giving up. She is relentless in her quest. She is only giving him a little respite, until next time. She decides to take the thirty-minute walk to the outskirts of town to visit the Bored Twins at their mansion. She had promised to take them to the town centre to witness some of the wonders of the festival.

She knocks at the kitchen door, but there is no response. She tries the door and it opens, but there is no one there. She walks to the girls' bedroom and to the parents' bedroom. The Bored Twins are not there either.

"Girls, where are you?" she calls.

The only response is that of multiple echoes of her own voice. She walks out to the garden. She wonders where the Bored Twins could have gone. She had expressly told them not to leave the house this whole afternoon because she would come to fetch them to sample the pleasures of the festival. They were clearly looking forward to the trip. They may just be playing a prank on her, one of their tiresome hide-and-seek games. She creeps towards the nearest rockery and looks behind it. The girls are not there. There are many other rockeries and ledges and fountains that have long dried out. This used to be a wonderfully landscaped garden in the days of the ostrich baron, made to look wild and natural in order to blend with the surroundings while at the same time standing out as a work of art. But now all its beauty is hidden in an overgrowth of tall grass and bushes. She dare not walk deeper into the garden for she is deadly scared of snakes.

"Where are you, girls?" she calls once more. "I am not in the mood to play your silly games!"

Then she remembers the cellar. It is their favourite hiding place that even their parents do not know about. She walks into the house once more and tiptoes all the way to the cellar. Her tiptoeing is to no avail because the floorboards creak and squeak all the way. In the passageway and on the steps to the basement, rats and other insects run in different directions. She hates creepy-crawlies and regrets coming all this way.

She opens the door, and there are the Bored Twins sitting on the floor, sulking! They tell Saluni that their mother has forbidden them to go with her to the festival even though their father had happily given his permission.

"Your mother can allow you to stray all over the countryside, yet she does not allow you to go to town with me?" says Saluni. "That is strange. I'll wait for her and find out why."

"She may come back late," says the smaller twin.

"It doesn't matter. I'll wait. We'll sort the matter out and then tomorrow we'll go," Saluni assures them.

"But tomorrow the radio man may not be there," moans the bigger twin.

She is referring to the local radio station, which has set up a booth at the main parking lot in town, where it broadcasts the activities of the festival live to the whole region. The presenters interview the performers, the out-of-town celebrities, the ordinary tourists and the organisers of the festival. The latter have assumed a celebrated stature in the community. Even the pastors who object to certain theatrical productions demand and are granted airtime. When Saluni noticed that there was a special slot for broadcasting music by the groups and individuals of Hermanus, she thought it would be a great idea to take the Bored Twins to the recording booth to be recorded on compact disc that would later be played on the radio. Not only would this give the Bored Twins the fame they deserve, it would also provide her with the opportunity to showcase her bluesy voice—previously enjoyed only by the girls and the denizens of the taverns—to the broader community. The man at the radio booth told her that recording sessions were being held all day long on a first-come-first-recorded basis. The Bored Twins were very excited to hear that their angelic voices would be heard on radio all over the district.

Saluni tells the twins that it is best to wait for their parents outside, since she is quite uncomfortable in the closed space of the cellar. Soon it will be dark, which will make things worse for her.

Saluni and the Bored Twins sit on the kitchen stoep, sulking. Saluni is able to sulk effectively because this afternoon she is almost sober.

When the parents finally arrive Saluni demands to know why the mother wants to deny her beautiful daughters the pleasures of the festival.

"Don't you remember that today we were supposed to record our singing on the radio?" she asks.

"That is why I don't want the girls to go to town," explains the mother. "It is this recording thing."

"You don't want people to know of the beautiful voices of your twins?" asks Saluni. "You don't want to share your children's healing voices with the world?"

"I don't want people to steal the voices of my children," says the mother.

Saluni looks at the father, hoping for an explanation that will make better sense.

"Don't blame me," says the father. "I have been trying to reason with her . . . to convince her there is nothing to fear, but she won't listen."

"Of course there is nothing to fear. Why would she think there is anything to fear?"

"She is fearful of those recording machines. She says the machines steal your voice. After singing to those machines you go home with only the speaking voice but without your singing voice."

Since no one can convince the mother otherwise, the sulking continues in the girls' room, where Saluni spends the night, with her trusty candle burning. There are no bedtime stories tonight. In the morning she puts the small piece of candle that has sur-

vived the night in her sequinned handbag, and sullenly leaves for
town to haunt the Whale Caller.

AT FIRST there is a creaking noise like the wheels of an unoiled
bicycle. It sounds as if it is just outside the Wendy house. Then
other sounds join in. More structured. More sonorous. They are
accompanied by a strong smell of salt and rotting kelp. The
Whale Caller knows at once that the sounds, like the compound
smell, come from the sea. The songs of the whales. The deeper
sounds are transmitted in tremors through the waves and the
rocks and the ground. He can feel the vibrations even as he sleeps
on his single wooden bed. The high-pitched sounds are carried by
the wind, with the smells of the sea riding on them. They penetrate the thin wooden walls of the Wendy house to massage his
body until it feels completely relaxed.

There must be a mass choir out there. There is a tremulous
bass that rises and falls as the waves drone in monotone in the
background. There is lowing and bellowing. There are deep
belches and screeching and gurgling. There are prolonged trom-
bone notes and sharp piccolo staccatos. Cymbals and brushes and
whistles join vibrating sopranos and flourishing trumpets and
subdued church organs. The Whale Caller is tempted to grab his
horn and run to the ocean to join the sublime choir. He listens for
some time, but before he can act on his temptation he is lulled
to a deep dreamless sleep.

In the morning he is not sure if he has dreamt the choir or if it
is really out there. If he has not, then there must be a whole invasion of whales in the waters of Hermanuspietersfontein. After his
ablutions and the ritual of spraying his body with essence, he
dons his new tuxedo especially for the choir that has given him so
much joy in the night. He selects Sharisha's special kelp horn and

walks to the sea. If Sharisha is not there to enjoy the tuxedo and the special horn, then he won't keep these items wasting in the Wendy house indefinitely. He will use them to welcome other whales, especially those that have given him so much pleasure with their nighttime music.

There is indeed an invasion of the southern rights. The Whale Caller can count up to twenty of them, including calves, spread over an area of a square kilometre or so. Some have come so close inshore that they are just outside the line of breakers from the beach. He stands in the morning mist and admires their stream-lined bodies, short stiff necks and enormous heads that may cover as much as a third of the whole body. He watches as the muscular tails lazily propel the huge bodies.

He hears the sound of a kelp horn, not at all like his, playing some kind of a Morse code. He knows immediately that it is the official whale crier of Hermanus, Mr. Wilson Salukazana, the gra-cious gentleman from Zwelihle Township. He is alerting the tourists to the presence and the location of the whales. People are beginning to gather. Cameras are clicking and camcorders follow the languid movement of the behemoths. Some of the creatures are playing with floating kelp, manipulating it so that the fronds rub over their backs. The Whale Caller knows that they are trying to remove parasites from their bodies. This is indicated by the callosities on the whales, which are pink or orange instead of white, a clear sign of the presence of lice.

The Whale Caller walks to his peninsula. He stands on the highest boulder and blows his horn. The whales suddenly become alert. They expel the air through their blowholes with greater vigour. He blows his horn even harder, and finds himself playing Sharisha's special song. A gigantic southern right erupts from the water, about a hundred metres from him. It rockets up in the air, and then comes crashing down with a very loud splash. As its head rises from the water again the Whale Caller's heart beats like a mad drum in his chest, for he sees the well-shaped bonnet that he knows so well, sitting gracefully on the whale's snout. White like salt. He breathes even faster when he sees the wart-like callosities on the head, also white like rough grains of salt. Not pink or orange like the callosities of other whales. They are distinctively shaped like the Three Sisters Hills of the Karoo. He blows his horn even harder, and the whale opens its mouth wide, displaying white baleen that hangs from the roof of its mouth. Not dark baleen like that of other whales. It is a smile that the Whale Caller knows so well. Sharisha's surf white smile! Once more she launches herself up in the air and falls in a massive splash. She performs these breaching displays in time with her special song that the Whale Caller blows relentlessly.

The Whale Caller changes the tune and Sharisha stops the aerial displays. She moves gently in a circle, the top of her fourteen-metre-long body gleaming in its blackness. The rest of the body below is greyish. Her skin is smooth. She breathes out white vapour from her double blowhole on top of her head and it rises up to five metres high, in a perfect V shape. Then she lies parallel to the water, and performs the tail-slapping dance that is part of the mating ritual. She lobtails repeatedly, making loud smacking sounds that leave the Whale Caller breathing more and more heavily. He blows the horn and screams as if in agony. He is drenched in sweat as his horn ejaculates sounds that rise from deep staccatos to high-pitched wails. Sharisha emits a very deep hollow sound. A prolonged, pained bellow. Then she uses her flippers to steer herself away from the Whale Caller. Breathlessly he watches her wave her flippers as she sails away.

The Whale Caller feels invigorated as he walks back from the peninsula. Even the sight of Saluni, standing near the green bench as if waiting for him, does not rile him. He smiles at her, for he is in a charitable mood today. But she seems to be in a foul mood. For the first time he feels the need to talk to her. But he does not know what to say, or how to begin. He just stands there grinning foolishly. She becomes suspicious of his motives. After all, he has never given her the time of day. You don't all of a sudden become friendly towards a village drunk unless you have some mischief up your sleeve.

"Don't mess with me now," she warns him. "I won't stand any nonsense from anyone today. A foolish woman deprived me of fame yesterday. I am pissed off!"

"See how beautiful they are! The whales, I mean. Just see!" says the Whale Caller, oblivious of her anger.

"A stupid superstitious woman."

"You see that one over there? The one sailing away? That one is Sharisha."

"You have given them names?"

"Only Sharisha."

Saluni looks at him questioningly, as if she doubts his sanity. Then she walks away, shaking her head pityingly. He is left only with the sweet mouldy smell that urges him to follow her. But he does not. Instead he decides to visit Mr. Yodd, to express his joy and give his thanks. And perhaps to gloat a little. As he walks down to the grotto the grey doves with black wings and the white seagulls with grey wings, all sporting matching red feet, share his excitement by hovering over him, and defecating on his head.

HOY, MR. YODD! Today you are talking to a fulfilled man. She is back. Sharisha has returned. She has braved man-created dangers to be with me. She has risked ships' propellers that slice curious whales at this time of the year. She has defied fishing gear entanglements and explosives from oil exploration activity to be here, Mr. Yodd. To be with yours truly. She has returned, Mr. Yodd, she has returned!

# TWO

THE DAY IS GREY from an unseasonable summer downpour, and the Whale Caller is relentless in his search for Saluni. He has been at it for days now, sniffing like a dog, hoping to catch her sweet and mouldy odour. The damp soil and the rotting kelp fill the air with smells of their own, making it impossible for him to scent her. He has returned to his old haunts, where Saluni used to materialise from nowhere with the sole aim of annoying him, but she is not there. He has walked the length of Walker Bay, which cradles Hermanus from Danger Point in the east to Mudge Point in the west. He has looked in the lagoons where tourists and adventurous locals carelessly joust with death in throwing themselves from high cliffs into the sea. In the lagoons that don't have high enough cliffs from which to dive, he has endured the deafening noise from the machines of motorised water sports enthusiasts. He has strolled on the soft white sands of Grotto Beach, the longest and largest of the beaches of Hermanus, stretching all the way eastwards to the mouth of the Klein River. He has visited other beaches as well: the Voelklip with its terraced lawns; the secluded Langbaai, popular with lovers and naturists; the Kammabaai, a haven for surfers;

the Onrus, also loved by surfers and body-boarders . . . the Plankhuis . . . the Hawston . . . the string of beaches with white sands. He has even taken his search to the Hoy's Koppie of his youth, the conical hill with caves, where he used to blow the kelp horn, sending the devout to feats of ballroom dancing on the rocky terrain and to bouts of speaking in tongues. Saluni is nowhere to be found.

He has not confided in Mr. Yodd because he knows that he will laugh at him and ridicule him. His search is mortifying enough without inviting further mortification from Mr. Yodd. He would not know how to answer if Mr. Yodd were to ask why he is looking for Saluni. Most likely Mr. Yodd does not even remember who Saluni is. Even as he trudges all over town and its environs he is not aware what power compels him to search for her with such desperation. Only that when she did not materialise for many days he became unsettled. He felt that something was missing in his life—the same kind of emptiness he felt when Sharisha had not returned from the southern seas. Yet Sharisha's spectacular breaching still graces the waters of Hermanus. Every morning he still stands on the highest boulder of his peninsula and blows his kelp horn that inspires astounding aerial displays. How can he feel a void when he has Sharisha all to himself? The sweet and mouldy smell!

He begins to blame himself. Perhaps if he had paid some attention to Saluni, if he had not ignored her so, she would not have vanished. He knows nothing about her, where she lives, what she does when she is not stalking him. He does not know where to look for her, save to wait at his own haunts, and at all sorts of touristy places, hoping she will show up. It doesn't occur to him to search in the taverns of Hermanus. That's where anyone else would have begun the search. Saluni is famous as a village drunk.

If the Whale Caller had paid a visit to the taverns and pubs of Hermanus—those that are patronised by fisherfolk, labourers and layabouts rather than the bars at luxury hotels—he would have known that her disappearance has nothing to do with him. He would have heard the story, told in toothless and frothy mirth, of how Saluni had developed a rash all over her body, as if she had rolled in poison ivy. The rash, however, had not been caused by poison ivy, but by a hairy millipede that the Bored Twins found outside their bedroom window and secretly placed in her bra one morning after she had spent a night of storytelling and celestial singing and snoring with them. In the morning she dressed hurriedly without noticing the millipede snuggling in her B-cup.

As soon as she walked out of the mansion the millipede began to take a walk in her bosom. She jumped up and down screaming. As she spun in the air and landed on the ground with great force the millipede crawled to what it deemed to be safer parts of her body, and tried to take sanctuary in any nook or cranny that it could find. She danced about in blind panic, ripping off her perpetual coat. The twins were standing just outside the kitchen door, laughing their angelic laughter and clapping their sweet little hands as she stripped her blouse, and then her skirt, all the while screaming and cursing the girls with their mother's genitalia for laughing at her. The millipede was wiggling all over her body since even the nooks and crannies were opening and closing quite violently in her frenzied dance. Soon the petticoat was off, and then the bra. She was waving these garments about, shaking them, hoping that whatever creature was hiding in them would drop off. The shaking became frantic until she collapsed on the ground, foaming at the mouth.

Only then did the Bored Twins realise the serious consequence of their game. They tried to revive Saluni by pouring water on her face, all the while crying, "Sorry, auntie . . . sorry, auntie." They were struck with terror when they saw a red rash erupting all over her naked body, right before their eyes. It seemed to be flaming where the millipede had walked, leaving a trail of hair that stuck out of her skin like red villi on a fruit. Her girlish breasts had the most hair and it looked almost like bristle.

After a minute or so she regained consciousness. The girls were relieved to see that she was not dead. They were all over her, confessing their crime, and accusing each other of initiating the prank. She gathered her clothes and put them on, without uttering a word to the Bored Twins, who kept on crying, "Sorry, auntie . . . sorry, auntie!" They were jumping all around her, hoping to hear her say that she had forgiven them. But she walked away without giving them a second look. She went back to town and back to the taverns. As she sat in a favourite watering hole, drinking wine and relating how the Bored Twins almost killed her in spite of her being a love child, her body was itching all over. She was obviously ill, and the habitués, despite the fact that they had found the story quite funny at first, became concerned. "Whose children are these who play such cruel games on the love child?" they asked. She found herself defending them: "I am sure they didn't mean any harm. They were playing. They wouldn't want to harm me on purpose. They are angels."


On this grey afternoon the Whale Caller's relentlessness weakens. He makes a determined effort to forget about Saluni for a while and pay more attention to Sharisha. He will resume the search some other day, for he cannot give her up altogether. At the very least he wants to know what became of her. For now he needs something that will raise his spirits . . . that will make him soar from the depths of depression in which he has been wallowing lately. And only Sharisha can do that. He goes back to the Wendy house to fetch Sharisha's special horn.

He does not need to go to his peninsula because there are no spectators today. They have run away from the rain that is threatening to fall again. They don't know how to deal with a wet summer, for this is a region of winter rains. He stands on one of the crags at Walker Bay and blows his horn. The whales are taking advantage of the privacy, and a group of them have assembled a hundred metres from where he stands. He performs a small jig, for he will have fun today without gawking eyes. Not only will he enjoy Sharisha's joyful splashes, he will have a whole spectacle of magical performances by the rest of the whales. Already they are performing without any prompting from him.

He blows his horn, punctuating each splash with a siren-like wail, but suddenly stops when he notices something odd. Usually the southern rights that are seen close inshore are females, sometimes with calves. But the whales today are distinctly males, about five of them. He has learnt to spot the elusive difference. While some are engaged in the most exhibitionist breaching, others are circling around a spyhopping whale. They are lobtailing, repeatedly slapping the surface of the water with their tails. The Whale Caller blows Sharisha's song when he sees the callosities on the head that is sticking out of the water—the snout of the spyhopping whale has a perfect bonnet of pure white callosities. It is, of course, Sharisha, and the males are competing for her attentions. Each one is displaying its best moves in an attempt to seduce her.

The Whale Caller is suddenly seized by a fit of jealousy. He yells at the males, calling them names and shooing them away from his Sharisha. He shouts: "Rapists! You are nothing but a gang of rapists!" But they do not pay any attention to him. They make a concerted effort to reach Sharisha. The Whale Caller blows his horn once again, and this time it surely catches Sharisha's attention. She thrusts her whole body out of the water in a graceful leap, and splashes down a short distance away from the horny males. He blows once more, hoping for another breaching leap that will take her away from them once and for all. But she seems to be teasing them. She seems to want them to come and have her. The Whale Caller feels betrayed. But he does not give up. He will yet get them away from her. His confidence in her increases when he realises that Sharisha is not really inviting them for any hanky-panky but is tricking them into taking one direction while she takes an evasive action in another direction. The Whale Caller cannot help laughing and applauding and shouting: "That's my Sharisha!"

But he has become gleeful too soon. A persistent male is in hot pursuit while others seem to give up hope. She flees into shallow waters, hoping that the male will give up the chase. But the male is eager to have her even at the risk of stranding himself. She rolls onto her back, and the male reaches her. She submits. They lie belly to belly and copulate. The Whale Caller tries to save Sharisha from this rape by blowing his horn and creating havoc in a discordant tune. The other males are not deterred by the discord; they charge towards the mating couple. The mating is brief and each of the males has her, then sails away. By the time the fourth male is lying belly to belly with her the Whale Caller has given up in exasperation. In no time the feast is over and Sharisha sails away; only her flukes can be seen above the water . . . sailing further and further away from him.

"They have done it! They have ravaged Sharisha!" mutters the Whale Caller as he walks back to his Wendy house.

He thinks about it at night, this ravaging of Sharisha. Perhaps it is a good thing for her. Unlike humans, whales don't indulge in such acts for recreation but for procreation. Sharisha will have a calf next time she returns from the southern seas. And he is blessed for he was there at its conception. He was a participant with his horn. He feels like a father already.

Then a scary thought strikes him. What if Sharisha is about to go back to the southern seas? What if what he witnessed yesterday afternoon was a final romp, a farewell orgy? Southern rights mate in winter. Like the rains, this friskiness in the middle of summer is unseasonable. Perhaps it is heralding her return to the southern seas, though others will be here for another month or two. Sharisha may be on her way to the southern seas already. He jumps out of bed, has a quick wash in a plastic basin, dons the black tie, grabs his horn and runs to the crag. It is dawn and he can hear the songs of the whales. Humpbacks, he concludes. The songs are structured and high-pitched. It can only be the songs of the humpbacks. They are communicating with other humpbacks that may be on breeding grounds hundreds of miles away, for their sound carries well under water. Southern rights sing their songs in a much lower frequency.

The Whale Caller is pleasantly surprised to see Sharisha close inshore, singing her big heart out. Once again she has learnt to sing like a humpback, a skill she had once acquired but unlearnt in the southern seas. How she does it remains a mystery, for only humpbacks are able to produce the pulsed clicks that Sharisha is producing now. There is a look of fulfilment about her.

The Whale Caller joins in the music with his kelp horn and to-gether they sing until the sun rises. Sharisha has indeed managed to make him forget Saluni.

SALUNI. She refuses to be forgotten. She is discovered sitting in front of the *Hermanus Roll of Honour*, above the Old Harbour with the brittle boats. She is guarded by two big grey guns on both sides of the stone column. Cannons of a bygone era. Both plaques of the roll of honour—nailed onto the column and freshly pol-ished by enthusiastic war veterans for the Kalfiefees—reflect a tired yellow light that forms a halo above her head. The sun has returned today. The first panel, older and duller, has eleven names, citizens of Hermanus who died in World War One (1914–1918), and another list of twenty-eight names of those who "gave their lives for freedom" in World War Two (1939–1945). The brighter panel has only four names, citizens of Hermanus who were killed in some war that is not mentioned. It is described only as the *Republic of South Africa Roll of Honour* (*1973–1979*). They dare not even whisper the name of the war, for they died on the border defending apartheid.

She looks as if she is part of the monument, surrounded by the spiky silver-coloured chain that enhances the monument's militariness. She sits on the ground, her head now buried between her knees. No more halo. She is exhausted from carousing with sailors till the early hours of the morning. She is a battle-scarred soldier nursing old wounds. The tourists who are congregated like New Age worshippers behind the monument ignore her. They are more interested in getting their turn at the orange telescope that is next to the marble altar with pictures of today's deities—a humpback and a southern right—and the sacred inscription: *Whale-Viewing Site—Indawo Yokubukela Iminenga.*

Saluni. She is merged with the monument and is in a world of dreams when the Whale Caller, on his way to Mr. Yodd, discovers her. At first he mistakes her for a mangy dog licking its wounds. But when he gets closer he sees the familiar red hair and red stilettos. And black fishnet stockings this time.

"Why did you disappear?" he demands, without ceremony.

She is startled only a little, and looks up at him. Her hangovered eyes betray amusement even though she pretends to be annoyed. She snarls at him: "Can't a lady take a nap without being rudely awoken by some . . . handsome . . . gentleman?"

The Whale Caller insists: "Why did you disappear?"

"From where?" she asks.

"From everywhere. You just vanished. People don't just vanish like that."

"Be a sport, will you? Get me something to drink."

"I have been looking for you everywhere," he says in anguish.

"Okay, now you found me."

Just like that. As if it was the most natural thing for him to look for her! As if she had been waiting there to be found by him! As if they have been looking for and finding each other all their lives!

"So please get me a drink of water," she says. "My throat is on fire."

"I'll do better than water. I'll get you something else to extinguish that fire."

He buys her a vanilla and caramel cone from an ice cream vendor. She snatches it as if it is something he has always owed her. Not even a "thank you." She licks it with exaggerated delicacy.

"Now that you have found me what do you plan to do about it?" she asks.

"I don't know. I was off to some place on some business," he says lamely. "I didn't imagine I'd find you here."

"And all along I thought you were a man of boundless imagination! What is the business *some place* that you are off to?"

He can't tell her about Mr. Yodd. That he was going to his grotto to confess about her. The whole thing would sound foolish to her. He feels awkward and doesn't know what to say next. She is now standing up and looking him straight in the eye. He is flustered and her amusement irritates him.

"So, what happened to you?" he finally asks.

"Nothing happened. I just got sick. Had a rash all over my body. Had to stay in bed for two weeks."

"Sorry to hear that," he says. "There must be some bug doing the rounds."

Then an idea strikes him: "Do you want to look at the whales? Let's go and see the whales."

"What for?"

"I thought you liked whales. I see you every day when I am blowing my horn. Before you had the rash, I mean."

"I don't come here to watch the whales. I come here to watch you."

She enjoys standing there watching him squirm in embarrassment. He realises that he looks foolish but does not know what to do about it. If he could he would wipe the smirk off her face.

"I like you . . . not the whales," she adds. "That horn of yours!"

"I must go now . . . somebody is expecting me."

But he does not go. He stands there timidly, watching her lick the ice cream and chew the cone with suggestive sensuality, all the while looking deep into his eyes. He would like to change the embarrassing direction of this conversation, but he is at a loss for words. She saves him by blurting out: "What's your fascination with whales, anyway? They look stupid."

Now he is offended.

"They are beautiful," he says.

"Beautiful? They have all those ugly warts on their ugly heads!"

"They are not warts . . . they are callosities . . . and they are beautiful . . . and . . . and those southern rights are graceful . . . and they are big."

"Not big enough. The blue whale, yes . . . if they were the blue whale, then I would respect them."

"How would you know about the blue whale? I am sure you have never seen one. They don't come close to shore."

"It is the biggest mammal on earth . . . that I know for sure. But these whales of yours, they are like toys . . . they don't tickle my fancy . . . they are too small for me."

He feels insulted. He walks away from her without another word. Why on earth was he searching for such an obnoxious person?

"If you were a whale you would be the blue whale," she calls after him, laughing.

He does not look back. He must get as far away as possible from such indecorous remarks. The sweet and mouldy smell follows him for a while but fizzles out as he gets further away from her cackling.

Without thinking much about it Saluni takes the direction of the mansion. She has not seen the Bored Twins for two weeks and she misses them: their peals of laughter, their singing, their storytelling. The singing, especially, has a healing effect, and she can do with some of that at this time. If they had sung for her at the worst moment of her rash, she is certain it would have healed quicker. But then she had misguidedly made up her mind that she never wanted to see them again, ever. Now she has forgiven the dear hearts. She yearns for them. Hopefully they are not out there in the marshes playing in the mud and plucking off the wings of butterflies, letting them suffer a lifetime of crawling without the benefit of flight. Or breaking the legs of the praying mantis, punishing them for feeding on other insects. Their parents are likely to be working in the vineyards. At harvesttime they leave home at five in the morning and only return after seven at night. If this is not the season for such work—Saluni does not bother to follow the cycles of the vine, except to imbibe what comes from the grape—the parents will be in the townships and villages of the district, collecting scrap metal in a donkey-drawn cart and selling it at the recycling centre. The Bored Twins, she feels, need her because they are all alone throughout the day. She cannot bear a grudge and let the little angels suffer.

The Bored Twins are not at home. Saluni coos: "Come home, Bored Twins, all is forgiven!" There is no response, except for the echoes from the mansion. Some of their raggedy dolls and assorted home-made toys are strewn outside. They must have been playing here not so long ago. They have strayed to the swamps in defiance of their parents. Saluni is not up to searching in all the swamps and marshes in the countryside; she goes back to town and to Walker Bay.

Saluni. She sits on a rock next to the emerald green water. She watches plankton floating among the ragged rocks and seagulls scavenging among humans. She is entertained by a group of seagulls feeding on the umbilical cords hanging from newborn seal pups.

THE WHALE CALLER DESCENDS to Mr. Yodd's grotto. The shadows have fallen on most of the crag. But the water in the shallows is still emerald green from the light. The depths are still blue. He peers into the grotto. No rock rabbits today. They can't be asleep so early. They must be out overturning garbage cans near the monument, spreading out a banquet for the scavenging seagulls.

HOY, MR. YODD. Have you ever heard of such an outrage? Too small for her! All of sixteen metres long and more than sixty tons in weight, and yet they are too small for the beauty whose face has been battered by wine. She is the kind that puts a premium on size, I see, and she finds Sharisha wanting. That mountain of a lady with the Three Sisters on her head, she disparages her. She finds every southern right wanting. She may as well find *me* wanting. You can't bank on the fact that she has called me a flattering name, which was more on the indecent side, if you ask me. You want to know what she called me, Mr. Yodd? She called me a blue whale. Don't laugh, Mr. Yodd. You don't think I have it in me to be a blue whale? Whatever you think, Mr. Yodd, she sees a blue whale in me. Very big and very strong. Pulsating with hot blood. Blue whales are not just the largest mammals on earth; they are the largest mammals that ever lived. Their size is legendary, the stuff of many tales. I bet it was a blue whale that swallowed Jonah. Jonah can't have been swallowed by anything lesser. Okay, I am a southern right man, as you rightly point out. Everyone knows that. The lady knows that too because she has watched me blow for the southern rights. But I can be a blue whale too if she wants me to be one. I can be her blue whale. And you know what, Mr. Yodd, I was born to be a blue whale, now that I think of it. Blue whales are not common. They are unattainable. Like me . . . can't get . . . can't buy . . . can't deposit! They are not for the land-bound. They are out there, hundreds of miles into the ocean. You don't toy with a blue whale, Mr. Yodd. Unless you are a Norwegian, a Japanese or an Icelandic whaler. Those whalers don't care if you are a blue whale or a sperm whale or any kind of whale. In the name of culture and tradition, they harpoon you . . . just as their forebears killed whales and reduced their blubber to oil in trypots. You can laugh as much as you like, I am a blue whale. Orcas? What are orcas? Killer whales, of course! It is just like you, Mr. Yodd, to bring up something like that just to rain on the blue whale's parade. Orcas! Ferocious they are, for they devour seals and dolphins without any mercy. Yes, I do know that they themselves are dolphins. Perhaps you stretch it too far when you say they are cannibalistic dolphins for they don't eat other killer whales. They eat the harmless man-loving dolphins. The trusting ones that man has always betrayed. Killer whales are much smaller than the blue whale, yet they have been known to attack blue whales and tear them to pieces for lunch. So what's the use of the blue whale's great size, you ask, if it can be eaten by a dolphin one-tenth its weight? And you say if I am a blue whale, then Saluni is my killer whale? Saluni will never be my killer whale. You can say that about her because you don't know her.

You are right, I don't know her either. But I have talked to her at least. She is a lady. She doesn't strike me as a killer whale. You are still laughing! You are laughing at me, Mr. Yodd! I suspect tears are running down your cheeks. And I can tell you, if you are doing what I think you are doing—rolling on the ground—you look undignified. Okay, okay! Maybe it's not such a great idea after all. Maybe I am not a blue whale at all. She got it all wrong; I am not a blue whale.

THE USUAL MORTIFICATION after confession. And this time he feels it weighing heavily on his shoulders. When you are carrying a load of mortification it is as if everyone you meet can see it. You want to steer away from people. You want the security of the wilderness. But it is not possible to have that in a town like Hermanus, especially at a place like Walker Bay. The eyes of the world are on him. The world has joined Mr. Yodd in his guffaws.

Sharisha. That will be the balm that heals his heart. Sharisha never judges him. Never makes fun of his insecurities. She will bring back his shattered dignity. He feels guilty that she, who is usually the subject of confession to Mr. Yodd, did not feature at all this time. Only Saluni. The whole confession was about Saluni. Once more he is attacked by feelings of guilt. Despite the weight on his shoulders he walks faster. He has a good idea where Sharisha might be at this time of the day. If she is not there he will blow his horn and play her song and she will manifest herself by breaching. Even if she is not that close to shore he will know it is Sharisha because when he plays the horn she breaches rapidly, up to fifteen times in a row, keeping to the rhythm of the horn. She doesn't have to be close to shore to respond to him because the sound of the horn, like the songs of the whales, carries for many kilometres.

He doesn't have to walk far, for there is Sharisha rubbing her head against the kelp. She must be irritated by lice. Normally Sharisha's callosities are free of lice; that is why they are surf white and not pink or orange or even yellow like those of other southern rights. It seems now lice are beginning to infest her, and the Whale Caller suspects it is from the randy males who had their way with her the other day. Although whale lice are quite harmless, they can irritate the joy out of a whale. Sharisha does look annoyed.

He stands there for some time, watching her struggle with the floating kelp. But soon his attention is drawn to a prolonged cough just below the crag. There is Saluni sitting on a rock, her feet in the emerald green water. Her coat is spread on the rock next to her, and her dress is up to her waist. With her thumbnails she is crushing lice from the seams of her petticoat. She seems oblivious of Sharisha, only a hundred metres from her. The Whale Caller walks down to her.

"Oh, so now you found me again!" she says. "You are not doing badly at this finding business."

"I was not looking for you this time," says the Whale Caller apologetically. "I was looking for Sharisha."

"Oh, Sharisha! The big fish you have named."

"She is not a fish," he says emphatically. "A whale is not a fish."

"A whale . . . a fish . . . same difference! You don't have to get so worked up about it. I wouldn't lose any sleep over it if I were you."

"Look at her, she is beautiful," he says with the pride of someone who has a stake in that beauty. "She is the queen of all southern rights. See her white callosities! See the regal wave of her flippers! See the bonnet of callosity on the tip of her snout!"

"How do you know the damn thing is female?"

"She is a woman all right."

"I can tell you I saw his thingy when he was jumping out of the water causing all that racket and disturbing the peace."

The Whale Caller chuckles in spite of himself.

"Even if she were male you wouldn't know where to look for *his thingy*."

"You don't want to admit that you have gone gaga over a male. And you are so big and strong and muscular and . . . hard . . . I hope. Nothing camp about you at all."

"I won't stand for this kind of talk," he says angrily. "You should be ashamed of yourself."

"It shouldn't bother you one bit. It is allowed. You were there when I was telling the pastors that it is even in the constitution of the country."

"I won't argue with you about Sharisha. I know what I know."

She goes back to the business of crushing her lice. Sharisha thrusts her massive body up in the air, dives back into the water and doesn't emerge again. She does this sometimes: dives in the water and stays many metres under the surface for up to half an hour without coming up for a breath.

"Don't you dare think that I normally go around carrying lice on my body," she says all of a sudden. "I am a lady, you know? I was sick. For two weeks nobody washed my things. With the damn rash my whole body was in pain. I couldn't do a damn thing for myself."

"I didn't say anything."

"Just so you know."

SALUNI. She arrives at the Wendy house. She has come to visit, but has no intention of ever leaving. That is why she is carrying a suitcase with all her worldly possessions. She has taken him up on his offer, made in a moment of weakness, to come over for a thorough sprucing-up that will destroy her lice once and for all. He welcomes her with a hot cup of cream of mushroom soup, and then prepares a hot bath for her. He pours in the water the pungent solution that is usually used as sheep dip.

"Look the other way while I take my clothes off," she says with a naughty twinkle in her voice.

"Actually, I am leaving," he says as he dashes out of the room.

"I was only joking! Come back! I don't have a problem if you watch!"

But he is already out. She curses his cowardice under her breath, strips naked and gets into the enamel bathtub. She screams that the solution is burning her body. He shouts back from the second room—used as a kitchen—that it is all for the best because it will kill all the vermin that is feeding on her body.

"You may come in and scrub my back if you like," she calls out.

"I would rather not," he responds.

"You are a shy one, aren't you?" she observes. "I like that in a man."

After the bath she spends the rest of the day wrapped up in a blanket because all her clothes—including those that were in the suitcase—have been soaked in the solution, and then hung on the washing line outside to dry. She goes to bed early in the evening, her body still burning from the solution. She finds it difficult to sleep, especially because it has been many years since she slept sober. Well . . . almost sober . . . because she did take a secret sip of the methylated spirits that he uses for cleaning his tuxedo. She lies awake for a long time, listening to him pottering about in the kitchen, and wondering when he will sneak into bed. But he never does. He spends the night in a sleeping bag in the kitchen.

The Whale Caller wakes up after midnight to see a light through the cracks of her door. He thinks that she has forgotten to switch off the light. He tiptoes to the bedroom and flicks off the switch near the door. As he tiptoes back to his sleeping bag he is stopped in his tracks by a shrill scream from the bedroom.

"I wasn't trying to do anything," he assures her. "I was just switching off the light."

"Never do that again! Where is the fuckin' switch?"

He rushes back into the bedroom to switch on the light. And there she is, standing on the floor, naked, looking quite witless and bewildered.

"Never ever do that again! I hate the dark! I do not sleep in the dark! I do not walk in the dark! I do not do anything in the dark, in case you are the kind of man who does it only in the dark! Do you understand me?"

"I would not want to do anything with you in the dark," he says defensively. "I was switching off the light because I thought you had forgotten to switch it off."

"Just never switch the light off again, that's all."

The Whale Caller apologises, and goes back to his sleeping bag.

When Saluni finally wakes up in the morning the aches of the sheep dip are gone. But her body is racked by something worse than a hangover—the pain of sobriety. A long-forgotten feeling! Her clothes are on the chair next to the bed, all neatly ironed. After a quick wash in the plastic basin, and an application of makeup from her sequinned handbag, she wears her green taffeta dress and her black fishnet stockings and her red pencil-heel shoes and her fawn pure-wool coat. Her wild red hair is restrained in a black net. Once more her former state of elegance has been restored. With it the mouldy yet sweet smell.

It strikes the Whale Caller that she has taken all the fuss over her in her stride, as if being pampered is her birthright. Not a word of gratitude. This does not bother him. It is just an observation for its own sake.

She has been around for three weeks, and he has got used to her presence and to her haunting odour. She has become his shadow, except on Bored Twins days. Once in a while she makes herself useful by collecting seashells and arranging them on the wooden wall, sticking them on with glue as some form of decoration. Or by cooking an early morning millet meal porridge which they eat with milk for breakfast. She cooks only when she is hungry and he is too occupied with other things to cook at that time. At most times she just sits there for the whole day and expects to be fed and groomed and mollycoddled. He enjoys brushing and disentangling her red locks. Sometimes he braids them crudely. This activity always makes her body tingle.

When she has been to the mansion and has brought back a bottle of wine, she spends the day following him doing his rounds with the whales, while she occasionally takes a sip from her bottle, and collects the seashells. She nurses the bottle: the Whale Caller has vowed that he will not buy her wine because he'd rather she stopped drinking.

Occasionally she spends the night at the mansion and comes back the next day quite radiant and euphoric. On such days she never stops talking about the Bored Twins and their beauty and their singing and how they are such angels.

"You are the one who always visits them," says the Whale Caller. "Why don't we ever see them coming here to see you?"

"They can't come to town on their own," Saluni explains. "Their parents work all day long. Their mother doesn't want them to come to town anyway, because she thinks someone will steal their voices. I go there to keep an eye on them because they are always all alone."

In the first week at the Wendy house she spent the evenings at the taverns drinking and singing with her mates. She staggered back to the Wendy house, sometimes at three in the morning. She found him asleep in his sleeping bag in the kitchen and never woke him up. Instead she crept into her bed, leaving the lights on. However drunk she might be, she never forgot to leave the lights on. In the morning he would patiently warn her of the dangers of walking alone at night. She would only laugh and say: "You are beginning to behave like a husband . . . which is rather sweet. It would be sweeter if you did other husbandly things too."

But by the end of the second week she had stopped going to the taverns, and she made a whole fanfare of it. She announced grandly: "I have stopped for your sake . . . to make you happy." So, indeed, he should be grateful for such a wonderful gift. Now she spends all her time between the mansion and the Wendy house, and between the Wendy house and the beach.

He has taught her to waltz to the songs of the whales. These are the most exhilarating moments of his life. Sharisha has gone back to the southern seas, but other southern rights are still here, providing the music. Sometimes a humpback visits and adds its thrilling notes. At dawn the Whale Caller wakes Saluni up and together they go to the Voelklip beach. Sometimes, more often of late, it is Saluni who wakes him up, since now she has got into the spirit of things. If the whales happen not to be there that dawn he calls them with his horn and they respond. He gets hold of Saluni and together they float on the sand as if they are riding the clouds, as he used to float, albeit on a rocky surface, during his days at the Church of the Sacred Kelp Horn.

At first Saluni was not too excited about these early morning frolics. But she decided to indulge him, especially after he had deserted her for the whole day and night to be with Sharisha on the eve of her departure.

Saluni had only been staying with him in the Wendy house for about ten days when one night the Whale Caller had a nightmare: Sharisha was being attacked by hordes of killer whales. The deadly orcas were concentrating mostly on the callosities, biting chunks away. The water around her was red. He woke up screaming. He knew at once that Sharisha would be leaving soon. Nightmares were her way of communicating that to him. He rushed to the bedroom and woke Saluni up to tell her of his fears. She was not pleased at all; especially because her head was pounding from a hangover. The previous night she had finished a whole bottle of wine brought from the mansion, while watching the Whale Caller cook his staple of macaroni and cheese. The drinking had continued while they ate the supper and while he washed the plates and pot. He had gone to sleep in the kitchen as usual, leaving her sitting on the bed, pretending to be in some tavern; singing colourful songs and cracking dirty jokes to herself, then rocking the Wendy house with her gruff laughter. To be woken up so early in the morning on account of bad dreams about whales was not something she was ready to entertain.

She shouted: "You and that ugly fish! I hope it goes away . . . forever! Maybe we'll have some peace when it's gone."

Without another word, the Whale Caller dressed up in his tuxedo, took his horn and left Saluni in bed nursing her precious hangover.

This time he went to his peninsula where he knew the curious could only watch from a distance. He blew his kelp horn, praying that Sharisha had not migrated yet. Her head emerged from the water, only fifty metres away. She rose out of the water and then crashed down with a loud splash. Refreshing droplets sprayed him. She rose again, turned in the air above the water, and then, with her back arched, fell backwards on the water, with a yet louder splash. Seagulls flocked to pick up from the surface of the water pieces of skin that she had shed as she breached. There would be some lice to pick up too, now that she had been infested.

Sharisha breached like that repeatedly, increasing the pace as the Whale Caller got more excited.

The rising sun found him sitting on a rock and blowing his kelp horn. Sharisha responded with her own love calls. She rocked in the water in a mating dance. The Whale Caller stood up and rocked on the rocks. He raised his left leg, turned and twisted on one spot, then stamped the foot down. He did the same with the right leg. He repeated this dance in rapid succession for a long time, whilst blowing the sounds of the whining wind. People gathered on the shore and watched. Even those who had regularly watched the Whale Caller at his antics with the whales had never seen anything like this before. He did not seem to tire. He just went on and on raising his legs, spinning his sturdy body in the air, and then stamping his feet on the rocks. Sharisha did not seem to tire either. She was creating a whirlwind on the water by making a complicated combination of rocking, breaching and lob-tailing. The rocking part—moving from side to side, and then forwards and backwards—fascinated the onlookers most for they had never seen a whale do anything like that.

By midday Saluni was getting very worried about him. She could hear the horn from the Wendy house. There was a particular timbre of sadness in it that she could not stand. The very thought that he was with Sharisha infuriated her. At first she wanted to go down there and drag him out of his foolish trance. But her pride would not let her do that. Instead she went to the mansion. Even as she was playing and singing with the Bored Twins, picking the tulips that grew like wild flowers among the shrubs, her mind was at the rocky peninsula, wondering what the Whale Caller and Sharisha were up to at that moment. She was confident that when she returned to the Wendy house in the late afternoon, the Whale Caller would be over his madness. He would be waiting for her with a bowl of macaroni and cheese, as he always did.

But Saluni had not reckoned with the power of the whirlwind that Sharisha was generating in the sea, locking the Whale Caller tightly in her embrace. The sun was about to set and the Whale Caller had not returned. Saluni swallowed her pride and went down to the shore. The biggest crowd she had ever seen at his whale-calling events had gathered. People were clapping their hands in accompaniment to the kelp horn. And to Sharisha's grunts and groans. It reminded Saluni of the charismatic church services that were sometimes held in circus-like tents by visiting superstar pastors. People babbling things whose meaning no one could fathom, then falling on the ground shouting the name of the Lord and foaming at the mouth. When they woke up they were saved and their road to Heaven was guaranteed. Only here the things they were babbling had nothing to do with the Lord. While some were egging the Whale Caller on, others were directing their encouragement to the whale. There were those who were just screaming and whimpering, as if they shared the ecstasy of the man and his whale.

Saluni decided to stop the whole circus once and for all. She tried to walk across the precarious rocks to the tip of the peninsula where the Whale Caller continued his dance oblivious of the world around him.

"Hey, what is she trying to do? She will fall into the water," said a breathless spectator.

"It's Saluni the village drunk," observed another. "She must be zonked as usual."

"Where do you think you are going, Saluni?" the people asked.

"To stop this whole nonsense," said Saluni, trying to keep her balance by stretching her arms out and stepping delicately on the sharp rocks.

"She's gone bonkers," someone said. "She is going to kill herself in her madness."

It was obvious that she would not make it, especially in her state of inebriation. She walked back to the shore and stood there in front of everyone. She shouted at the Whale Caller: "Come on, man, stop your rubbish with that fish and come back home!"

But the Whale Caller did not come home that evening. He did not come home that night either. The spectators went to their homes and to their hotels to sleep. Sharisha and the Whale Caller continued their dance unabated. Deep in the night the wails of his horn could be heard, sometimes sounding like a muted cornet and at others like a "last post" bugle, and then picking up again in the fast-paced scatting of a demented jazz singer. In the cool breeze of the night, and with the absence of spectators, the dance became even more frenzied. His horn penetrated deep into every aperture of the whale's body, as if in search of a soul in the midst of all the blubber.

The next morning the dance continued. Spectators returned and found the Whale Caller drenched in sweat. Both his horn and Sharisha were groaning deeply like out-of-tune tubas. Both were breathless as the dance seemed to be slowly fizzling out.

It was almost midday when Sharisha sailed away waving her flipper and the Whale Caller found his steps back to the shore. The crowd was going crazy, screaming, making catcalls and applauding. As soon as he reached the shore he fell on the ground in utter exhaustion. He was drenched in sweat and other secretions of the body. The front and the seat of his tuxedo pants were wet and sticky from the seed of life.

He opened his eyes and smiled at the wide eyes that were looking at him from above. The people went even wilder with applause. Saluni was among them. But she was not participating in all the excitement. She just stood there, arms akimbo, shouting at him: "You have shamed yourself . . . and me!"

"The people of Hermanuspietersfontein don't seem to think so," he said softly, and promptly fell asleep right there on the ground. The crowd gathered around them and some wondered who the people of Hermanuspietersfontein were.

"He means us," one of them offered helpfully. "It is what this town used to be called . . . after the shepherd and teacher who came down the mountain past the Hemel-en-Aarde valley and set up camp here almost two hundred years ago . . . before the land was stolen from the Khoikhoi."

"It is a foolish name. It belongs to an old world. Does he miss the past?"

"He does not care about the origins of the name," said Saluni defensively. "He just likes the old name. He says it rolls nicely on the tongue."

"He may think he hasn't got a political agenda by insisting on a name that no one uses anymore. Everything in South Africa is political."

"What has that got to do with his dance? I ask."

The people were arguing about the merits of the name as they left. They had forgotten all about the satisfaction he had given them with his dance. Saluni remained there, sitting on the ground guarding him. If she had had the strength she would have carried him back to the Wendy house.

It was after this experience that Saluni decided to go along with his mad suggestion that they should welcome the dawn of a new day with a waltz on the beach. She felt that perhaps if she indulged him, and sometimes even pampered him—within reasonable limits, of course, for a man can easily get spoilt if he is too pampered—he would forget about Sharisha. So, that first morning she reluctantly went to the beach, and to her surprise found that she actually enjoyed it. She caught on very fast, and soon enough she was floating as well as the Whale Caller.

Now the dance has got into her, to the extent that she is often the one who wakes the Whale Caller up even when he is too lazy to go waltzing in the morning. She hopes that their discovery of something that they can do together will make him appreciate her more, and will bind them together, until she becomes indispensable. It also helps her keep a close eye on him lest he gets entangled with another whale. Unfortunately she can't be with him all the time, because sometimes she needs to quench her addiction to the Bored Twins. She needs the healing voices that cleanse both her body and her soul. But she also needs the wine with which the parents reward her occasionally. Of late the bottles are becoming scarcer, because the vineyard owners are under pressure from the workers themselves to stop the practice of paying them with bottles of wine. The vineyard owners are now gradually resorting to paying their labourers with the normal currency that is legal tender in the rest of South Africa. And this is not good news for Saluni.

She goes to the mansion, spends the day with the Bored Twins and returns empty-handed. Even though the Whale Caller has refused to buy her wine on previous occasions, she asks him all the same, and once more he says no. She pesters him as he potters around the Wendy house, but he stubbornly stands his ground.

"You can't do this to me, man," she pleads. "You stopped me from going to the taverns where my mates bought me all the wine in the world."

"You stopped for your own good," says the Whale Caller.

"I stopped for you, man . . . I did it for you . . . Now look what I get."

The Whale Caller ignores her and continues to look for things to occupy the hands that are unable to stay idle. He sits on the bed and polishes his shoes.

"I will drink all the methylated spirits in the house if you don't buy me a bottle of wine."

"Ah, you have been drinking my methylated spirits! I was wondering why a bottle that used to last me for months is now getting finished so quickly."

"Please don't make me beg, man. I hate begging."

"I should have known it's you! I don't clean my suit that often. Since she left I don't get to wear it at all."

"Everything is about the fish, eh? Even when it's not here! What about me? What about my feelings? What about my needs?"

"Even when I used to light a primus stove with methylated spirits . . . before I had this Wendy house wired for electricity . . . the methylated spirits lasted longer than it does since you came here."

"I am a love child, man," she screams almost hysterically. "You can't do this to me; I am a love child!"

She blurts out the story of her conception, as she has told it numerous times before in the taverns of Hermanus—with the variations that the habitués of the taverns know so well. To the Whale Caller, of course, the version he hears today is the first one.

She was conceived on a rainy day by a beautiful teenager who was involved in an illicit love affair with a married man. Under a corrugated iron roof whose noise in the rain swallowed their moans of pleasure. Rain changed to hail, and at that moment the man hit the right spot and the seed was planted. The young woman was completely smitten with him, and hoped that now she was carrying his child, she would have him all to herself forever. But it was not to be. When the older man refused to leave his aged wife for her, she was devastated. She fell into a deep depression. She was consumed by the flames of love until she lost her mind. And indeed troubadours (they are a constant!) composed songs about her unrequited love. The child was born, and was named Saluni. She—Saluni—was only six months old when her lovesick mother poured petrol all over her body and immolated herself. To this day, Saluni says with a dramatic gesture, she remembers quite vividly the yellow flames that consumed her beautiful mother in the same manner that she had been consumed by love. She is a love child, she repeats, and as a love child she cannot be denied whatever her heart desires.

It is a romantic story that overwhelms the Whale Caller with deep feelings for her. Who would not love a love child? Who would be cruel enough to deny a love child a measly bottle of wine? He goes to a nearby hotel off-sales store and buys her a bottle of expensive wine, for he believes the cheaper autumn harvests are not good for her health; they will corrode her insides. But after just one sip Saluni complains: "This wine is no good. Too smooth. It's for sissies. It's like drinking water. Next time you give me the money and I'll buy real wine."

The Whale Caller ignores her whining and occupies himself with pressing his tuxedo even though he had already pressed it yesterday and the day before.

Besides dancing at dawn there are other things that Saluni and the Whale Caller do together. They go to the biggest supermarket in town to "window shop," as they call it, for food. This began as Saluni's project; her attempt to initiate him into what she refers to as civilised living. It started with decorating the walls with seashells. Then she bought a vase and a tablecloth from the flea market that is held on Saturdays at the parking lot. She brings tulips from the mansion and arranges them in the vase on the wobbly table. She rearranges the flowers every day, according to their colours, and as she does so the Whale Caller feels his own life being rearranged.

Civilised living includes a number of rituals against which his whole body rebels. But he goes along with them, especially because she reminds him all the time that she went along with his waltz at dawn. All of a sudden eating has become a ritual. Before this the Whale Caller used to eat in order to fill his stomach and didn't attach much importance to the process. He could eat standing outside the Wendy house watching the distant waves, relaxing on the bed or even walking to Walker Bay. Now they sit down at the table. The table itself looks like an altar, with a white tablecloth, flowers and a candle. Although in most instances their diet comprises pasta and cheese, she makes a whole ceremony of eating it, in a number of courses—the same macaroni and cheese served as a starter, entrée and dessert—for she is keen to teach him how to eat a meal of many courses, which she says they are destined to do one day. Whenever he starts mumbling a complaint she reminds him: "We were born for better things. At least I was."

He learns table manners, although he suspects that the whole ritual is geared towards arousing him. He is well aware that in the "civilised world" the ritual of eating is some kind of foreplay. That is why gentlemen and ladies have candlelight dinners before bedding each other. He remembers from his travels along the coast that in the African languages he came across the crudest word for sex, which literally translated into "eating." In this garish language of the gutter a man eats a woman. The Whale Caller surmised it should have been the other way round—although that still leaves his body cringing from the rawness of it all.

The eating rituals extend to "window shopping" at the supermarket. This entails strolling along the aisles, stopping at the shelves displaying food they like, and then eating it with their eyes. They walk together pushing a trolley. Saluni stops in front of a shelf containing cans of beef stew. She looks at the pieces of meat, tomatoes, carrots and potatoes swimming in brown onion gravy on the label. She swallows hard as she eats the stew with her eyes. Then she moves on to the next shelf, and this one is stacked with cans of corned beef with a picture of the beef, potatoes and fried eggs sunny-side up. And then to cans of chicken à la king in thick mushroom sauce. Food fit for a queen. She gormandises it all with her greedy eyes. She takes a look at the Whale Caller, who has been staring at canned ravioli in tomato sauce. She is disgusted with him.

"You can't eat that," she says. "We came all the way so that you can eat good food, not what we eat every day at home."

"We don't eat ravioli every day."

"What's the difference? We eat pasta. Pasta is pasta even if it has bits of mince in its stupid little envelopes."

"It is good food to me."

"Come here, I'll teach you good food," says Saluni, dragging him by the shirtsleeve and stopping at a shelf of smoked oysters in cottonseed oil. "Eat!" she commands, and drags him to a shelf of smoked mussels, and then to white crab meat. For dessert they go to a section that has fudge brownies and peanut butter crunch bars and angel food cakes, all pictured seductively on the boxes.

By the time they walk out of the supermarket they have satisfied their tastes, now they go back home to satisfy their hunger with macaroni and cheese.

"I am ravenous," says Saluni. "I am ready for your macaroni and cheese."

"Perhaps we should introduce a new system, Saluni," suggests the Whale Caller. "We should start with macaroni and cheese first, and then take our eyes to enjoy the supermarket delicacies . . . with full stomachs."

"It sounds like a brilliant idea," says Saluni doubtfully. "But if our stomachs are full, are we still going to enjoy eating the food with our eyes? Are we still going to salivate?"

"We can only try," says the Whale Caller.

"We can only try," agrees Saluni. She is pleased that he has finally got into the spirit of the eating ritual, in the same way that she got into the spirit of the dance.

They walk quietly for some time, and then he mutters to himself: "It beats me who would want to buy canned oysters and mussels when we can have the real stuff, fresh out of the water."

"If we have the real stuff right under our noses, why don't we ever see it on our dinner table?" asks Saluni. "Why do we only see macaroni and cheese?"

"Because, Saluni, old-age pension money can go only so far. Plus I like macaroni and cheese. It's as decent a meal as you can get."


It's been more than a month since Sharisha migrated to the southern seas. Autumn still carries smells of warmth. Soon it will be winter, and then the rains will fall. Saluni is an almost fulfilled woman. She no longer has the need to waste her life away in the taverns of Hermanus. She has the Whale Caller now. And she has the Bored Twins. She has the wine too, either from the mansion or from the Whale Caller, who has got around to buying her the occasional bottle of plonk, according to her demands. However, she suspects that though Sharisha has been gone for such a long time, her aura still hovers in the air, especially in the bedroom. Hence her lack of complete fulfilment.

The Whale Caller continues to sleep in the sleeping bag in the kitchen. But today Saluni is determined that their relationship will be consummated. She will no longer throw hints as she has been doing these past weeks. Hints don't get through his thick gleaming pate. She will drag him kicking and screaming into bed. And indeed, after taking a bath she gets into bed and calls him to the bedroom.

"I am tired of your nonsense, man," she says.

"And now what have I done?"

"It's what you have not done that concerns me."

He is mystified.

"What have I not done?"

"Tonight I am going to make you cry for your mother," she threatens.

The Whale Caller is scandalised. And filled with fear.

"You do want to cry for your mother, don't you? I haven't met a man who wouldn't want to cry for his mother. Come on, man, you can't deny me the joy of making you yell for your mother. I am a love child."

Such talk makes the Whale Caller very uncomfortable. And very embarrassed. But at the same time it makes him want her. Especially the part about being a love child. He wants nothing more than to make love to a love child. Without further to-do he strips naked and shyly creeps into bed. She shifts against the wall to create more space for him on the single bed. Her body immediately charges him with electric currents. But images of whales interfere at that moment of excitement and he goes limp. Still he manages to convince himself that the whales are blameless, even though he can almost touch them as they float before his closed eyes. The fault for his limpness can only lie with the sweet and mouldy smell, even though tonight it is quite subdued. He tries very hard to obliterate both the smell and the whales from his mind, and focus more on the warmth and the softness of her body. For some time it seems things will work. But at a crucial moment the image of Sharisha appears. His weak manhood becomes even weaker until it dies completely as Sharisha lobtails in the sea of his mind.

"Is there something wrong with me, man?" asks Saluni.

"It is not you."

"It is that stupid creature, is it not?"

"At least you no longer call her a fish."

"That stupid *fish* has castrated you."

She spits out the word *fish* as if it were invective. He winces.

"In any case," says the Whale Caller, "sex is overrated. I don't need it. I can live without it. Ever since coming back from my travels around the coast I have lost all appetite for it."

"If that is the case, go back to your sleeping bag and have wet dreams about your bloody fish."

Even as she says this, she knows that it contradicts her true wishes. However, she does not want his sinewy body to provoke her into utter madness for nothing. He apologetically gathers his clothes from the floor and slinks out of the room.

She realises that the only way she will ever possess this man and restore his manly functions is to get rid of Sharisha. But how do you get rid of a whale? She closes her eyes tightly and a hazy image of the past emerges. She sees genteel women walking on Cape Town's promenades wearing long colourful dresses. They are perfectly shaped because of the corsets made from baleen. Some are shading their heads from the sun with umbrellas whose ribs are made of baleen. Down on the rocks by the sea men are fishing and their rods are made of baleen. The beautiful corseted women are bringing them picnic baskets. She looks at them longingly, for if she had lived during their time she would have been one of them. She would be there with the Whale Caller. There would be no Sharisha, for her baleen would have been part of her corset and umbrella. Some of it would have been part of the chairseats in her beautiful seaside cottage.

In today's world, with all the foolish laws that protect these useless creatures, what do you do with a stubborn whale that refuses to let loose your man's very soul? You cannot just go to any old whale and kick it around and beat it up with your stilettoheel, shouting that it must leave your man alone. Whales don't take kindly to that sort of thing.

She decides to bide her time. In the meanwhile, in the mornings following the nights her body has been raging, she hunts for mating seals on the rocks and sand hills for her own gratification. She sits on a rock and watches them. She finds it titillating that the females can make love to their males only a few weeks after the birth of their babies. Sometimes a couple is mating while another female is giving birth on the rocks, with seagulls waiting to feast on the placenta and the umbilical cord.

THE WHALE CALLER SITS on the green bench and watches Saluni frolic in the shallows. The wind is blowing her hair in all wild directions. She dances with the wind. She raises her arms and flaps them in some imagined flight. She takes off and soars higher than any bird has soared. She soars to the clouds. Her perpetual coat fails to weigh her down. And then from the clouds she dives back into the water to resume her dance with the wind. The shallows are a perfect place to express her elation. There are no whales to mess up her day and all his attention is on her. She is truly beautiful, he observes, in spite of her ravaged face. He grudgingly admits to himself that indeed the village drunk's presence at the Wendy house and at the seaside has brightened his life, especially during an off-season like this when the whales have migrated to the southern seas.

She has no cares in the world. She does not worry about what the next day will bring. She is a transgressor of all that he holds sacred: moderation, quiet dignity, never raising the voice, avoidance of vulgar vocabulary, never flaunting desires of any kind, frugality. Created in sin, she is such a wonderful sinner. A glorious celebrant of worldliness. He envies her for that. He would like to transgress once in a while . . . to be as carefree as she is . . . to be taken over by that wanton spirit! She has often egged him to stop being so stiff and taking himself so seriously. Go out on some hedonistic binge! But his fear is stronger than his desire for pleasure. People were made for different things, he tells himself. Saluni was made to be recklessly happy. He was made to be cautious. And to be patient.

Whereas she always demands instant gratification of life, he would rather have delayed pleasure, for it carries in it something more solid. Momentary pleasure is flimsy and is for the light-headed ones such as Saluni. True pleasure must be restrained. Whenever Saluni complains of boredom because she thinks there is no variety in their lives or they don't have much "fun," except for the waltz and the window shopping, he answers: "Tomorrow is just as good a day as any. We can still be happy tomorrow. You don't gormandise pleasure as if there is no tomorrow." She, on the other hand, suspects he is conserving his energy for the return of the whales . . . for Sharisha.

"Don't just sit there, man! Come fly with me!" she calls out.

"Those waves don't look friendly today," he warns her. "Better be careful."

"You are just a coward," she says. "You don't want to come and play in the water in case you actually enjoy it and become happy! I have never known anyone so scared of happiness!"

She stands on a smooth rock that is surrounded by water. She is looking in his direction and doesn't see the returning tide.

"Hey, look out!" he shouts.

But it is too late. The tide sweeps her away. Her eyeballs almost pop out in bewilderment, which leaves the Whale Caller in stitches. She disappears in the waves and then pops up again, raising her hand as if she is waving. He waves back, still laughing. As the waves toss her about she reminds him of a breaching whale. Although she is just a speck compared to the smallest whale that ever visited Hermanus, she begins to assume the demeanour of a playful whale. And this sends him into a further paroxysm of laughter. Until he realises that Saluni is not clowning about. She really is in trouble, wrestling with the waves. And they are getting the better of her. For a while he had forgotten that Saluni was not Sharisha and that not all women are at home in the sea like Sharisha. He kicks off his boots and runs in her direction. He dives into the water. He is still laughing when he swims back to shore with her.

She is both angry and puzzled as she gasps for air and throws up the salty water. She has never seen him laugh this much. Come to think of it, she has never seen him laugh at all. At best he chuckles. And here he is, having a good laugh at her expense.

He places her on the sand and takes off her coat. He pumps the water out of her stomach. Thankfully she has not swallowed that much. She vomits bits of the macaroni and cheese that she had for lunch.

"The damnable coat," he says as he continues to pump. "It almost killed you."

"You don't like my drinking," she says between the heaving and the groaning. "You don't like my coat. What else don't you like about me?"

"Your stubbornness," he says. "You could have died in there. You should have seen yourself. You were quite a sight."

"You think this is funny, do you?" she asks, and then a stream of curses—mostly about his mother's genitalia—escapes her beautiful but chapped lips.

"I don't mind if you call me names," says the Whale Caller. "But you don't curse a dead woman who never did you any wrong."

"And you don't laugh at a drowning woman who never did you any wrong," she shouts, spitting out the last morsel in her mouth.

He cannot help laughing one more time at the memory of her helpless body being tossed by the waves. This infuriates her and she breaks out into another round of colourful profanity.

"We are being observed all the time, Saluni," he says, adopting some measure of seriousness. "We must behave appropriately at all times. Garbage must not come from our mouths."

"And who is observing us?"

He is rather vague about this, as if the question has caught him off guard.

"Perhaps it is your big fish," suggests Saluni. "You are always dreaming of your big fish."

"Whales are not fish!" he moans.

It is her turn to laugh.

"The Bible says they are fish so they are fish."

"The Bible says no such thing."

"It says Jonah was swallowed by a big fish."

To steer Saluni away from insulting Sharisha he decides that the person who is watching them is Mr. Yodd.

"And who is Mr. Yodd? Another one of your whales?"

"Perhaps it is time I formally introduced you to Mr. Yodd," says the Whale Caller. "But first we need to get rid of this!"

He grabs the coat and drags it across the sand. He rolls it into a big ball and throws it into the water. Saluni yells at him as the waves toss it about until it cannot be seen anymore.

"I want my coat back," she screams, stamping her feet like a spoilt child. "You go get my coat back!"

"No, I won't," he says, with the firmness of a father talking to a naughty child. "You are more beautiful without that coat. Come with me, I want to show you something."

"No, I won't, not until you give me my coat back."

He grabs her arm and drags her along to the Old Harbour and down the crag to Mr. Yodd's grotto. She is taken by surprise by his firmness, and sulkily she allows herself to be dragged along. He kneels before the grotto, but she refuses to do so. She just stands there and stares at him in defiant mien, her cheeks filled with air like a balloon signalling her anger.

◆

HOY, MR. YODD. She is Saluni. We are just walking the road together, Mr. Yodd. We do not have a destination. We'll see how far it takes us. We'll see where it takes us.

◆

AS THEY WALK UP the crag from the grotto he is wondering why Mr. Yodd did not laugh at him this time. He had only listened to his brief confession without any comment. Was it because of the presence of Saluni, who had refused to kneel down? Such confessions are a self-flagellation, and it doesn't help if Mr. Yodd decided not to humiliate him. He needs his dose of mortification and is disappointed that none was forthcoming from today's confession.

Saluni on the other hand is still livid. The water is beginning to evaporate from her clothes and she is shivering from the cold. She wonders why he called her a fellow-traveller without a destination—a slight from the man she regards as the love of her life. What about Sharisha? Does he think he has a destination with Sharisha? She fumes even more when she remembers her coat. She feels naked without her coat.

This is a new side of him she has not seen before: first the laughter, and then the firmness! There is hope yet. Life will be perfect the day he surprises her with another kind of firmness— where it matters most.

Strangely she feels as if a burden has been lifted off her shoulders. She feels free. The freedom of the naked!

Although—ostensibly to get back at him for the coat and the laughter—she ridicules the foolishness of talking to rock rabbits at a nondescript cave, she is curious about the ritual of confession. She is secretly fascinated by the unseen confessor. The Whale Caller professes to hate the rituals she is trying to introduce in his life, yet in his own way he is a creature of ritual. Often she secretly follows him as he goes to confess. He does not know she is there listening. She stands against the wind for she knows he can smell her. Sometimes she doesn't hear what he tells Mr. Yodd because the wind takes his words in another direction.

One day she decides to take the plunge and confess. She brings with her oblations of tulips from the mansion. She arranges them around the mouth of the grotto as she addresses Mr. Yodd.

HOY, MR. YODD! Harvesting the clouds must be left to those who have big wings. I used to fly, Mr. Yodd. To soar to the highest skies. To live up there in cloudland. Until he brought me back to earth. To walk firmly on the ground. Without staggering. So that the ground knows who I am. The ground needs to respect who I am. Who am I? I am Saluni, and I have taken you over. Maybe not taken you over as such. I just want to have a piece of you too. He does not know it, but I have watched him talk to you. Once he dragged me here and I rubbished the very notion of the confessional. The place, yes, but also the mortifying confessor and the very act of confessing. He does not know that since then I have followed him. I heard him confess all sorts of things about me to you, Mr. Yodd. And about that behemoth he calls Sharisha. In the same breath: me and Sharisha. The eternal triangle: man, woman and whale. I can tell you I am not going to be part of any triangle. The fish must go. Ha! It galls him when I call his whale a fish, so I will call it that until he gets rid of it. I have heard him confess, Mr. Yodd. I said to myself: One day I'll confess about him to Mr. Yodd too. Then I didn't know what he gets for his confessions, but I said to myself: If he can confess about me, so can I about him. And here I am, Mr. Yodd, for the first time, kneeling in front of your cave . . . or grotto, as you prefer it to be called. You know, Mr. Yodd, I have been living with him in his little Wendy house for three months now. I have decided to find rhythm in some of his madness. You are part of that rhythm. That is why I have adopted you. I don't know what you will do for me, but I have adopted you. I am a lady, Mr. Yodd, and I am beautiful. Why doesn't he touch me? Why does he turn his back on me? Thanks for the correction: he does not turn his back. It would have been better if he did, for I would still feel his flesh. Why does he insist on wasting his nights in that confounded sleeping bag? Is it because of the light? Some people are fearful of the light. They like to do things in the dark. I, on the other hand, am a child of the light. I am a love child, conceived in the daytime. It had to be daytime because those were stolen moments. The man would have to go back to his wife and the young woman would have to steal back to her parents. I am a child of the day, Mr. Yodd. That is why I am fearful of the dark. That is why I ran away from the Free State farmstead where I was born and spent a lovely carefree childhood. Under the big sky the nights poured themselves on me, and drenched me with darkness. Darkness suffocates me. But it was not only from darkness that I was escaping. I am an exile from thunder. I walked from the Free State through the Karoo because our summer rains over there are accompanied by thunder and lightning. I was fearful of thunder. I had heard that the Western Cape is a place of gentle winter rains. I managed to run away from thunder, but couldn't escape darkness. Darkness follows day everywhere. Darkness follows me to the end of the earth. I thought I had escaped darkness forever since I knew that there were streetlights in these cities. I remember the freedom I felt when I first came here: with lights in the streets. I could walk from tavern to tavern at all hours of the day and night. But where I lived before I joined him in his Wendy house . . . they didn't have such lights. I had to rely on my trusty candle. Oh, so you find this quite hilarious? I have heard of these tricks of yours, Mr. Yodd . . . the laughter that is intended to mortify. You might as well stop it because it does nothing to me. I refuse to be mortified by you or by anyone else. Instead, your laughter makes me want to laugh back at you, as I am now doing. I do not need the self-flagellation as he does. Mortification will rebound, Mr. Yodd, and hit you between the eyes!

SHE CLIMBS BACK from the grotto. Stiletto-heels were not made for crag climbing. She is therefore holding her shoes in her hands and is walking in her stockinged feet. Near the whale-viewing site she finds the Whale Caller waiting. She walks past him, pretending not to see him.

"What were you doing down there?" he asks.

"Oh, nothing!" she says, without stopping. He follows her.

"But you were talking. Who were you talking to?"

"Oh, to no one in particular!"

"You were talking to Mr. Yodd, weren't you?"

She does not deny it. She just keeps on walking.

Now he has no doubt that this is the woman for him.

She sits on the concrete bench near the war monument to put on her shoes. He sits beside her. There is a silence between them. After a while she stands up again and walks on the tarred road past the big parking lot and away from the Old Harbour area. He follows her. About half a kilometre away she takes off her shoes again and walks down the paved path that leads back to the sea. He follows. She sits on the green bench near the path, a few metres above the water. He sits down too. There is silence again. He is looking straight ahead as if something on the horizon has grabbed his attention. She looks at him intently as if she is studying the contours on his face, and bursts out laughing. He looks at her and bursts out laughing too.

"You laughed," she says.

"You laughed first," he says.

"I always laugh. You never do," she says.

"You have brought laughter into my life," he says.

There is silence once more. The world is at peace with itself. American armies are not invading third-world countries, making the world unsafe for the rest of humanity; terrorists are not engaging in the slaughter of the innocent in high-rise buildings and at holiday resorts; criminals have ceased their rapes and murders and robberies; dictators of the world have given up dictating; warlords have laid down their arms; politicians have learnt to be truthful and have stopped thieving. The world *is* at peace with itself. Across a small rift, not far from where the couple is enjoying the peace of the world, a cultus of tourists is engaged in the ritual of gorging quantities of seafood and gallons of wine. They are sitting in the open-air restaurant whose portico juts into the sea on stilts. They are at peace with the world.

A song can be heard among the waves below the restaurant.

"Did you hear that voice?" asks Saluni.

"I didn't hear anything," says the Whale Caller.

"You can hear your whales a hundred miles away but you cannot hear a boy only a few metres below us?"

"Human voices are not like the voices of whales," he says apologetically.

In all fairness, the voice comes only in waves because the wind blows it in the opposite direction, and then suddenly when the wind subsides the voice carries to the couple on the green bench. The Whale Caller strains his ears and finally can hear something.

"It is Lunga Tubu singing to the waves," says Saluni.

"Who is Lunga Tubu?"

"He is here at least twice a week. But you never see him because you only see whales."

There he is, Lunga Tubu, standing on a rock and singing to the tourists on the portico above. An occasional offering of a coin is thrown in his direction. He has to catch it before it drops into the water. He has become very adept at it. The tourists seem to enjoy this part of the game most: when he jumps up to catch a coin, without missing a beat. Kindlier souls throw the coins in the clear water on the side of the portico, for him to gather after a few songs.

The Whale Caller can now hear his song very clearly: *Softly a serenade, whispers I love you, Santa Lucia, Sa-a-anta-a-a-a Lucia-a-a-a-a.* It is a boy's voice, and has not yet broken. Yet it is so canorous that it lifts the Whale Caller to his feet. He applauds and shouts: "Bravo! Bravo!"

Unlike the Bored Twins, whose voices are those of angels, Saluni explains, Lunga Tubu's voice is of this earth. It is a voice of a humble twelve-year-old boy from Zwelihle Township who comes down to the sea on weekends and public holidays to sing for his supper.

It seems to the Whale Caller that Saluni's influence has now made him hear the songs of humans as well. It has also made him see things that he has never noticed before, although they have been around him all the time.

The head waiter appears on the portico and shoos Lunga Tubu away. But the boy continues his song. Saluni has seen this ritual many times before and finds it quite funny. The Whale Caller, on the other hand, is disgusted that a boy with such a pleasant voice is being driven away so unceremoniously.

"He says the boy steals his tips," explains Saluni.

"But the boy didn't even get within ten metres of the restaurant. Does he think the poor boy has long invisible hands?"

"He thinks that if the tourists didn't have to throw some coins at Lunga he and the other waiters would be getting bigger tips."

The head waiter disappears into the kitchen and returns with a fat man who is either the owner or the manager of the restaurant. The man walks down the wooden steps on the side of the portico, shouting abuse at Lunga Tubu. He picks up pebbles and throws them at the boy, who is now running away.

"Run this way, Lunga, he won't dare come to bother you here," shouts Saluni.

The boy runs to the green bench. He is tiny and emaciated.

"What did you do to that man?" asks the Whale Caller.

"Nothing," says the boy. "He doesn't want me to sing near his restaurant."

Saluni explains to the Whale Caller that Lunga Tubu's presence here destabilises the serenity of Hermanus—a sanctified playground of the rich. Lunga Tubu is disturbing the peace of the world. His tiny frame nags the delicate souls with what they would rather forget: that only a few kilometres away there is another world that is not at peace with itself—a whole festering world of the disillusioned, those who have no stake in the much-talked-about black economic empowerment, which is really the issue of the black middle class rather than of people like Lunga Tubu. While the town of Hermanus is raking in fortunes from tourism, the mothers and fathers of Zwelihle are unemployed. It is a world where people have lost all faith in politicians. Once, they had dreams, but they have seen politicians and trade union leaders become overnight millionaires instead. Only tiny crumbs trickle down to what used to be called "the masses" in the heyday of the revolution.

Of course only a liar can claim that things are as bad as they were during the days of apartheid, Saluni is emphatic about this. More people have been housed than ever before. Even shacks in informal settlements here and in the inland provinces have been electrified. Services such as telephones and water have been provided even in the remote villages. But in a country with such high unemployment, this has come with new problems. People are unable to pay for these services.

One little "empowerment" that exists in Zwelihle is the indigent tariff. Poor families that qualify for this tariff are relieved of paying for utilities and municipal services. But the city fathers and mothers are quick to disqualify a family as soon as it owns a fridge, a geyser or some other appliance that may be deemed a luxury. If they can afford a fridge, common wisdom dictates, they can afford to pay their utilities bills. The inspectors of the municipality discovered once that Lunga Tubu's family owned a range of electrical appliances and gadgets. The family was immediately disqualified from the indigent tariff. It did not matter to the bureaucrats that these appliances were hand-me-downs from his mother's employer in "the kitchens." Hence he has to sing, not only for his supper and his fees at Lukhanyo Primary School, where he is doing Grade Six, but for service arrears as well. And this is the most crucial of his expenses. Many citizens of Zwelihle have had their houses auctioned away because of service arrears.

"There is no place you do not know in Hermanus, Saluni," observes the Whale Caller. He is obviously quite impressed by her command of the politics of Hermanus. "There is nothing you don't know in this district."

"People in the taverns talk," says Saluni. "And I have been to every tavern worth its name in the district. Until you came along."

"*You* came along."

"*You* searched for me."

The Whale Caller studies the tiny boy in front of him. The boy is grinning expectantly.

"You sing well, boy," says the Whale Caller. "What do you want to be when you grow up?"

"A whale caller," says Saluni impishly.

"An opera singer," replies the boy.

And he is determined to be one, whatever obstacles may be put in his way. He sings in a school choir. But one day he will surpass his heroes: Luciano Pavarotti, Plácido Domingo and José Carreras. He then rattles off the history of the three tenors, and tells the Whale Caller about some of their great concerts. The Whale Caller himself has never been one for music, except the songs of the whales.

Lunga Tubu breaks into a rendition of "*O sole mio*," and then follows it with "*La donna è mobile*." There are tears in the Whale Caller's eyes. Saluni looks at him, shakes her head and smiles.

"That is very sweet," she says.

The Whale Caller is clearly offended. He gives Lunga Tubu some banknotes without even counting them and abruptly walks away.

"Hey, what's wrong now?" asks Saluni, running after the Whale Caller. "It is okay, man, you can cry."

# THREE

THE WHALES HAVE BEEN gone for many months, and the taverns of Hermanus miss their love child. She has been gone for almost as long as the whales. Many rumours circulate, ranging from the mundane to the sublime. She stowed away in an oil tanker. She was seen at the Cape Town docks drinking with a bunch of Mediterranean seafaring types who took a fancy to her and persuaded her to sail the world with them, smuggling crude to third-world countries with black-market economies. She is hibernating with a new rash after the Bored Twins placed ten hairy millipedes in her bra—five in each cup. Others saw her in conference with a bevy of watermaids—beautiful women with lower bodies of fish—in the deep of the night. She has joined them in their undersea queendom. She is in the process of metamorphosing into a watermaid.

These stories change every day, like the story of her own conception: one day she is seen riding on the back of a dolphin which swims with her to the horizon, and the next day she has joined a cloister of nuns and has taken the vow of chastity, or has been discovered by a talent scout and now she sings the blues on a cruise liner.

There are those who know a different truth. They are the very few who have found reason to venture to the beaches, to Walker Bay and the Old Harbour—areas often shunned by the true-blooded citizens of Hermanus as being too touristy. They have seen Saluni, they claim, waltzing in the morning with a strange man who blows a kelp horn for the whales. No, not Wilson Salukazana the whale crier from Zwelihle, who is employed by the town council to alert whale watchers as to the presence and location of whales. Everyone knows the whale crier. He has been seen in newspapers and on television. Everyone in the world who has a camera has photographed him. The whale man seen with Saluni is a different one, the bald brawny silver-bearded man in blue dungarees or black tie who does not relish an audience when he blows his horn, but merely tolerates it because there is nothing he can do about it. The one who calls whales to himself and spends the nights dancing with them. Saluni is often seen with him. Loitering on the beach like the strandlopers of old. Strolling down supermarket aisles. Smiling broadly. Sometimes even holding hands! Yes, the very Saluni that they thought they knew so well! The love child.

But the habitués of the taverns do not want to believe these rumour-mongers. Their story is pooh-poohed as the most ridiculous ever invented in the Western Cape and beyond. If Saluni were anywhere near Hermanus, they argue, she would not have deserted her eternal greatest haunts—the taverns of Hermanus. A lady who prides herself on elegance—however threadbare and old-time it may be—cannot become a strandloper. There is more romance in joining a noviciate or a band of smugglers, in belting out the blues on passenger ships, in riding dolphins and in transforming into hallowed water beings.

Saluni has indeed transformed into a watermaid of sorts. Her body has not turned into that of a fish, but on sunny days she spends many hours with her feet immersed in the emerald green shallows. Even on a day like this where everything is just a mass of greyness and one can't tell where the sea ends and the sky begins, she sits on a rock playing with the water and making monotonous splashes with her feet. When days are grey, water also assumes dull colours. Not blue. Not emerald green. Misty purple. Oily brown. Or just grey like the day. The Whale Caller sits on the green bench above and watches her as he used to watch the whales. He can only see her back. The wild wind blows her red hair in wild directions, making it look like the hissing serpents of Medusa. But he knows that from the front her face will not turn every living thing beholding it into stone. It is a ravishing face, though the elements and the wine have taken their toll on it.

He is alarmed at the intensity of his feeling for her, so violent that it wants to burst out of his chest. It has never happened like this before; even with the buxom women in the hamlets he passed through when he used to travel the coast. Those were his happy-go-lucky days. He indulged his youthful fancies and moved on. Sometimes he lingered for a few months or even years when the ambience was convivial enough. But ultimately he moved on because no strong attachments were ever established in his adventures and misadventures with the female folk. This feeling that is actually making him physically ill is a new experience, and in spite of its debilitating effect it illumines his face. His whole body feels light as if he is levitating, though he is actually sitting firmly on the bench.

Saluni is very much aware of his physical illness. She shares a similar malaise, with slight variations, though she sometimes doubts if his is directly related to her. She believes that it is likely to be caused by someone—or rather something—else. Her doubts worsen whenever he sits on that bench and has a faraway look in his eyes. She suspects that on those occasions his mind is populated by images of Sharisha lobtailing and doing all sorts of crude things in the ocean. Although the name of Sharisha has not featured in their conversation for many months, she silently bears a grudge against her. She blames her for the sad fact that she and the Whale Caller have not consummated their union.

Her thoughts are on this lack of consummation as she withdraws from the water to sit on the moist sand a short distance away. Drawing deeply from her historical memory, she chants spells from the binding rituals of those wonderful pagan epochs. She commands through binding hymns that her beloved should be subject to her will and act according to her wishes. With sand she builds an effigy of her beloved, in the manner that the lovesick moulded such effigies in old Egypt and Greece—a male pursuit in those ancient cultures—and still mould them in the enchanting voodoo rituals of some Africans. In her sequinned handbag, which is lying on the sand next to the stilettos, she finds a matchbox. She uses the matchsticks to pierce the sandman in the arms and the legs and the heart, chanting the binding hymn that the beloved will come to her running, burning with desire, and she will drag him by his beard and even by his genitals, until he surrenders himself completely to her. She tortures the sandman with her "needles" until the Whale Caller feels the pain where he is sitting, and has seizures. He does not know the immediate source of this further violence on his body, except for the fact that the mere sight of Saluni has been giving him feverish outbursts lately.

Although the fever has caused him great discomfort in the general area of his groin, he would like to believe that it has nothing to do with carnal desires. His position since his return from his wanderings and the discovery of the pleasures that can be derived from whales is that there are things that are more beautiful and less messy than copulation. The most important is just being at the same place at the same time with the object of your affections, breathing the same air and smelling the same smells. Doing little things for each other rather than to each other. He loves doing little things for Saluni although she never seems to notice them. He does all the giving and she is a thankless receiver. He rejoices in generosity and has stopped being puzzled at her lack of any expression of gratitude.

Once there was an outburst about it. He had returned quite late from collecting his monthly pension because of the long queues at the mobile pay point since such payments are all made only one day of the month. Thousands of old-age pensioners and disabled people had been queuing for hours, especially those, like the Whale Caller, who do not have bank accounts to which the money is directly transferred by the state. He had been standing in the queue all day long, and could not even dash away for lunch lest he lost his place. He was very hungry and was looking forward to a nice hot meal when he got back to the Wendy house. But Saluni had not cooked any food. She was just sitting on the bed filing and painting her nails.

"You did not cook? Why?" asked the Whale Caller.

"I was not hungry," she responded.

"You go to the Bored Twins and when you come back there is a meal waiting for you."

"What have the Bored Twins got to do with it, man? What are you on about?"

"Whenever you come back there is food waiting for you, Saluni. Did you think I cooked it because I was hungry?"

"Don't get so worked up about it, man. It's only food."

"If I cooked only when I am hungry there would be no meals in this house."

The Whale Caller sulked as he brought water to the boil on the hot plate. It was no big deal to cook macaroni and then to sprinkle grated Gouda on it while it was hot. It took less than fifteen minutes. But it was the principle of it all that he was concerned with, and he was infuriated by the fact that Saluni didn't seem bothered at all. She tried to introduce some small talk about their next window-shopping expedition, but he did not respond.

"Oh, I see," said Saluni, "you want a woman who will cook for you? You didn't bring me here to be your maid, did you?"

"I didn't bring you here at all. You brought yourself."

"But I am not your servant."

"I am not your servant either, but I do cook for you. Did you think I was doing it because I was your servant?"

"So now you are nitpicking, are you?"

"I look after you because I care, not because I am your servant. I expect the caring to be mutual."

Saluni only laughed. He vowed to himself never to raise the matter of Saluni's selfishness again. Now he has learnt to live with it. It is how Saluni has been created. She means no harm by it. She just has never known how to look out for the next person. He watches her with pride as she chants her binding spells. He can't hear what she is saying. He thinks she has invented a new childish game.

The grey sky darkens, and Saluni stamps on her sandman, chanting more binding spells. His body convulses, which he tries hard to hide though his face is mapped with pain. Mercifully the pain evaporates as soon as she stops the manic dance. In Saluni's fit of unfulfilled erotomania the flattened effigy has joined the other grains of white sand that will become sand castles in a few months' time when the winter rains have stopped and the warmth of summer has returned. She grabs her stilettos and handbag, and walks up to the bench.

"It looks like rain," she says.

"It smells like rain," he says.

"Perhaps we should go home."

"You might have to carry me on your back," he says. "My whole body feels sick."

"I know."

"How do you know?"

"Somehow we make each other sick. But don't worry, you will get over it."

"I don't want to get over it. It is a beautiful sickness."

They slowly walk back to the Wendy house.


It is raining in big drops that are typical only of the inland provinces. The kind of drops that leave you with a migraine when they hit your head. Not the gentle rain of the Western Cape. The sound is particularly loud on the pine roof of the Wendy house. The dark clouds make for a premature night. Saluni reaches for the switch. She strips naked and then dives into bed. The Whale Caller sits on a kitchen chair listening to the rhythms of his ailment and of the rain.

Thunder and lightning . . . another unusual feature of today's weather! A rolling sound relayed from one possessed drummer to another. In crescendos, segues and diminuendos. Some drummers rumbling in the distance, others clapping rapidly just outside the window. Shaking the Wendy house to Saluni's utter panic. She buries her head under the blanket and screams. But the head cannot stay covered for long as she is afraid of the darkness. The Whale Caller rushes to the bedroom, sits on the bed and tries to allay her fears by holding her tightly to himself while caressing her back. For a while she is petrified. But soon she becomes animated. And is as breathless as the relentless rain. He is not sure whether it is from the thunder or from the caress that has now turned into a massage.

"Do not be afraid," he says. "Nothing will happen to you. I'll stay with you till this whole mayhem is over."

He kicks off his boots and gets into bed with her.

"Not with your dungarees on," she says into his ear.

He gets out of bed and takes his clothes off. Not just the dun-

garees. Everything. On his own volition too! His gigantic naked-
ness leaves Saluni wide-eyed. He jumps back into bed. She is still
stiff with fear but her mischievous bone cannot help tickling him
in the armpits. He bursts out laughing. He clings to her to save
himself from her tickling; she clings to him to save herself from
thunder. The smallness of the wooden single bed works in their
favour.

"Is this tickling business supposed to be foreplay?" he asks,
raising his voice above the pounding rain. The thunder now
sounds quite distant, which seems to loosen her body. She is now
more relaxed.

There is hope for humanity yet: the Whale Caller has actually
uttered the word "foreplay" without flinching or cringing.

"All my life with you is foreplay," she says. "By the time
evening comes I am dripping wet. I have been waiting for a long
time, man. You can only have so much foreplay."

She exudes the smell. Even more so than ever before. The
sweet and mouldy smell of his mother. Making love to Saluni
would be as disgusting as making love to his mother. The thought
gives him the erection of the world even as he recoils from its re-
pulsiveness. As he fumbles around he discovers that every square
inch of her body is an erogenous zone. Even the split ends of her
hair ignite with his touch. All the gratitude she has been with-
holding is saturated in her body and now is ready to gush out into
his sinews, making them almost explode.

"Today I am really going to make you cry for your mother!"
says Saluni.

And she does make him cry. It begins as a whimper that rises
into a scream. If it were not for the rain and the distant thunder
passers-by would think somebody is murdering him in that
Wendy house. He is begging for mercy and pleading with his
mother to come and save him. But soon enough another voice—
presumably the murderer's—joins the moans. This second voice

begins by singing the blues—a breathless form of scatting. The murderer and the murdered then become indistinguishable as they are both begging for mercy from each other. The poor passers-by would be perplexed to hear the murderer and the murdered babble in tongues, much as the people used to do at the Church of the Sacred Kelp Horn when the Whale Caller blew his horn to a climactic frenzy.

A dying scream joined after a few beats by another dying scream. Then silence. They cannot believe the intensity of what has just happened.

"I bathed myself in you, Saluni," says a breathless Whale Caller. "Your waters of life mixed with mine to wash our souls. It was a wonderful cleansing ceremony, Saluni, and I am cleansed."

"It is something you cannot do with Sharisha," jokes a breathless Saluni.

"You do not know that, Saluni, you do not know that."

After this breathless murder he declares that he would like to be her slave forever and ever more, world without end, amen.

MANY BREATHLESS DAYS FOLLOW breathless nights. Some are grey like the first day of the cleansing ritual, while others are sunny. Some have the wetness of the source of life; some are as dry as the Karoo. They may be stormy, or sometimes calm. Cold or sweltering. But they are all breathless.

SALUNI. She has bloomed like the tulips of the mansion and the cracks on her face have smoothed out. It is as if the bees that are always buzzing around the tulips have filled the crevices with the bee-glue that they collect from buds to patch up their hives. The face has the glow of faces that have been cleansed with the propolis of the bees.

When the Whale Caller first heard her bluesy voice she had three addictions: the wine, the Bored Twins and the Whale Caller. That was in November. In the last seven months she has gradually discarded two vices and has remained with one: the Whale Caller. Of course, it is not quite accurate to say she discarded the Bored Twins. She just found herself needing their opiate presence less and less as the cleansing ceremonies with the Whale Caller became more frantic. When she was still a haunting shadow to his kelp horn rituals with the whales she used to go to the mansion every other day. Every day even. She was highly dependent on them for the elation that even her regular plonk could not give her. After she joined him at the Wendy house and they developed common rituals such as window shopping and dancing to the music of the whales she found herself going to the mansion only once a week. Sometimes once in two weeks. And then carnal desires were satisfied and she forgot to go to the mansion altogether. She wanted to be enveloped in his aura all the time, climaxing every few minutes at the memory of the next cleansing ceremony in the looming night. A memory of an analeptic future! He, on the other hand, seemed to spend his days in a daze. He did not even notice that there were no longer any fresh tulips in the house, and that the last bunch stayed there until it wilted and the water in the vase became slimy green and smelly with the rot.

She gave up wine, a decision that was difficult, but was helped by the fact that even when she had gone to the mansion she rarely came back with a bottle of wine as she used to in the past. Vineyard owners had now adopted a new tendency of paying their workers with actual money instead of bottles of wine. The father of the Bored Twins would only have a bottle of wine when the boss was in a celebratory mood and the market was saturated with the cheap brands of autumn harvests from his vineyard and those of competitors. Saluni was now going to the mansion with very little expectation of wine. She went solely for the elation.

This meant that she had to pester the Whale Caller every time she wanted a bottle of wine. "After all," she would remind him, "I stopped going to the taverns for you." She had never found herself in this position before, where she had to beg for a bottle of wine on a daily basis. Back in the old days she would just walk to a tavern, regale them with stories, threaten them with her being a love child, and they would ply her with as much wine as she could imbibe—which was quite a lot considering her small body! On the other hand, the Whale Caller found it unacceptable to feed her habit, which he detested in the first place. But he understood what it was to be addicted, and reluctantly bought a bottle, perhaps once or twice a week, which was still a strain on his meagre resources. And then the cleansing ceremonies! She needed no other intoxicant but him. Of course there were withdrawal symptoms. In the same way that there were some when she gave up the Bored Twins. Irritability mostly. A headache. Nausea. Obsessive behaviour.

Perhaps the latter is not a withdrawal symptom for it continues to this day. Perhaps it is part of her enchantment with ritual. When they went to the beach in the morning—not to waltz, since in June the whales took their song to the southern seas a thousand miles away, but just to walk in the freezing morning breeze—she went back to the house five times to make sure that the door was locked. On the way she elegantly puffed on a cigarette with her long black slender holder. She dropped the butt on the grass and stepped on it. But after walking for fifty metres or so she went back to make sure that the butt was completely extinguished lest it set the grass on fire. She did this three times, until the Whale Caller voiced his irritation.

Now she lies on her back on the bed looking at the ceiling while waiting for the Whale Caller, who is in the kitchen pottering around as he is wont to do every night before he comes to bed. As if he is gathering courage to face another night of untrammelled passion. She does what she does every night before she sleeps: counts the wooden panels on the ceiling of the Wendy house. He walks in and catches her at it. He laughs. She is quite piqued because he continues to laugh even as they snuggle up in the small bed. She starts from the beginning to count the panels, very deliberately this time and very much aloud so that she can be heard above his foolish laughter. Then she turns her back on him and sulks until she falls asleep. For the first time since the cleansing rituals began a month ago it is his turn to be left high and dry in the limbo of unfulfilled desire. He vows to himself never to make fun of other people's silly compulsive habits again.

In the morning Saluni is still sulking. She announces grandly that she is going to spend the day with the Bored Twins at the mansion. She is fussing over her looks as if she is going to see a lover. She wears the green corduroy pants and black knee-high pencil-heel boots that he bought her at the flea market as a peace offering after he threw her coat away. As she brushes her hair she mutters that it is cold outside and some evil person threw her coat into the ocean. She is wearing a flimsy pink sweater and she wonders aloud whether the evil person will now generate some heat around her as she walks all the way to the mansion. And if the evil person thinks that the corduroy pants and the boots make up for the lost coat, then the evil person is quite mistaken. The Whale Caller pretends not to hear any of this. He is surprised at this sudden decision to go to the mansion because since the cleansing rituals took off in earnest she has not even mentioned the Bored Twins. He knows that for some reason he is being punished, and he feels threatened by the Bored Twins. He has always felt uneasy about her relationship with the angelic girls. He is well aware of her previous addiction to their aura. He fears that going back to them will spark her relapse into the addiction. He nevertheless packs her a lunch of their staple in a "scoff tin," which is not really a tin but a plastic container. A bright smile replaces the sulks. She gives him a goodbye peck and minces away to the countryside.

Her sweet and mouldy smell lingers in the house, leaving the poor man with further unfulfilled desires.

When Saluni is away he discovers that he no longer knows how to be on his own. He tries very hard to remember what he used to do with himself before Saluni invaded his world. He only knows that during the season of the whales he spent all his time with the whales. But when the whales had migrated to the southern seas what did he do? And why is it impossible to do whatever he used to do now that Saluni's presence has become his habit? He wanders on the beach like the strandlopers of old. Or perhaps more like a lost oversized urchin. Whereas the strandlopers were beach-combing, his wanderings are quite aimless.

Saluni feels lost too. But she is determined to break the dependence on him that is taking hold of her like a narcotic. She wants to recapture part of her old life—at least that part that will not threaten her relationship with the Whale Caller. The Bored Twins are that part; though she knows that he is not exactly enamoured of them. But surely he will consider them a lesser evil than the taverns of Hermanus. She is so steeped in these thoughts that she does not realise that she has almost passed the mansion.

She is surprised to find the Bored Twins, who are normally high-spirited children, confined to their room.

"You don't care for us anymore, auntie," they greet her feebly. "You don't love us anymore."

"What gives you that idea?" asks Saluni.

"You don't come to play with us now," says one of the girls.

"It is because of what we did to you," says the other twin. "But we said we were sorry, auntie."

"It is not because of that. I've long forgotten about that. I was just busy lately. Things are not the same in my life . . . but, oh, you wouldn't understand! Tell you what, I promise I'll come and see you much more often."

"I know," says the first twin. "It is because Papa no longer gives you bottles of wine. But it is not his fault . . . really . . ."

"Nonsense! I don't drink wine anymore. Even when I did, I didn't come to see you for the bottles of wine."

The room has an unangelic stench of fever. One of the girls is sleeping on the mattress and is sweating so much that the sheet is wet. Their parents have left them alone, despite the fact that the girl is hot and cold and sometimes delirious. The girls tell Saluni that their parents had to go to work in the vineyards even though both the mother and the father also have the flu. It is the fate of all "piece-job" workers, Saluni knows: no work, no pay; no pension; no sick leave; no maternity leave, let alone the luxury of paternity leave; no compassionate leave even if your loved one is dying. The parents had to choose between staying at home to nurse the girl back to health, and then all die of starvation; or going to work and praying the girl will not be dying at home while they harvest the grapes. The consolation, of course, is that it will be one quick death, and not the slow death of the whole family.

Saluni knows immediately what to do. She has seen in the wild garden a minty shrub whose power she learnt from the people of the inland provinces. In the villages and farmlands beyond the mountains every homestead grows this medicinal herb. From the early days of humanity in these parts grandmothers have used this herb to relieve the symptoms of flu and to bring down the temperature. Saluni gets the shrub from the garden and boils it in water on a primus stove—not in the kitchen, but in the girls' bedroom.

She takes the boiling water from the primus stove and puts it on the floor. The shrub is still in the water. It has turned brown from the cooking. So has the water. She instructs the girl to kneel over it and covers both the girl and the steaming pot with a heavy blanket. The girl screams and tries to struggle out of the blanket.

"Take it easy," says Saluni. "Otherwise you'll scald yourself."

The girl's muffled voice can be heard whining under the blanket: "It's too hot in here . . . the steam is burning me."

"You are going to kill her, auntie . . . you are going to kill her," screams the twin who is fortunate enough not to have caught the fever from her sister. She is trying to pull Saluni away from the blanket, which she is pressing hard to the floor with both hands and both knees so that neither the steam nor the girl will escape.

"Nonsense," says Saluni. "This will help her instead. She needs to inhale the mentholated vapours and sweat the fever out. You'll see, in no time she will be fine again."

After all the steaming the girl falls into a deep sleep. When the parents return in the evening they are amazed at the improvement in her condition. She is almost her sprightly self again. Saluni teaches them how to prepare the remedy for their own flu, and after inhaling the vapours they feel much better as well. It is too late for her to walk back to the Wendy house, so she decides to sleep with the Bored Twins. This will also help her monitor the sick girl and to steam her some more if the flu becomes stubborn.

When the time for sleeping comes she panics when she remembers that she has not brought her candle with her. She is now used to the electrified luxury of the Wendy house and has become too careless about darkness. There is a candle somewhere in her sequinned handbag, but she left the handbag at the Wendy house because she had not planned to sleep over. The girls' parents agree to indulge her with a candle since she has helped their little girl so much. As soon as she gets into her bedding she feels something hard and rough touching her body. She screams when she discovers that she is sleeping on a snake. She jumps up, to great laughter from the girls. One of the girls reaches for the snake and dangles it in front of her.

"It's only a rubber snake, auntie," she says, still laughing.

"Never again play such tricks on me," shouts Saluni. "Do you want me to die of a heart attack?"

"We don't want you to die, auntie," says the sick twin. "We love you."

"Sorry, auntie," says the other twin. "Sorry, auntie."

When night falls and Saluni hasn't returned the Whale Caller becomes jittery. He knows that she will not walk in the countryside in the dark. He blames himself for being insensitive to her neuroses. Perhaps that is why she had gone to the Bored Twins. Now, because of him, Saluni might have relapsed to the bottle. She might be spending the night singing rude songs with sailors and layabouts in the taverns of Hermanus. Worse still, she might have deserted him forever, and this sends a cold panic galloping in his guts. He is tempted to go and search for her, but decides against it when he realises that there are hundreds of taverns dotting the district. He would not know where to begin.

The night is too long. The bed that broke its virginity that breathless night of murder and thunder is lumpy and uncomfortable, asserting its own longing.

At dawn his body itches for a waltz, even though in winter there are no songs of the whales. If Saluni were here they would be dancing a cappella. After sunrise he decides to go to the mansion and find out if Saluni did go there. And if she did, he would like to know where she said she was going when she left the mansion. If she did not get to the Bored Twins at all, then she had lied to him. There must be another lover. When and how it happened he has no idea, as Saluni has been with him all the time these past few weeks. Since the first cleansing ritual they have been inseparable.

He has a general idea where the mansion is located. He remembers seeing it once or twice at a distance many years ago. He follows the road out of town in a westerly direction and trudges on until he sees the white building shimmering in the morning sun. From this distance its dilapidation is not noticeable. As he gets closer, the tulips that are blooming in the wild garden dazzle him with their wild colours. The flowers grow in clusters of deep purple, white, pink, yellow and red. Some petals combine different hues. There are red petals with yellow edges and violet petals with white edges. Saluni has told him the story of how the tulips were cultivated by the ostrich baron in the 1920s. He had inherited the bulbs from his forebears, who had in turn received them from the first in line—the son of the tulip baron who had long ago exiled himself to the Cape of Good Hope after the crash of the tulip market in Holland and the suicide of his father. The first in line had sailed with the bulbs to the Cape for sentimental reasons. He had no intention of starting a tulip business in the "new world," but instead had secured himself clerical employment with the Dutch East India Company. He planted his bulbs in his little garden, and when his children—both those from his Dutch wife and from Khoikhoi and Malay slave mistresses—were all grown up they dug out some of the bulbs and planted them in their little gardens. It happened like that over the generations, for almost three hundred years, until the time of the ostrich baron.

Tulips flower in spring, but these have developed erratic habits. They blossom any season they feel like blossoming, and they do it all at the same time, upstaging every other plant in the wild garden. And when they have decided to bloom, sometimes after hibernating for three years without a peep of colour from them, they are relentless. They spread all over the garden and are not deterred by the wild shrubs and grasses and the prickly pear and other cacti that otherwise reign supreme in the garden. But they never grow beyond what used to be the borders of the original ostrich baron's garden.

The Whale Caller can hear shrieks of laughter from the garden. The voices have hollow reverberations like drops of water
dripping from the roof of a cave into a rippling pool on the floor.
He is overwhelmed by inexplicable elation. There is a strong scent
of peace in the air despite the commotion that he can hear from
around the corner. As he walks closer new odours assail him—the
pungent smells of history coming in a whoosh from the broken
windows of the mansion. The sweet and mouldy smell he knows
so well comes floating gently to him, overpowering the variety of
smells that permeate the air. And then he hears her voice: "I got
it! Don't let it get away!"

Saluni and the Bored Twins are having a wonderful time chasing goats. These animals occasionally invade the garden since they
are partial to the cactus that grows on what used to be rockeries.
Saluni has got a goat by the hind legs, letting its big udder dangle
indecently. She lifts it up and one of the Bored Twins grabs a teat
and squeezes the milk into her mouth. The goat is struggling and
trying to escape and milk splatters all over her face. Saluni lets it
go and runs to help the second twin, who is chasing another goat
that has an even bigger udder. After a relentless chase they catch
the goat, overpower it, and successfully milk it into the girl's
mouth.

The Whale Caller watches for a while. Saluni sees him leaning
against the wall and shouts excitedly, "Come on, man. There is
milk for you too."

The Whale Caller hesitates a little. She beckons him once more
and he joins the chase. He becomes the girls' hero when he helps
them catch and subdue the wildest of the animals. They cheer
and applaud and go crazy over its teats. When they have had their
fill they spray each other with the milk. He also has his turn suck-
ling the warm milk. This is his first experience of goat milk and
he finds the strange taste quite enjoyable. Then the girls spray

him with the milk. Saluni watches all this with a big smile on her face.

"Let us not waste the milk," the Whale Caller says, with streaks of milk mapping his face. "Remember that these goats have their kids to feed as well as providing the farmer with milk."

"They are just wild goats," says one of the twins. "They don't belong to a farmer."

"You don't know that," says Saluni.

"They belong to someone all right. That is why they don't have their kids with them," says the Whale Caller, letting the goat free and jumping out of its way. It kicks violently, throwing one of the twins to the ground. They all laugh at her. They help the fallen girl up and Saluni introduces them to the Whale Caller.

"A whale caller? What does a whale caller do?" asks the smaller twin.

"Is he your husband?" enquires the other one.

"Boyfriend! Remember Aunt Saluni told Mama that she was not married."

"You ask silly questions," says Saluni, brushing the dust from the Whale Caller with her hands.

"I came to fetch you, Saluni," says the Whale Caller. "I waited for you for the whole night. I was worried about you, Saluni."

"Why did you wait for her, Mr. Whale Caller?" asks the bigger twin. "Why were you worried about her when she was with us?"

"He is her boyfriend, silly!" says the smaller twin. "He is supposed to worry."

The girls find the notion that Aunt Saluni may have a boyfriend quite funny, and they giggle, jumping about, clapping their sweet little hands and chanting: "Aunt Saluni has a boyfriend . . . a boyfriend. Aunt Saluni has a boyfriend . . . a boyfriend."

Saluni stands there, arms akimbo, displaying a toothless grin.

The Whale Caller's body moves to the rhythm of the chants despite himself.

The girls clamber on him, and play with his silver-grey beard and marvel at his bushy chest, hunting for little fairies that they claim are hiding there. He in turn is spellbound by their beauty and their angelic voices. But what strikes him most is the wonderful fact that the girls smell like earthworms.

"Your face is glowing," observes the smaller twin.

This only confirms what he has earlier observed when he was looking in the mirror trimming his beard. Ever since the cleansing rituals his face has acquired a smooth glow. Saluni is not the only one who has a propolis face.

When Saluni and the Whale Caller decide to go, the Bored Twins sing for them. They are transfixed. At the end of the song they try once more to go, but the twins break into another song that transfixes their visitors once more. This happens over and over again until late in the afternoon when the girls either get tired of singing or just get bored. Only then are the visitors able to go.

Saluni and the Whale Caller are euphoric as they walk back home. Euphoria tends to make one almost levitate in the air, but their gait is heavy because of the goat milk that still fills their stomachs almost to bursting point, even when so many hours have gone by since the early morning adventures with the goats. He sees their long shadows and cannot believe that he allowed the Bored Twins to hold him captive for such a long time. It would have been a wasted day if it were not for the reward of euphoria. Now he understands Saluni's addiction to them. The girls are Euphoriants! This fills him with fear, for he is dead scared of happiness. He makes a deal with himself: he will stay away from the Bored Twins as much as possible. He will imbibe them only occasionally, but will not allow any dependence to develop.

Saluni is babbling effervescently beside him about her folly of having given up the Bored Twins for almost a month. After all, they are just sweet little girls who need her company only in the daytime when their parents are at work. There is no harm in resuming her regular visits to the mansion. There is no need for him to feel so insecure, she advises him, because the Bored Twins will never replace him. There is room in her big heart for him and them.

He is convinced that Saluni has relapsed.


Saluni. It is the final month of winter this year and once more she has become a junkie. She cannot have enough of the Bored Twins. She leaves the Wendy house in the morning and spends several hours with them almost every day. She used to sing only when she was drunk, but now she joins them in full sobriety, and together they belt out hymns that they have heard on the radio. The fact that they do not know most of the words never deters them. They make up their own words as they go along. Words about goats and beetles and tulips and rain and Mama and Papa finally coming home. Saluni has also taught them censored versions of the songs she used to sing in the taverns.

This afternoon, like most afternoons, she returns to the Wendy house babbling in euphoric tongues. The Whale Caller is sitting on the chair moping and feeling sorry for himself. She sweeps him to his feet and dances around him, waving his arms like a bird in flight and then like the dying swan of classical ballet. As she falls to the floor she breaks out laughing and, kicking her legs up, she rides an invisible upside-down bicycle. The Cutex cannot restrain the runs in her stockings and more of them appear as she pedals even harder. Such undignified behaviour always embarrasses the Whale Caller, especially when it goes beyond the bounds of euphoria into the terrain of trancelike ecstasy, as if she has eaten the petals of the bell-shaped moon flowers that create hallucinations.

"You look ridiculous, Saluni," he says. "What will people say when they see you like this?"

"Come on, man," she says, "don't be such a sourpuss. Do something crazy for once in your life. Take me in your arms and lose yourself in me."

The Whale Caller is scandalised.

"It is daytime, Saluni!"

"So what? Who says madness is only for the night?"

That is another thing with these visits to the mansion. Euphoria has other side effects on her. It sharpens her appreciation of him and their mutual rituals. It makes her insatiable. It carnalises him to oblivion. To the point that he finds this euphoria too taxing on his robust physique, and he has come to dread the nightly cleansing rituals. Not that he wants to do away with them altogether. No. He would rather die. He merely wants the rate and the pace reduced, so that he can catch his breath, and replenish his body with more strength and more juices for better-quality ritualing next time.

He helps her to her feet.

"Poor man," she says. "I was only joking. I don't want to be hard on you. You are such a sweet boy it would not work in my favour if I killed you."

"I think you must take it easy about going to the Bored Twins," he says.

"Oh, no! Not again, man. We talked about that, didn't we?"

"Yeah, but you are overdoing it now. Do spend some days with me, Saluni. I don't only want to see you at night."

Saluni agrees not to go to the mansion the next day. And she occupies herself with reviving civilised living. She has been neglecting quite a few things in the house lately, she realises. For instance the man has gone back to his old eating habits. He does not sit at the table that is covered with a white tablecloth as she has taught him. No candlelight. Sometimes he even sits on the bed holding a bowl of macaroni and cheese to his chest and munching away, quite oblivious of her disgust.

"I must take you to a restaurant, man, so that you can see how people eat there," she says.

This brings a mocking chuckle from the Whale Caller.

"Since when can we afford eating out?" he asks.

"We go out window shopping for food . . ."

"We used to, before you took to going to the mansion every day."

"Hey, we still do when I return early enough."

"It is not enough," moans the Whale Caller.

"You never knew that you would end up liking it like this, did you?" she says excitedly. "Then we'll window shop, hey? We'll window shop as much as you like. What do you say to that? As much as you like. Then we'll go to the best restaurants in town and window eat there. I'll teach you how."

On Friday evening when the socialites of Hermanus go dining and dancing and theatring, Saluni and the Whale Caller are also getting ready for an evening out. He polishes his black shoes until they reflect the light from the naked bulb that hangs on the ceiling. He wears his tuxedo and is happy for the opportunity. Since Sharisha left it has been lying fallow in the box under the bed. Of course once in a while he takes it out to press it, but the satisfaction from that activity does not come close to the one he derives from actually wearing it for a purpose. Saluni brushes his beard. Then she slips into her green taffeta dress, fishnet stockings and red pencil-heel shoes. Her red hair is held in a black net. Her face is heavily made up with crimson lipstick and violet mascara. She sprays perfume all over her body—even on her head and legs.

That is one thing that troubles the Whale Caller—Saluni's strong perfume. Some mornings when she feels particularly like a lady she sprays herself with it, and its strong smell fills the room. It stings his eyes. He coughs, unable to breathe, and then sneezes for a long time. Often he rushes to the door to breathe the fresh air outside. Sometimes he is still in bed. He covers his head with the blanket. But the perfume is so strong that it penetrates the blanket. He is afraid to tell her that her perfume makes him suffer so. At first he thought she was trying to disguise the sweet and mouldy smell. But soon he realised that she was not aware of the fact that her body exuded such an odour. Fortunately the ugly scent of the perfume never lasts for any length of time. Soon the sweet and mouldy smell hangs in the air long after she is gone.

They walk out of the door, and out of the gate. They tread genteelly on the pavement, arm in arm. He inhales the cold breeze from the sea with relish and rejoices in the soft fragrances of rotting kelp. He has fond memories of this ambience because at this time of the year when Sharisha was enjoying the krill in the southern seas the smells became a balm to his yearning soul. He is amazed at himself that he no longer yearns even though Sharisha has been gone for so long. He would not even have thought of her had it not been for the smells from the sea. They have walked only a few yards when Saluni extricates her arm from the genteelness and trots back to the Wendy house.

"It's locked, Saluni. Please let's not waste time," he calls after her.

"Just to make sure, man, just to make sure," she calls back.

She does this twice or thrice, and he waits patiently. Finally she defies the urge to walk back to check just one more time, and they stroll down the road.

They walk past American-type fast food franchises—the day

calls for something classier than whopping burgers, deep-fried thick-battered chicken and slick pizzas that bear little resemblance to the original Italian peasant fare—and then turn into a street that prides itself on its restaurants. They stop for a while at the window of a hotel restaurant with a sushi bar, and watch the patrons sitting on cushions or mats on the floor like a congregation of some New Age religion, eating delicate oval-shaped balls of rice rolled in fish. On the low tables there are tiny bowls of different dark sauces. Other worshippers are sitting at the bar drinking some whitish sacramental drink and eating similar fare. There are chunks of white, grey, red and pink fish displayed on flat wooden rectangular rice plates. She explains to him that the fish is eaten raw, and he says that is not to his taste. Fish can only be decent when it is coated in spiced batter, fried in plenty of oil, and then eaten with golden brown chips, in the traditional manner of the Western Cape.

"You can talk about macaroni and cheese," says Saluni, "but you don't know anything about fish."

"I used to live on fish when I walked the coast," he tells her. "I lived in fisherfolk villages where they knew how to fry the fish."

At this point the maître d' sees them standing outside looking through the window debating the merits of his food. He goes out and invites them in.

"We have the best nigiri in South Africa," he adds. "Yes, in this little town of Hermanus we beat top restaurants in Cape Town and Johannesburg. Our secret lies in the fact that our fish is fermented in salt and our rice is seasoned with a sweet vinegar mixture, as sushi originally used to be created in ancient Japan."

The Whale Caller is looking at him closely, wondering how it is possible for a man to work up so much enthusiasm for mere fish and rice. Saluni declines the invitation for them both and tells the maître d' that they would rather enjoy his decorative delicacies with their eyes from a distance.

"We also serve sushi that doesn't include sashimi . . . that doesn't include raw fish . . . if that's what you are squeamish about," the man says. He is persuasive, but Saluni explains once more that they are only interested in eating his food with their eyes, if he doesn't mind. The friendly face changes in a flash.

"Of course I mind. You make my customers nervous watching them like that. Please go and be spectators somewhere else," he says as he angrily walks back into the restaurant.

"I wouldn't like to be watched when I eat either," says the Whale Caller. "Eating should be a private matter. Like sex."

He startles himself with this last observation. His worst nightmare is becoming a reality: Saluni has debauched him, to the extent that a simile like that can roll out of his mouth unprovoked. But all this is lost on Saluni.

"As if it is something sinful," says Saluni. "If they want to eat in private they mustn't come to a restaurant."

The maître d' draws the blinds and the remote diners are left facing white kimono-clad outlines of Japanese beauties and leafy bamboos on a red background.

"Oh, man! What did he do that for? I wanted to taste some of that sake," wails Saluni.

"Sake?" asks the Whale Caller.

"The wine," she explains. "It is made from rice. I understand it is wonderfully powerful. As strong as the man next to me."

"Don't even think about it," he warns her. "Otherwise I might find you swimming in the bottle again and wasting your life in the taverns."

"You look so cute when you worry about me," she says, cackling.

There are other restaurants. Each one boldly advertises some foreign cuisine, ranging from Indian and Chinese to French and Italian. But their curtains are drawn.

"Perhaps we should change our dining strategy next time,"

says Saluni. "We should dine in the daytime. Curtains are bound to be open in the daytime."

"Perhaps we shouldn't dine at all," says the Whale Caller. "We should be sitting in front of a warm heater at home."

"Don't give up so easily, man," she says. "You'll see, you'll like it once you get the hang of it. Just like the window shopping."

They are about to give up despite Saluni's exhortations when they chance upon a Cape Dutch house at a corner of a nondescript street. It is the only restaurant that unashamedly boasts of specialising in South African cuisine. Everyone knows that in the Western Cape when they talk of South African cuisine they mean the Cape Malay food that is a result of the melting cultures of Indonesia, India, Malaysia, Khoikhoi and Dutch. The same kind of interbreeding that brought into existence the wonderfully coloured people of the Western Cape. As in the rest of the restaurants at this time of the night, this one's thick maroon velvet draperies are drawn as well. But at one of the windows there has been some carelessness since there is a big gap between the curtains through which Saluni and the Whale Caller can see inside.

The glass reflects their own images because of the glare from the streetlights. Therefore they have to press their faces against the panes in order to have a good look at the chefs standing in a row—the high priest and his acolytes—cutting roast lamb, beef, chicken, pork and venison behind a long buffet counter of crayfish, langoustine, perlemoen, curries, rotis, samoosas, colourful salads, pies, boboties, sosaties, pickled snoek fish, masala fish, rice, and sweetmeats such as temeletjies and the syrupy doughnuts known as koeksisters. The priests do everything in full view of the worshippers, many of whom watch in admiration as they brandish their big knives about, slicing the roasts with pomp and ceremony. Sosaties are braaied over an open fire, while the worshippers ceremonially walk the length of the altar, serving their fancy onto their plates. Then they walk to their tables, also set up like altars, each one with a candle burning idly. Worshippers are in couples. Youthful upwardly mobile lovers and jaded old-world couples from the houses of retired millionaires that dot the district. There are hardly any tourists at this time of the year.

"I find this worshipping of food obscene," the Whale Caller whispers.

She gives him an acid glare and says, "You should count your blessings and taste every dish instead of complaining."

"After all, sooner or later it will be digested and will surely become stools. Then it will be scorned and despised. People forget that only a few hours back they were venerating it."

"You are the only human being outside the doctor's rooms who talks of stools. Normal people talk of shit, man. Not stools. Not faeces. Not waste matter. Pure unadulterated shit!"

"Ja, whatever you call it, Saluni . . . whatever you call it."

"You didn't rebel like this when I taught you window shopping. You ended up liking it."

"Because it was private, Saluni. Not like here where people have built special temples for the ritual of eating . . . where eaters enact pagan rites of mating."

"Now you are getting carried away, man," says an astounded Saluni. "No one is mating anybody here. You are beginning to have wonderfully dirty thoughts . . . like me. People are just eating, that's all."

"It's not just eating, Saluni. You and I know that with these people eating is part of lovemaking . . . part of . . ." He cannot bring himself to say it.

"Foreplay? You once uttered that word, man. What went wrong now? I thought you had got over your primness."

"In private, Saluni. It was uttered between you and me . . . in the privacy of our bedroom."

"I still don't see the difference, man. We eat at supermarkets with our eyes . . ."

"Here, my dear Saluni, we are voyeurs of an orgy. This is where I put the full stop, Saluni. I am not going to be part of this window eating anymore."

He steps aside. Saluni continues to stand at the window and to gormandise each of the dishes. But there is no fun in it if she can't share the experience with him. The food tastes like paper. She is disappointed in him, and says so. He apologises and explains that this deification of food is a new experience for him. He eats to sustain himself, because if he does not eat he will die. His habits of eating are quite rudimentary. When he used to walk the coast he only needed to get fish, braai it on the open coal with maize on the cob and eat it. There was no ceremony. When he returned from the coast it became easier and cheaper to boil macaroni, sprinkle it with shredded cheese and eat. Again there was no ceremony.

"You hate ceremony then, do you?" mocks Saluni. "But you are a creature of ritual. Like me, you are prone to ceremonial actions. You cannot pretend otherwise."

The evening has been a disaster, and they walk home without a word to each other. She walks in front, almost trotting, and he follows leisurely behind. He is beginning to regret his outburst. Perhaps he should have just gone along with the ritual. It never hurts to be accommodative. But if he did Saluni would have expected them to visit the restaurants every weekend. Just as they visit the supermarkets at least once a week. He enjoys those visits. No one knows that they are eating from the displays of canned and boxed food. It is therefore private. Supermarkets are not temples built for the purpose of worshipping food. One buys the food and takes it to the privacy of one's home. He can never bring himself to enjoy the vulgarities of public eating. He will just have to find a way of making it up to Saluni.

The next morning, after their ablutions, he brushes her hair and braids it into two long ropes. He files her nails and polishes them with Cutex. While he is at it he uses some of the nail polish to stop the runs on her nylon stockings. Indeed on the following days he pampers Saluni even more. In the mornings he goes to the flower market and buys her a flower—whatever flower is the cheapest that day. He takes her to the town centre to listen to blind buskers playing love standards on their violins, guitars or saxophones.

Nights rock the Wendy house, even on red days.

Although she never outrightly expresses gratitude to the Whale Caller for anything, she claims she is the happiest she has ever been, but he can see that something is missing in her life. She mopes around and is down-spirited. She looks depressed, and he knows why. The Bored Twins.

"Why don't you go and see them," he asks out of the blue one day. "I think they are missing you too."

"And then you are going to bitch about it? No, I am not going."

"When did I bitch about anything, Saluni?"

"I know you don't like them, and God knows what those little angels ever did to you."

"It's not that I don't like them, Saluni. I just don't want you to be so dependent on them. I don't mind if you see them once in a while. Not every day. I need you too, Saluni, you know that. Some days I need to spend the whole day with you."

She goes to the mansion. And euphoria returns to her. He continues to pamper her, which depletes his financial resources—especially the daily flower that he insists on buying despite the abundance of tulips and the offerings on the collection plates of the blind musicians. But he does not mind. What matters is that they are both happy and many days pass without a single quarrel between them. She indulges him by talking to him sweetly, in a bluesy musical voice, and by being generally pleasant to him even when she thinks he is being stiff and stupid.

One afternoon on her way home from the mansion she visits Mr. Yodd. It is not a spur-of-the-moment decision. She has been planning the visit the whole day. And for the whole day a conflict has been brewing in her head as to whether to go or not to go. She brings with her a bunch of tulips from the mansion and walks down the crag to the grotto. This time she kneels down on some jagged stones and arranges the tulips around the small entrance as a propitiation rite. The stones under her knees are far from comfortable, and she wonders how the Whale Caller managed to kneel here—sometimes for hours on end. Perhaps it was part of his mortification: the very quest to put the flesh to death that made him deny himself the pleasures of fish, even though he could afford it, and live on an unchanging insipid diet. He may not frequent Mr. Yodd anymore, but he is still a flagellant at heart. The quest that today makes him deny himself the Bored Twins, despite himself.

Saluni can hear some squeaking and rustling sounds inside. Perhaps the rock rabbits are fighting. Or nursing babies. Or just enjoying one another. All these may sound the same to the uninitiated. A rock rabbit peeps out to see what has cast a shadow at the entrance of their abode. It sees the tulips, grabs some of them and dashes back into the grotto without paying any attention to Saluni. These are the woes of winter. In the absence of tourists the dustbins are empty and the rock rabbits have been reduced to the indignities of eating unseasonable flowers.

⏦

HOY, MR. YODD! It is true. We forget about you when our boat is sailing in calm seas. We remember you only in times of storms. That is why we create deities in the first place, Mr. Yodd. To remember them in times of upheaval. We conjure them into existence so that they can explain our own existence—and therefore our troubles—away. Where is he? He does not need you any-more. He is a fulfilled man and can survive without mortification. He wakes up every morning, reaches for the mist and wraps him-self with it like a blanket of the mountain people. He is ensconced in the comfort of the mist and his body has forgotten its previous need for your flogging laughter. I have taken you over because I feel that you cannot just sit in your little hole going to waste. Par-don me, Mr. Yodd . . . in your grotto. Someone must confess to you and I am here to do just that. I am not just doing you a favour, perhaps feeling sorry for you now that he has given you up. I need to confess. He won't like it when he finally gets to hear of it. There is no reason for him to be insecure about it. Sometimes he can be such a big baby. But I do want to nurse his sensitivities. He claims now you belong to me. I never knew this selfish streak in him. He thought he was going to hog you to himself, and when I discovered you and decided that you can serve my purposes as well he throws all his toys out of the cot and vows he will have nothing to do with you. Is this the real reason he no longer comes? It is the real reason. I do not go around inventing reasons for him. Okay, it is not the mist. This is the real reason. Perhaps you are right when you say he didn't really mean it. There were upheavals in our lives when he said it. We were snapping at each other. You may be right, I was the snapper. We were still trying to find each other, that is why. Now that peace and harmony reign I do not want to upset the delicate situation. Yet I feel that a confession is necessary. And it is a simple one: we are too happy to survive each other. There is no anguish in our lives. That is the reason I am here. I worry myself sick because there is no anguish. True love is supposed to be accompanied by profound pain. Yet in our lives things seem to be so easy and smooth. What happened to the pain that used to rack us? Perhaps I am beginning to lose him. That must be it. I am beginning to lose him . . . to Sharisha, as you sug-gest. You had to bring the big fish into the picture. We are at the

door of August and the southern rights will soon return. Now
that you have done me the favour of bringing the matter up, this
thought brings anguish into my life. What is left for me to do is to
bring anguish into his life too. Then we'll both wallow in anguish.
You are right, Mr. Yodd. My anguish is enough to cause him anguish. I can feel our relationship gathering anguish on both sides
already. It is indeed true love. You are a genius, Mr. Yodd. Laugh
as you may, I knew you would do the trick. Laugh as you may, I
am going home to smother him with love. Laugh as you may, I am
going to drag him out of the mist and suffocate him with love and
therefore with anguish until he has his fill of it.

SALUNI. She is laughing mockingly as she walks up the crag, im-
itating the confessor's derisive laughter. Poor Mr. Yodd. He lost
his temper because his laughter did not bruise her. He tried to rub
salt on her self-inflicted anguish by chanting over and over: "Sharisha will be back soon! Sharisha will be back soon!" Chanting in
the same rhythm as the Bored Twins when they tease her about
something. About having a boyfriend, for instance. His voice,
however, had the swishing harshness of a cat-o'-nine-tails. His efforts became pathetic when she chanted back: "Saluni fears nobody! Saluni will crush your little Sharisha to pieces!" When he
broke into a laughter that would have shamed a stone she cackled
back at him. That's when he lost his temper and asked her to va-
cate his sacred grounds once and for all.

His laughter is a flagellum. But this woman is so thick-skinned
that she does not bleed at all. Not a single weal appears after the
hardest flagellation. His efforts are wasted on her. Her indiffer-
ence disempowers his laughter. He would rather have the Whale
Caller anytime. The Whale Caller knows how to glory in penance.
Not only does the flagellum send him into fits of mortification,

even mere chastisement does the trick. Flagellation had become an addictive drug to the Whale Caller, until this arrogant woman featured in his life and took it over. How did Mr. Yodd lose his hold on him? Mr. Yodd still puzzles over how Saluni became such a compelling drug that she was able to replace him.

She cackles on until she reaches the top, where she stands and faces down the crag challengingly. She will be back, she assures herself. Mr. Yodd has not heard the last of her. Her eyes stray past the emerald green shallows to the blue depths. Then she sees it. Something that brings shivers to her body. Not shivers of fear. Shivers of anger. There is the head of a whale at some distance sticking out of the surface of the blue depths. It is spyhopping, searching as if it has lost sight of its companions. From the callosities on the snout, the so-called bonnet, Saluni can tell that it is a southern right.

So, they are back! Mr. Yodd must have known that the southern rights were back. It is the end of July and they are gradually returning, until they peak in September and October. They will have her to contend with. Especially those that have wicked designs on her man. Who knows? It might be Sharisha herself who is crudely spyhopping out there. Saluni is prepared for a battle. She wanted some anguish in her life, but this is an overdose of it. She has always known that this day would come, but realises now that she has not prepared herself for it.

She practically runs home in her stockinged feet since she is carrying her pencil-heel shoes in her hands. She finds the Whale Caller pressing his tuxedo in the kitchen. Although occasionally he occupies himself in this manner, she suddenly suspects that there is a sinister motive for it this time. He must be aware of the return of the southern rights. His ears are keen for their songs. He must have heard them in the night and said nothing about it. Perhaps that is why he is displaying a smug smile.

"You have come from the mansion," he says, "yet you don't

bring home any euphoria. Were the Bored Twins not there to-day?"

"It wore off as soon as I saw what you were up to," she says, gearing for war.

"I am not up to anything, Saluni," he says. "What happened to you?"

"Don't pretend you don't know. You didn't tell me that they were back. You were hiding it from me."

He looks at her suspiciously.

"Did you go to Mr. Yodd today?" he asks. "You look like some-one who has come from Mr. Yodd rather than from the Bored Twins."

"Of course I did."

"I think you have got the trick, Saluni. Imbibe euphoria from the Bored Twins, and then tone it down with Mr. Yodd's sombre-ness. Trust you to think of something brilliant like that. I should try it sometime."

"And I saw your damn whales too!"

"Well, Saluni, it is the season. But that shouldn't upset you at all. I find it exciting that the whales are back. Now we'll be able to dance to their songs at dawn."

He puts the iron on the ironing board and reaches for her, sweeping her away in an impromptu waltz. She resists and pushes him away. There is a smell of anger and resentment in the room.

"Didn't you miss our morning ballroom at the beach?" he asks amiably, hoping to pacify her. "I know I did."

"More like you missed your rude nightlong dances with Sha-risha."

"So it is about Sharisha, is it? Was it Sharisha that you saw?"

"How the hell would I know? All whales look the same to me."

"Were her callosities pure white? Did she have a perfect bon-net? Did she have callosities that look like the Three Sisters? Did she have a baby with her?"

"You are salivating already. You know what? You can go back to your confounded Sharisha for all I care."

She storms out of the door and out of the gate. She walks for a while, not quite sure where to go. She would go to a movie house if she had the money. She would stay for a double feature so that he panics and goes out searching for her. He would go from tavern to tavern asking drunken sailors if they had seen his lover. None of them, of course, would claim to have seen her. He would walk for the whole night in the cold, searching and weeping. He would catch a terrible cold, flu even, and would be in bed for the whole week sweating and delirious. It would serve him right.

On a lamppost she sees a poster about a healing session that is being conducted by a visiting evangelical pastor from America. She walks to a soccer field where a circus-like marquee has been erected. This is where she is going to while away time until the man at home fries in worry. The hymns are lively and welcoming. Inside the tent a young charismatic preacher is preaching against the sins of the flesh: fornication, incest, sodomy and the like. He reads from Genesis 16 about a woman called Sarai who gave her Egyptian slave to her husband, Abram, to produce children since she herself could not conceive. The slave conceives and becomes arrogant, wanting to usurp the mistress of the house. "In the manner that maids do even today," he adds this rider, to relate these ancient events to the modern lives of his congregation, some of whom are maids and have surely been involved in some hanky-panky with their masters. There are the madams too—as the employers of the maids are called—for such gatherings where people are healed and saved know no class boundaries. The madams in the congregation feel vindicated by the sermon. The preacher outlines with relish the conflicts between Sarai and the beautiful slave woman, embellishing them from the wealth of his imagination. When he has squeezed all the salacious juices from that story the congregation sings one verse of a hymn about the wrath of the Lord on all fornicators, and then the preacher turns to the Second Book of Samuel. He elaborates on the adulteries of King David and the children who were born out of them. He sounds like a gossip columnist rejoicing in the carnal lapses of a president. The congregation is fired with divine fervour. He seizes the opportunity to move them even to greater heights by returning to Genesis and reading God's command to the crowd that has now become so enthralled that many of the men and women are foaming at the mouth: "You shall desire your husband and he will rule over you . . ." They are screaming and testifying in tongues. After a while Saluni is bored by their antics. The message being propagated here is not the kind she would like to entertain. The night is going to be long. The preacher is sure to find more Old Testament scandals to keep his congregation fired up. He is testifying about Lot's daughters and their incestuous shenanigans that are graphically recorded in Genesis 19 when Saluni sneaks out of the tent. She seems to be the only one who has not been moved by the spirit. She is well aware of what will soon happen in that tent. Pairs in the congregation are gravitating into each other's arms, aroused by the sacred texts.

She walks back to the Wendy house and goes straight to bed. The Whale Caller timidly joins her. There is no cleansing ceremony tonight.

The following morning Saluni decides not to go to the mansion so as to make sure that the Whale Caller does not get into any mischief. She does not tell him that. She just follows him everywhere he goes. He finds this rather amusing and enjoys having her around. She follows him for three days—during which he avoids going to the beach lest he exacerbates her suspicions. But soon the urge to see the Bored Twins overpowers her and she goes to the mansion.

It is early in the morning but the girls are already playing in the dirt. She herds them back into the house and insists that they take a bath before they can play outside. She finds that they prepared themselves a breakfast of corn flakes and milk as soon as they woke up, without even first washing their hands and brushing their teeth. No one is ever there to teach them this basic hygiene because the parents leave home very early before the girls wake up and come back late in the evening. Sometimes the girls are already asleep when the parents return. Whenever she can, Saluni tries to teach them some of these rudimentary things—so that they can be ladies, she tells them.

After the bath she gives them a few pointers about the art of making one's face up. She takes out a lipstick, eyebrow pencil, face powder and mascara from her sequinned handbag and they all have a go at making themselves up. The girls do not take this exercise seriously. They just smear the lipstick on their cheeks and make silly patterns with the mascara and the eyebrow pencil. Saluni sees how much fun they are having and asks them to make her up with a silly face too. They all look like circus clowns.

Then they go to play outside. There are no goats to chase today, but there is always something interesting to do in the wild garden. The tulips are hibernating, just when it is about spring. Saluni finds this erratic behaviour irritating because she had hoped to pick a few to brighten the Whale Caller's life in the Wendy house. Not a single one of the plants is in bloom.

Saluni and the Bored Twins play hide-and-seek among the rockeries. The girls are not very good at hiding but Saluni pretends that she can't find them. Hiding behind an aloe, the smaller twin sees a snake slithering out of the house, and then cascading down the three steps of the kitchen door. It tries to gather speed, but cannot move fast enough on the grassless patch between the door and the rockeries. The twin chases it, catches it by the tail and lifts it up. It is quite helpless with its head dangling down.

The bigger twin joins her sister in the excitement, poking the eyes of the snake with a stick.

"Aunt Saluni, look what we found," cries the bigger twin, as they both go looking for Saluni excitedly. She emerges from where she was hiding and sees the snake, still dangling from the raised hand of the smaller twin.

"Oh, no!" Saluni says, laughing. "You won't catch me with your pranks this time! I know that is a rubber snake."

"It is not, auntie," says the smaller twin.

"It is a real snake, Aunt Saluni," confirms the bigger twin.

"You wouldn't be holding it like that if it were a real snake," says Saluni. "Even a blind person can see that it is a rubber snake."

The twin throws the snake at Saluni. She catches it, still laughing. It quickly coils itself around her arm. She is paralysed with terror. Then she falls down screaming and rolling on the ground. Her thigh bleeds from a wound that has been caused by a sharp stone on which she fell. The snake slithers away. Fortunately it is a mole snake that feeds on house mice and hasn't got any venom.

Saluni has fainted on the ground and is bleeding. The twins are now panicking. They try to shake her awake while crying: "Sorry, auntie . . . sorry, auntie!"

As soon as she regains her senses she jumps up and runs like the wind. She does not even think of picking up her shoes that are lying on the ground. She just runs as if something terrible is chasing her, until she reaches the Wendy house. The door is locked and the Whale Caller is not at home.

She suspects that he has gone to Walker Bay to consort with the whales, and she goes there. And indeed there he is, sitting on the green bench, watching a whale sluggishly working its way to join two other whales at some distance. He is wearing his tuxedo and is holding his horn.

"You locked me out of the house, man!" she screams.

He is startled out of his reverie and gives her an amazed stare.

"What's with the wild look and a clown's face? You look like a gorgon."

"How do you expect me to get into the house when you lock me out?"

"I didn't expect you back so early," he says. "You never come back this early when you have gone to the Bored Twins."

"Yes, I can see that you didn't expect me this early. So this is what you are up to when I am not there? I suppose that is your fish!"

"It is Sharisha, if that's what you mean."

"Then why are you not jumping about playing that stupid horn?"

The Whale Caller just stands up and walks away. Saluni shouts after him, telling him he has no right to walk away when she is still talking to him. But he is not in a mood for an argument. He chooses not to hear Saluni's shrill voice, even though it comes from only a few feet away, and redirects his thoughts to Sharisha. Sharisha never nags him about anything. He is wondering, though, what could have happened to her. There is something unusual about her.

The song is the same, although it sounds low and tired. That is how he came to the bay this morning. Just after Saluni had left for the mansion he heard the familiar song. He did not think twice about changing into black tie, grabbing his favourite horn and rushing to the bay. Sharisha was there all right. And was alone. He was a bit disappointed. He had expected her to return with a calf, after the pillaging that happened to her months ago, a few days before she left for the southern seas. Perhaps none of the males had been strong enough to plant the seed.

He played the horn. Sharisha responded unenthusiastically.

There was none of her usual breaching and lobtailing. She just floated on the water like a big dirigible that had fallen from the sky only to be tossed about by lazy winds on the surface of the ocean. She didn't seem to propel herself and depended on the whims of the waves. This purposeless and directionless whale was not the Sharisha he knew. Southern rights are lethargic by nature and are the most buoyant of whales, but at this point Sharisha— the very one who had been the most active of all southern rights in the Whale Caller's experience—seemed to be taking lethargy and buoyancy to extremes.

Then he saw it. As Sharisha made a feeble attempt to respond to his horn he saw the gaping wound on her side. He knew at once that it had been caused by a ship's propeller on her way from the southern seas. The law forbids fishing boats from coming closer than three hundred metres to a whale. However, whales are very curious people. They actually take their nosy selves to the trawlers and even to big passenger liners. Many have lost their tails or have died in their encounters with boats. Sometimes they get entangled with fishing gear because they play with it like kelp, using it to remove the irritating lice from their callosities. Perhaps Sharisha did have a baby after all. Perhaps it was entangled or sliced to pieces by the same boat that wounded the mother.

These thoughts are interrupted by Saluni, who is pulling the tail of his jacket in three angry jerks.

"Don't you dare ignore me, man, when I talk to you," she screeches. "Your fish is back and now you think you can treat me like rubbish!"

"I don't treat you like rubbish, Saluni."

"Then what do you call this . . . sneaking away to be with your fish? Somebody is bound to do something drastic about that fish. It is bound to end up on someone's dinner table somewhere in Japan and there'll be peace in the world."

"She has been wounded, Saluni. Didn't you see the gaping wound? You cannot but feel sorry for the poor creature. Don't be so heartless, Saluni."

"What about my gaping wound? Who feels sorry for me?"

She lifts up her dress to display the gaping wound on her thigh. He is alarmed.

"What happened to you, Saluni?" he asks anxiously.

"Why would you care what happened to me?"

"And your shoes . . . where are your shoes?"

"I lost them. I fell and I lost the shoes."

"Come, let us go home," says the Whale Caller, holding her hand and trying to help her up the crag. "I have gentian violet and bandages at home. I am going to nurse that wound and you'll see in no time it will be gone."

But Saluni pulls away from him.

"Go and use your stupid gentian violet and bandages on your stupid whale, man," she yells. "Just leave me alone."

He watches her as she limps down the crag to the sea. She confronts Sharisha, who has now joined two other whales almost two hundred metres away.

"Don't mess with me, man," she shouts at her. "I tell you, don't piss on my parade!"


August is the month of peach blossom. It is the month of sugarbirds and sunbirds. It is the beginning of the whale-watching season, though if one is fortunate one can see a whale or two even in the middle of winter. Whale watchers and sundry tourists are beginning to trickle back into Hermanus. They will peak in two months, although one can already feel the presence of the few who are already in town. One feels their presence in the prices that suddenly rocket through the roofs of the stores and restaurants even before one sees their funereal figures wandering in a daze with binoculars and digital cameras weighing heavily on their necks. They look like reliquary figures of a sadistic deity.

The Whale Caller grieves. Not because of the tourists. He is used to them at this time of the year. He can tolerate them for the next seven months, until the pilgrimage comes to an end in January and February. He has always carried on with his business of living even when they crowded around him, scrutinising him as though he was some curiosity. He grieves because of the new ways of watching whales. Despite the fact that the town is well suited for watching whales from its many cliffs, some entrepreneurs have introduced boat-based whale watching. Although the first permit for this kind of whale watching was issued by the government some six years ago, the Whale Caller has only just become aware of this activity since the boat operators had focused their business in open waters that were a distance away from his bluff haunts. This year for the first time he notices a mission of tourists in a boat sailing towards a whale. He has heard that there are strict regulations governing boat-based whale watching. For instance, the boat is not allowed to follow a whale at a speed of more than three and a half kilometres per hour. It must not get closer than fifty metres to a whale (no longer the three hundred metres of fishing boats), although if a whale inquisitively approaches the boat, then the fifty-metre rule no longer applies. The Whale Caller has seen tourists getting off the boat and excitedly boasting of how they actually touched a whale when it came alongside a boat and peered at the passengers. The boaster knew that touching whales was strictly prohibited, but people do it all the same on those boats. People enjoy it when they agitate the whales, even though they know that they are not allowed to do that. This troubles the Whale Caller. He has never touched a whale. He has never even touched Sharisha, except with his spirit—with his horn. There is no doubt in his mind that soon this boat-based whale watching will be abused. And no one will be out there at sea to enforce the regulations. Soon the ultimate prize for a boat trip will be the touching of a whale. And the entrepreneurs will claim that they did keep the fifty-metre distance but the whale approached them. They will blame it all on the whale. As far as he is concerned these boat-based whale watchers are no different from the whalers of old. They might as well carry harpoons and trypots in those boats.

The Whale Caller is grieving on the home front too. Saluni is giving him a hard time about Sharisha, though he tries every day to demonstrate to her that she—Saluni—is the most important person in his life. He has nursed her wound even as she rebelled against it. She is bent on punishing him by not letting it heal. When he has taken the trouble to clean it, and to apply gentian violet to it so that it doesn't become septic, she tries to wash the medicine off. Gentian violet is very stubborn though, and the wound remains purple for days, until he applies the medicine to it again.

When her lost shoes miraculously materialised one day when she returned from the mansion, a heel was broken. He took them to the shoemaker even though she rebelled against that too. She wanted to see him suffer as she hobbled along with one heelless shoe and one with a long pencil heel. Such is her displeasure with him. Even the effect of the Bored Twins doesn't seem to last that long on her anymore. By the time she gets home all the euphoria has dissipated. His mere silence is provocation to her because it means he is thinking of Sharisha. A simple question from him, such as: "Did you have something to eat at the mansion? Should I prepare some food for you?" invites a deadly glare and the response: "Why don't you go and ask your stupid fish?"

He is caught between two hard places. Sharisha does seem to have a yearning for the carefree romps of the past. Yet something is stopping her. The yearning is only in the eyes. Even her lobtailing, once a vigorous mating dance, is languid. Her whole demeanour is listless. Saluni on the other hand is castrating him with her tongue, to the extent that even the nightly cleansing rituals have fizzled out. They are now a fading memory, another source of irritation on her part. She says they don't happen anymore because Sharisha is back. His mind is full of dirty thoughts about whales throughout the day, to the extent that he is left enervated when the night demands action. He says Saluni's own words and not Sharisha should take the blame. "How do you expect a meaningful performance from me when there are these tensions between us?" he asks.

"I forbid you to see that whale again," says Saluni, in her best edictal tone.

But the Whale Caller does not respond.

"If you want us to go back where we were," she says, now pleadingly, "promise me you will never see that whale again."

The Whale Caller is unable to make such a promise. But he does not say so. He keeps quiet instead. His silence means consent to Saluni.

At night he lies awake, without the benefit of even the smallest cleansing rite, and therefore without the wonderful exhaustion that sends the celebrant into a cataleptic slumber. Saluni is in deep sleep. He wonders what Sharisha could be doing at that hour. He hears the songs of the whales at some distance. He listens hard for the slightest hint of Sharisha's voice, but he can't catch it. He wakes up and drapes a heavy blanket around his naked body. He tiptoes out of the house, and heads for Walker Bay. The moon is shining and he can see dark specks on the horizon. The whales are too distant for him to identify Sharisha. He didn't bring his horn; otherwise he would be calling her.

The following night he drapes his blanket around himself again, without wearing any clothes lest their rustle wakes Saluni up. He tiptoes out of the Wendy house. It is too easy. Saluni sleeps like a hibernating mole, especially when she has been run-

ning around with the Bored Twins all day long. He takes his horn
with him. This time he goes to his peninsula. He cannot see any
whales. He blows his horn. At first he blows it softly. Cautiously.
When nothing happens he blows it a little louder. He can see a
speck on the horizon, which becomes bigger as he continues to
blow the horn. It takes a long time for the speck to become a
whale, and a longer time for the whale to become Sharisha. He
tries a few steps of their dance, but Sharisha's response is a feeble
lobtailing. There is no spectacular breaching. No display of baleen
in a gigantic smile. He performs his usual dance, blowing the horn
with as much vigour as he can muster. His blanket falls off. It is
blown into the water and the waves sweep it away. He continues
to dance naked. Sharisha just floats there, looking at him wistfully.
He stops the dance. He is exasperated. He squats on a rock and
just watches her.

A voice startles him: "I stopped going to the taverns for you.
Now you do this to me? And shame on you, dangling your naked-
ness for every whale to see!"

Saluni is standing right behind him. Unheard by him, she has
walked over the precarious rocks to the point of the peninsula
where he is brooding. She is barefoot, like him, and wears a morning gown on top of her nightdress.

"You promised, man . . . you promised!" cries Saluni.

"I didn't promise anything, Saluni."

"Oh yes you did. You promised you would stop your stupid
dances with the whales. Whoever heard of a grown man stealing
away from the warm bed of his lover to spend the whole night
hopping about on the rocks blowing a meaningless song on a kelp
horn for some stupid whale he has named Sharisha?"

It is fortunate that Hermanus is asleep and there are no spectators to witness a naked hirsute man being frogmarched home by
a wisp of a woman in sleepwear.

In the Wendy house Saluni sits on the bed and weeps.

"I am a love child, man," she says. "You can't treat a love child like this."

Then she spits out the story of her conception. It is the story the Whale Caller has heard before, troubadours and all, except for the fact that in this version her mother dramatically shoots the lover. She never goes to jail because the judge decides that it was in self-defence. The woman was defending her honour and the honour of all the women of the world who have been chewed like bubblegum and then spat out when all the sweetness was gone.

The Whale Caller has never seen her weep before, and this makes him feel very bad about himself. She becomes so lovable when she shows her ability to be vulnerable. It is a new side of her. A desirable side. She is taken by surprise when he lunges at her and rips her sleeping garments off. The Wendy house rocks as it has never rocked before. As they achieve ceremonial ecstasy she is oblivious of the fact that his rigid body has pressed against her wound and it now oozes a pink mixture of blood and pus.

The next day she has lost all her softness and is determined to fight Sharisha on Sharisha's own turf. While the Whale Caller lingers in bed, savouring the memory of the night's rituals that continued right up to the morning, she wakes up, cleans her wound with gentian violet, puts on her high-heeled boots and his heavy army-issue coat, and goes to town. She buys a bottle of cheap wine, drinks from it in big gulps and walks to Walker Bay. The place is already teeming with early morning whale watchers. There are some whales, out there in the distance. She walks along the crag until she reaches his peninsula. There is Sharisha floating mindlessly, just as they left her last night. Saluni vows to herself that she is going to show Sharisha something she will never forget. She drank the wine for her, to make this showdown as momentous as only Cape plonk can make it. She is going to defend her mating rights like a ferocious bull seal—especially after the earthshaking rituals of last night.

"I tell you once and for all, stupid fish," she shrieks at Sharisha, "just leave him alone! You no longer have any stake in him!"

Then she opens the buttons of the coat and flashes Sharisha. She is not wearing anything under the coat. The purple wound glares at the hapless whale. She flashes her one more time. Sharisha only stares at her. A better idea strikes Saluni. She turns her back on the sea, lifts up the coat and moons the whale. Sharisha lazily turns, as if to show Saluni that she too has a wound. She sails away.

"That will show her," mutters Saluni as she walks off.

The few people who have watched her antics with increasing curiosity reward her with applause. She merely sneers at them and walks back to the Wendy house.

As soon as she enters the Whale Caller smells the fumes of wine.

"You are drunk," he says, accusingly.

"You would be too if you drank a whole bottle of wine," she says, giggling.

"After last night, Saluni . . . I thought we had worked things out."

"I caught you naked with a fish, man," says Saluni. "One night of heaving and panting does not erase that . . . especially because you refuse to repent."


In the three months that follow the Whale Caller agonises over Saluni's return to the bottle. She has lost all interest in the waltz at dawn. She has even lost the appetite for the window-shopping expeditions. She comes home drunk every night and sleeps until midday. Soon after lunch she leaves the house. She visits the Bored Twins. Or she whiles away time annoying Mr. Yodd with her refusal to be mortified. Or she goes to the taverns—a very sore point with the Whale Caller. She is doing all these things to punish him, since she can no longer make him suffer with her wound. It had finally healed.

The Whale Caller also agonises over Sharisha's lack of enthusiasm for the dance. He had thought the main reason was the wound. But now it has healed, yet she is as lethargic as ever. And is growing fatter by the day. He has tried every trick in the book to arouse her. When everything has failed he remembers the ritualised eating that is part of the mating game, first introduced to him by Saluni as civilised living. He has participated in Sharisha's mating games that are in line with whale culture, now she must participate in the human version of the mating ritual. He hopes that by bursting out of his conservative shell and making a public display of public eating Sharisha will be aroused to action once more.

He rents a small round table and a chair from the marketplace stallholders. He bribes a waiter from the restaurant that juts into the sea on stilts to lend him the best silver and crystal just for a few hours. The waiter smuggles the cutlery and the wine glasses out of the premises with the garbage and the Whale Caller pretends to be a dustbin scavenger and fishes these items out. He places the chair and the table on a small rocky island just off his peninsula. He sets the table with the white linen from the Wendy house and with the silverware and crystal wine glasses. He lays a table of seafood and the best of Cape chardonnay bought from the same waiter, and smuggled out of the restaurant wrapped in aluminium foil via the dustbin. It does not matter to the Whale Caller that the seafood may be leftovers from those diners who do not care for doggy bags. As for the wine, he will only use it as libation since he is a teetotaller.

He is in black tie. He looks like the jackass penguins that dot the rocks. He sits on the chair and blows his kelp horn. He blows some of the best mating calls he has learnt over the years. Sure enough Sharisha leaves the company of two other whales a dis-

tance away and languidly sails to the Whale Caller. He lights a
candle, borrowed from Saluni's sequinned handbag, and sits down
to dine on a meal that has been prepared elegantly in a gourmet
manner. Sharisha sails about fifty metres from the island, occasionally waving her fluke. Then she spyhops in big circles. While
he eats the seafood, he pours the wine in the glass, sniffs it, and
then throws it into the water as an offering to the spirits that rule
the sea. The very spirits that ate his father and that must now
heal Sharisha from whatever ails her.

The wind is the bearer of Lunga Tubu's voice. There he is
standing below the stilted restaurant singing *"Santa Lucia."* His
voice rises above the waves even when they are at their loudest.
The waves strike the rocks, creating white surf that stops at the
boy's feet and becomes the clear water in which he stands. The
Whale Caller can see his corrupt waiter from the restaurant shooing the boy away, throwing objects at him. He runs away, but as
soon as the waiter returns to his duties at the restaurant, the boy
returns to his spot and brazenly serenades the tourists, the Whale
Caller and Sharisha once again.

Suddenly Sharisha emerges from the spyhopping and swims to
join the two whales that have been waiting anxiously a short distance away. The three swim further away, but they do not get far
before the two whales rally around Sharisha. The Whale Caller
can hear deep bellows that carry in waves under the water to
where he sits with an unfinished meal. Sharisha sinks under water
and disappears for some time and then emerges again. There is
a struggle happening here, and it dawns for the first time on the
Whale Caller that he is about to witness a birth. He nearly
punches himself when he realises that all along her lethargy was
due to the fact that she was with child. He should have suspected
that. After all he was there when it all started last December, just
before Christmas. And indeed it is December again, just before
Christmas. The gestation period of southern rights is eleven to

twelve months. How silly of him to have expected Sharisha to return with a young one after only six months, and how truly silly
not to realise that there was no live young one yet because she was
still carrying it in her womb!

He stands up and blows his horn and dances around his altar.

He is not the only one who has become aware of the birth. The
cliffs of Hermanus have suddenly come alive with spectators who
are training their binoculars on Sharisha and the two midwives. A
whale giving birth is not an everyday sight. Not only do southern
rights mate in winter off South Africa, they give birth the following winter, off South Africa again. Sharisha bends the rules once
more. She mated in full view of the Whale Caller under the glare
of the December sun. And here she is again, birthing in the summer sun, to the accompaniment of the kelp horn and Lunga
Tubu's rendition of Pavarotti, Domingo and Carreras. The voice
that is yet to break has now added Mario Lanza to the repertoire.
The Whale Caller blows his horn harder, in an attempt to over-
whelm the young singer. Only his horn has the right to be part of
the miracle.

He does not hear Saluni's raspy voice, shouting at him and
calling him a no-good loser. She is standing at the tip of his peninsula. When she can't catch his attention she wades her way
through the waist-high water to the island. He stops playing for
a while as they face each other.

"You have no shame," she says. "You even stole my candle for
this rubbish."

"I told you . . . remember, I told you," says the Whale Caller
breathlessly, "and you didn't believe me. You said Sharisha was
male . . . you saw 'his' thingy, you said. Have you seen a male giving birth?"

"Who says the fish is giving birth?" she asks dismissively. "It
just wants your attention, that's all. And you and all these stupid
people have fallen for its tricks. You are all a bunch of suckers.

When you have finished making a fool of yourself you'll find me at home. And don't you bother waking me up. There'll be no cleansing ceremony for you ever! At least not from me!"

She wades back to the peninsula.

"She is giving birth, Saluni. That's what she is doing over there."

She stops and glares at him.

"You are lying, man," she says. "You are such a liar. Liar! Liar! Liar!"

She runs blindly through the water, and almost falls. Then she stops and glares at him again just before she reaches the tip of the peninsula.

"And by the way," she says, "I am going to the tavern. And don't you dare complain about it."

The Whale Caller watches her disappear among the people who are precariously crowding his peninsula. Then he goes back to blowing his horn.

The struggle continues until late in the afternoon. Just before dusk the child is born under water, but close enough to the surface for the spectators to see the tail coming out first, and then the whole body. The newborn calf is helped by the midwives to come up to the surface for the essential breath. It is white and the Whale Caller estimates that it is about five metres long. The midwives are very protective. They help the young one as they all follow Sharisha to a sheltered bay at a nearby estuary where she nurses the baby and for the first time it suckles.


June. The southern rights have long migrated from the breeding grounds in the warm waters of Hermanus to the cold feeding grounds in the southern seas. When the whales left in January Sharisha refused to go. She lives at the sheltered bay near the estuary, a haven she used to share with other calving mothers. But they are all gone now. Except Sharisha. By the end of February the last of the off-season whales were gone. Saluni was hoping that finally she would have peace of mind and the Whale Caller would regain his sanity, but Sharisha surprised even the Whale Caller when she decided to stay in Hermanus all year round. This, of course, presents a change of lifestyle on her part. For instance, during the whole breeding period there was no feeding. She relied on the blubber she had accumulated from the last feeding season in the southern seas. Now it is time to eat once more, and she misses the regular diet of krill and plankton that is found in the polar regions. Like Bryde's whales, which normally remain in these warm waters throughout the year, she feasts on schooling fish—another source of excitement for the people of Hermanus. Feeding activity by southern rights is a rare sight off the coast of the Western Cape.

Saluni seems to have given up on the Whale Caller. She leads her life, he leads his. They meet at night, share the same bed, but only their behinds touch. They wake up in the morning, go through the motions of ablutions, and then go their separate ways. She goes to the mansion or to the taverns. Or even to Mr. Yodd. He goes to the sea, to follow the movements of Sharisha and her baby, and just to watch them in wonder. He plays the horn sometimes and Sharisha responds by flapping her flippers. But most times he just enjoys watching the two of them. The baby seems to grow bigger every day. It has changed from white to a dark grey. Its callosities are beginning to take shape, and they promise to look like the mother's. The baby likes to ride on Sharisha's back, much like the way African women carry their children.

The Whale Caller enjoys watching Sharisha open her mouth in the broad smile that displays the baleen that looks like teeth. Then she scoops up a mouthful of water and, using the baleen as a sieve, strains the plankton from the water. It is different from the plankton of the southern seas, but since she has decided to stand her ground and not migrate, she will just have to acquire a taste for it.

Sometimes Saluni appears above the crag as he watches mother and child. She descends in a deliberate manner, making sure that he sees that she is ignoring him. She goes to where Lunga Tubu is sitting, near the stilts of the restaurant, taking a break from his singing and running away from waiters. She fusses over the boy, mothering him in full view of the Whale Caller. She aims to demonstrate to the misguided man that she has people she cares about too.

The Whale Caller is oblivious of her demonstrations. Especially now that Sharisha has begun to sing again—perhaps teaching the young one the art. He often joins in with his kelp horn. He becomes enraged when loud underwater bangs produced by seismic surveys interfere with the songs. Oil and gas explorations are carried out at this time of the year, since the government and the exploration companies believe it is safe; there are no whales to upset.

Despite these disturbances, the Whale Caller lives inside the song of whales. It is soothing inside the song, with fresh aromas that heal. He remembers telling Saluni once, long ago, when she was expressing her fear of the dark, that it is never night inside a song.

# FOUR

ANOTHER SEASON. Once more they return. The whales. They find Sharisha still nursing her calf near the estuary; the Whale Caller still spending many hours of the day entranced by them; and Saluni still sneaking about, trying very hard to catch his attention, then sauntering past him only to smother whoever happens to be within reach with excessive friendliness. Lunga Tubu is often the victim of these displays, which are really performed for the Whale Caller's benefit. The boy is not particularly fond of being fussed over by Saluni, and looks forward to the hours the Whale Caller is not in sight, for he has observed that it is only then that he gets some respite.

In one of these mothering sessions Lunga Tubu tells Saluni that the radio station people have returned and are now setting up a makeshift recording studio at the Market Square. It is, of course, Kalfiefees time again and the festivities have begun. Lunga Tubu will take his Pavarotti, Carreras, Domingo and Lanza to the festival at the Market Square, where he will earn more money from the tourists than the few coins he gets from the diners at the restaurant on stilts. But most importantly, this year he will get his voice recorded and the whole of the Western Cape will then know of his "tenor" that he renders in an unbroken contralto or even soprano voice.

The boy's enthusiasm gives Saluni ideas. She remembers how she was foiled by the Bored Twins' mother last year. She could have had her fame as well. Her voice could have ridden the air-waves if it were not for the foolish superstitions of the woman. She vows that this year nothing will stop her. She cannot record alone because she suspects no one will take her seriously. She can't sing with Lunga Tubu because he sings the kind of music that leaves her cold. In any event, even if she were to convert the boy to a more decent kind of music, the boy would totally hog the mike. He is the kind of person who'd like to grab all the limelight for himself, and wouldn't give her the least opportunity to break into a solo. She needs the angelic voices of the Bored Twins to give her bluesy voice credibility. Yes, she definitely needs the Bored Twins, and this year she will take them to the studio whether their mother likes it or not.

But first she must try to talk sense into the mother. She makes sure she has a candle and clean underwear in her sequinned hand-bag, and goes to the mansion. She knows that the parents always return after dark, so she will have to spend the night.

The Bored Twins are not home. They must have gone to the swamps to play with the frogs. She sits on the steps going up to the front door and waits. She occupies her time by counting the ants that have formed two long trails, one composed of fast work-ers heading in the direction of the rockeries and another of slow workers going in the opposite direction carrying heavy loads of meat carved with their mandibles from a dead lizard. This trail disappears around the corner. She wonders where they are going with all that food and what distance they can cover with loads heavier than their own weight before they get to their abode, but is too lazy to stand up and find out.

The trail gets thinner as the last bits of the rapidly dwindling lizard are carted away, and then there are no more ants to count. Saluni amuses herself by imagining the panels on the ceiling of the Wendy house and counting them. Then she counts everything in the Wendy house. The bed, the portable electric stove they call the hot plate, the cups, the plates, all the seashells pasted on the wall, the table, the Whale Caller brooding on the kitchen chair. That Whale Caller! He has a lot to learn about women. She is going to make him suffer with her absence until he kicks that behemoth out of his life. Soon he will turn around and ask for her forgiveness and, of course, she will make him plead and beg and pray before she grandly forgives him. And then they will live happily ever after.

It is almost sunset when the girls return. They have been out for the whole day and they smell of the sun. As usual they are excited to see Saluni. They are even more excited when she tells them of the radio man, but their faces fall when they remember that last year their mother did not allow them to record for fear that the machines would steal their voices. Saluni assures them that somehow this year things will work out differently. The girls should not worry their pretty little heads because she will devise a plan. Anyway, it is possible that the mother has since changed her views on the matter, and will allow them to go with her to see the Kalfiefees in town.

The girls cannot contain their joy. They must start rehearsing immediately. They teach Saluni a new song that they have composed at the swamps. It is about croaking frogs in their green and brown colours and how the girls caught them and pierced their eyes with sharp sticks and set them free to hop about in wonderful blindness. It is a haunting melody. They tell Saluni that the song is all about the fun they had at the swamps today. The blinded frogs will live peacefully because now they won't be bothered by the bright rays of the sun. They won't have to run away from danger, because they won't see it. They will therefore be safe since danger catches only those who run away from it. This dissertation on blindness resonates with Saluni, but she does not make any comment to the authors.

She, in turn, teaches them new songs. She would have liked to compose a song lamenting the dying whaling tradition since the seas are polluted with the ugly creatures that are of no use to mankind and expressing the hope that one day they will all strand themselves. Unfortunately, unlike the girls, she is not much of a composer. So she teaches them censored versions of tavern songs and hymns that have been adapted to serve secular desires. The rehearsal goes on into the night under the full moon whose light is so bright it erases the stars.

When the parents finally return in their donkey cart they are pleased to see Saluni. It is gratifying to have a visitor when the father has caught a guinea fowl. Such a delicacy becomes tastier when it is shared with others. He tells them how it happened. "A miracle," he says. "A gift of gourmet meat falling right into my hands."

"Who gave you the gift, Papa?" asks one of the twins.

"The farmer, silly," says the other twin. "The vineyard owner."

"God!" says the father.

He was shouting at the donkey to get cracking and it was just plodding along in the moonlight, too stubborn or tired to respond even to his whip. Then a car approached, blinding them with its bright lights. It must have disturbed a sleeping guinea fowl because as soon as it had whisked by the big bird flew from the nearby field right into his arms. He does not know how he managed to catch it since his eyes were still blind from the headlights. It must have been blind as well. He had to throw away his whip to catch it. Such night gifts abound on these roads. A rabbit, and once in a while a springbok, that has been foolish enough to run in front of the headlights only to be run over. Usually the roadkill is too messy to take home. Sometimes the game is not mashed into the road but knocked to one side by a bumper and is good enough to skin and take home. But never before has game fallen right into his outstretched hands.

"It just shows how great the Lord is," says the father.

The mother quickly boils water and Saluni helps her pluck the guinea fowl while the father dunks the girls in a metal bathtub full of cold water and scrubs the mud from their angelic bodies with a sponge. They always rebel at bath time and scream and bite their father's hands. He in turn slaps their hands until they calm down and realise that the more they make things difficult for him the longer the agony of the bath will last. They giggle and turn the whole thing into a game by lathering the father's arms and the stubble on his face as he scrubs their bodies. Bath time for the twins is always a messy business with the water ending up all over the floor.

"The Kalfiefees is on again," says Saluni as she cuts open the guinea fowl and scoops out its intestines with her hand. "It hasn't lost its magic."

"We wouldn't know about that," says the mother. "We are working people."

"I could take the twins there while you are at work. How's that, man?"

"You know I don't like my girls to go to town. It is not safe for little girls."

"They roam the countryside . . . on their own."

"The countryside is safer than the town."

"I'll look after them, man. They will be with me all the time."

"I know you mean well, Saluni. But I can't allow it."

"You know people make a lot of money during the Kalfiefees. They dance . . . they sing . . . and the stupid tourists give them money. I know a boy there who is making a lot of money singing for tourists. Lunga Tubu. And his voice is not even angelic. It is a voice of this earth. There is money for the taking in town . . . especially if you have a beautiful voice like the twins."

"So that is what you want, Saluni, to make money from my children?"

"I don't want their money, man. I just want to record with them. You heard us singing just now, when you came home. You heard how good we are together. We can be world famous, man. The twins and I can be world famous. You have read about the children who become stars. They build houses for their mothers. They buy cars for their mothers. They take their mothers overseas for holidays. You won't have to go to the vineyards again, man. You won't have to hawk scrap metal and bones."

"I forbid it, Saluni! I forbid it," screams the mother almost hysterically. "They will steal my children's voices."


This is the second full moon in the same month—it only happens once every three years. It is a blue moon. The Whale Caller is as blue as the moon. Even though there is very little communication between him and Saluni these days, he does miss her when she is not there. Especially when she spends the night away from the Wendy house. Perhaps at the mansion. Or even at the taverns. She comes and goes without telling him where she has been or where she is heading. He surmises from the wine fumes that she has been to the taverns, or from euphoria that she has been to the mansion. The euphoria, of course, is never shared with him. She becomes euphoric alone in the corner, giggling to herself and sighing repeatedly, and then gets into bed, turning her back on him. Sometimes she is gloomy and he suspects that she has been to Mr. Yodd. Even though she manages to defy Mr. Yodd's attempts at flagellation, she cannot but be gloomy after confessing at the grotto. He knows that Mr. Yodd never gives up. As long as she continues to go there bearing oblations of fruit and flowers Mr. Yodd hopes he will finally manage to humiliate her with his laughter.

On this blue night the Whale Caller sits under the blue moon at the tip of his peninsula. He is bathing his body in the smells of the night while waiting for dawn to bring Sharisha and the child from the estuary to the open sea. In the meantime he blows his kelp horn softly, practising a new song he has composed for the mother-and-child dyad. It is a variation on Sharisha's song, but now with trills and warbles that are repetitive enough to make an impression on the young one. His only audience is a lone dolphin that is digging out prey in the sand under the water with its bottle nose. It must be the blue moon, the Whale Caller concludes, that has deceived the dolphin into foraging in the deep of the night. The blue moon does many strange things. Hopefully it will bring watermaids frolicking on the surface of the water, dancing to his kelp horn. Saluni. She used to be a watermaid during their happy moments. He used to watch her playing in the sea. Saluni. Where could she be on this blue night?

At sunrise the Whale Caller sees a distant silhouette of a whale followed by a calf. It can only be Sharisha. The child is eleven months old and Sharisha no longer indulges it by carrying it on her back. Instead it has learnt to keep up with her. He blows his new song and the whales slowly sail towards the peninsula. They take their time, occasionally stopping to play with the floating kelp, pushing it and tossing it back and forth. And then touching and nudging at each other. The Whale Caller enjoys it immensely when the child mimics everything that Sharisha does. When she sails with her mouth open, exposing the baleen that looks like long piano keys, the child does the same. For some time the two sail towards him displaying these broad smiles.

When they get close enough Sharisha teaches the child a new trick: tail-sailing. Although this is a display especially for the

Whale Caller, it is quite different from the tail-slapping, the mating ritual that used to be a crucial form of bonding between the
Whale Caller and Sharisha. In tail-sailing Sharisha stands on her
head in the water with her tail sticking above the surface. The
child does likewise, and it is as though they are in competition to
see who will remain in that position the longest. The Whale
Caller stands up and laughs, clapping his hands, with his kelp
horn under his arm. And then he whips it out and blows it in a
celebratory flourish.

Saluni arrives and catches him at this unguarded moment
when he is so carefree and jubilant with only the two whales as his
audience now that the dolphin has left the space to them. She
wonders why this man is never so carefree with her. What is it
that she is supposed to do to make him prance about as he is doing for the stupid whales? She finds the effect they have on him
pathetic and she hates them even more for doing what she has
failed to do. The Whale Caller sees her and suddenly stops in
embarrassment and sits down on a rock. The whales take their
cue from him and stop their tail-sailing antics. Instead they
float about, now communing with their perfectly V-shaped
blows. There are hollow sounds in two-part harmony as mother
and child produce clouds of vapour by expelling air and tiny
drops of mucus from their lungs through each pair of blowholes.
There is no way the child can outdo Sharisha's big and prolonged
blows.

Saluni gingerly crosses the treacherous neck of the peninsula,
coming very close to where he sits. He longs to talk to her but on
previous occasions when he has taken the initiative to open up di-
alogue she has lashed back either with chilly silence or some hurt-
ful remark that is directed at whatever object is in sight but is
really meant for him. He expects her to do her usual thing, walk
by flaunting her slim figure, and then smother someone else with
love. But it is too early in the morning and there is no Lunga

Tubu to mother. There will not be any Lunga Tubu for the whole day. For the whole week even, since he spends all his time at the Kalfiefees where there are better pickings.

The Whale Caller pretends he is oblivious to her presence and focuses on the blows of the whales. She has a brilliant idea. Although it now comes as her own original idea, it was first suggested to her by Mr. Yodd at one of her regular confessions. *Change the tactics. If you accommodate his obsession with the whales, you might beat Sharisha at her own game.* From now on she won't show any hostility towards Sharisha in the presence of the Whale Caller. She will wage a subtle war. Psywar! She will make life difficult for the behemoth when no one is watching, and be friendly towards it when he is around. She will not utter another word against Sharisha to the Whale Caller.

She stands in front of the Whale Caller and smiles. He is not sure whether it is safe to smile back. This may be a trap. She may be inviting him to smile back in order to mow him down with her tongue. He shifts his position and focuses on the two whales. She playfully skips to a new position so that once more she stands in front of him, smiling.

"Come on, man," she says. "Don't be such a sourpuss. It is a beautiful day."

"You've come from the Bored Twins then and not from the taverns?"

"What has anything got to do with it? It is a beautiful day and your two whales are beautiful. I like the water spouting out of their heads."

"Beautiful? Since when, Saluni? You scare me when you say such things."

"Since I decided there is no point in fighting you about your Sharisha. After all she is only a fish. I am all woman. Sooner or later you will realise that you need a woman in your life more than you need a fish."

"A whale is not a fish, Saluni. It is a mammal . . . like you and me."

"Like you, maybe, but not . . . Okay, like you and me. I am not going to argue about it, man. I am not going to argue about your whale ever again."

The Whale Caller finds this hard to believe. But, naturally, he is pleased.

"They mean you no harm, Saluni," he says. "And you are right. They are beautiful. Their blows are like a synchronised dance."

Then he tells her about the origins of the whale's blow. It is a story from across the vast Indian Ocean, from a people who share their love for southern rights with the Khoikhoi people who lived along the shores of the present-day Hermanus way back then when everything here was young and just as young in the continent of Aboriginal Dreaming. It was all so young that the ice was still melting and water was rising, covering the land and threatening to drown all the creatures. They wanted to escape but did not have any canoes to cross the vast expanse to the other side. They heard of Whale Man, who was the only one who had a canoe.

But Whale Man was very selfish. He did not want anyone to use his canoe.

"Let us just take the canoe," suggested Starfish Man. "Otherwise all we animals will perish in the water."

"Whale Man is very big and strong," said Koala Man. "Who do you think among us here would dare take his canoe without his permission?"

"Leave everything to me," said Starfish Man.

And there was Whale Man pulling his canoe with a rope!

"Hey, Brother Whale Man," said Starfish Man. "I see on your callosities that you are being bothered by lice. I can help you. Come over here, Brother Whale Man, and put your beautiful head on my lap. I'll scratch it and you'll feel very good. I'll get rid of all the lice on your head."

"You are a good neighbour, Brother Starfish Man," said Whale Man, tying the rope of his canoe to his leg and settling his head on Starfish Man's lap. Starfish Man scratched his head and massaged it until Whale Man was drowsy. He felt very good. In the meantime Koala Man had cut the rope, tied it to a boulder and dragged the canoe away. All the animals climbed into it and rowed away, with the muscular Koala Man doing most of the paddling.

"Is my canoe still fine, Brother Starfish Man?" asked Whale Man.

Starfish Man hesitated a bit and then said, "Oh, yes, it is still there. Don't you feel the weight when you try to move your leg?"

Whale Man moved his leg and the rope snapped where it was tied to the rock. He jumped to his feet only to see his canoe moving away into the distance. He realised that he had been tricked by Starfish Man. He lunged at him, but Starfish Man ducked, picked up a rock on the ground and hit Whale Man on the head twice, making two holes close together. Blood gushed out, which made Whale Man raving mad. He grabbed Starfish Man and beat him with his fists and with stones and with sticks and with everything else he could lay his hands on, until Starfish Man lay flattened on the rock. Then he took Starfish Man and threw him into the water, where, to this day, he lies on the sand.

Whale Man dived into the sea and swam as fast as he could, trying to chase his stolen canoe. But it had already reached the other side, and all the animals had disappeared into the woods. Before Koala Man joined the other animals where they were hiding he pushed the canoe into the water and it floated away. It is still floating somewhere out there in the seas of the world.

Whale Man has not given up his search. That is why, to this day, he can be seen searching the oceans for his stolen canoe, blowing water from the head wounds inflicted by Starfish Man, way way back in Dreamtime.

The idea of Dreamtime has Saluni laughing delightedly. This

is the husky but girlish laughter that the Whale Caller has missed all these days. She is now sitting on his lap. For some time they are silent, watching Sharisha and her child spouting rhythmically through their blowholes. The rays of the sun splash rainbow colours on the spray.

"You have many wonderful stories from that part of the world . . . about shark callers . . . and now about Whale Man and Dreamtime . . . and how whales got their blows," she says in childlike awe.

"Oh, I have many Dreamings, told to me by travellers from those big islands during the days when I used to walk the coast."

"Perhaps in another life you lived in the Dreamtime," she says, burying her fingers in his bushy chest and allowing them to explore the sinewy contours. Despite the weather being so cool, he breaks into a sweat.

"Let's go to the Wendy house . . . now . . . please!" he pleads.

"It is daytime, man," she says teasingly. "You know how you feel about things that should happen only at night."

He is almost out of breath: "It does not matter. Daytime can be Dreamtime too. We can make it Dreamtime. We must go now."

"Go ahead," she says. "I'm coming. Get ready. It will be an earthquake."

He hesitates because he does not know why she wants to remain behind alone.

"Go, man, go," she says. "I'll be with you in no time. I just want a bit of time to . . . make my body ready to receive you. You won't understand, man; it's a woman thing. Just go and before you know it I'll be there."

He walks back to the Wendy house. First she makes certain that he is truly out of sight, and then she gets into the water and takes a few steps towards the whales. She stops to confront Sharisha, who is about fifty metres off in the blue depths.

"I say leave him alone, you foolish fish," she shouts. "He is mine!"

She turns her back to the whales. The level of the water is just below her knees. She lifts up her wet dress and lowers her underpants to the knees. She moons Sharisha, slapping her bottom and screaming: "Take that, you lousy fish!" And then she pulls up her underpants and walks away, leaving the poor whale looking scandalised. The calf is oblivious of what is happening and is breaching away.

Sharisha looks at Saluni as she walks away from the peninsula and then she leaps out of the water in one massive breach to land next to the young one. They sail away, back to the sheltered bay near the estuary.

At the Wendy house the Whale Caller sits on the bed waiting impatiently. He is naked and his manhood is staring at him with its single eye, enquiring why it is being subjected to this punishment. A wet Saluni glides into the room with pomp and ceremony.

Her prophesy is fulfilled. There is an earthquake.

HOY, MR. YODD! You are a clever one, aren't you? Your strategy paid off. Now the sickness has returned in our lives. We inflict wonderful ailments on each other again. Yes, I did dismiss it at first. It is difficult sometimes to know whether one should trust you or not. You are the past master of shaming. How does one know when your advice should be taken seriously, or if it is just a trick to mortify somebody? This time it paid off. Obviously there is a heart somewhere there, Mr. Yodd, otherwise why would you go out of your way to help me? Oh, I see! It is for your own selfish reasons. You enjoy my oblations, but you hate the fact that your laughter has no effect on me. You want him back here for a dose of flagellation. You long for him. You think that if I bring happiness into his life he will feel guilty enough to want to confess. He will have the urge to dilute it with mortification. He will come for your laughter. You are merely using me for your own ends, Mr. Yodd. Guess what? I am using you too. He has given you up, Mr. Yodd. You will never see him again. You have tried to draw blood from me with your laughter. You have failed so many times but you continue to laugh at me whenever I come here. I can hear you laughing, Mr. Yodd. Don't deny it now. And, oh, I have brought you more oblations! Tulips? There are no tulips at this time. I know there should be, but they are not there. They bloom when they feel like it, irrespective of what season it is. I have spread out fruit at the mouth of your grotto—peaches and litchis, apricots and pears. Rock rabbits are already taking them inside. Some can't wait before they take a bite. You need to discipline your rock rabbits, Mr. Yodd. They must never partake of oblations before they present them to the master. Breathless times have returned, Mr. Yodd. Breathless times have returned.

❧

SALUNI. She is determined to record with the Bored Twins despite the Whale Caller's reservations. He feels that the mother's wishes should be respected. Her main concern is that soon the Kalfiefees will be over and the temporary recording studio of the radio station will pack and leave town. Once more fame and fortune will escape her. It mustn't happen again, not this time.

Early in the morning she arrives at the mansion. The parents have left at dawn and the Bored Twins are still in bed. She tells them her plan about the secret mission to go to town to sing for the world. Their parents must never know about it. The twins are very thrilled to be entrusted with such a secret and they promise that they won't tell. They do not rebel when she gives them a bath and grooms their hair. She sprays them with some of her perfume from the sequinned handbag. She dresses them in their white frocks. Once more they look like angels. She looks all over the room for their sandals and finds each one in a different place.

The three singers walk to town, confident that fame is beckoning at last. The Bored Twins walk awkwardly now they are shod because they are used to going barefoot. But Saluni insists that they wear the sandals because no one goes to town barefoot.

They practise the songs as they trot along. People stop and listen. Others decide to turn from their journeys and follow them. Labourers digging a trench on the roadside switch off their pneumatic drills, drop their tools and follow them. Soon there is a crowd of people trailing behind and alongside them. They are overwhelmed with euphoria, especially in those parts where Saluni is silent and the Bored Twins are singing on their own. Saluni's voice, though pleasantly throaty, does dilute the euphoria since she is not a Euphoriant.

By the time they arrive in town the attendant crowd has become so big that it blocks the traffic. At first the traffic police think it is a demonstration. There are often demonstrations during the Kalfiefees season, mostly by evangelicals and sundry charismatic and fundamentalist types who do not like this or that performance because it will consign the beautiful town of Hermanus to the fate of Sodom and Gomorrah, or by people from the margins of society who demand a share in the wealth that is generated by God's whales. However, if this is a demonstration it is a strange one. No one in the crowd shows any anger. No one is chanting slogans. People are merely frolicking like spring lambs and giggling or even guffawing as if someone is tickling them. When the traffic police try to control them, announcing over a megaphone that people should keep to the pavements since cars have the right of way on the road, everyone cooperates. Some even start hugging and kissing the police, who now believe that some madness has finally caught up with the good folk of Hermanus. Perhaps they have been chewing the petals of bell-shaped moon flowers. But as soon as the police hear the voices of the girls they are caught up in the madness too. They join the crowd and jubilantly accompany it on foot, on motorbikes and on horseback. A police car with a wailing siren tries to lead the way without really knowing where the crowd is going. Twice it takes a wrong turn, but the determined sergeant drives back again to rejoin the crowd until they arrive at the Market Square where there are stalls for different products and services, including the makeshift recording studio where live broadcasts on the activities of the Kalfiefees are also being made.

Most of the crowd has to remain outside since there is not enough room for a big audience in the studio. Those who are able to get in give Saluni and the Bored Twins a prolonged standing ovation after the performance. The radio man is pleased. He tells Saluni: "As you know we are recording community singers and groups to broadcast to Hermanus and the neighbouring areas only during this festival. However, you and the girls are so good that I am going to cut a demo."

Saluni has no idea what a demo is. The radio man explains that it is a CD that is meant to demonstrate to the record companies how good the singing is. Some record company may be interested and may sign a lucrative contract with them. He offers to be the agent and manager of the phenomenal trio: *Saluni and the Bored Twins*. He promises to come back in a few months' time, after doing the rounds of festivals, with a few copies of the CD.

"Unfortunately it can't be sooner," he says, "because festivals are very trendy these days. There are oyster festivals and trout festivals and peach festivals . . . and most of them are crowded into the second half of the year. I have to cover them all for the radio station. Only after that will I be able to focus on your music career. And you can be sure, baby, I am going to take you places."

"A few months? Can't we get the CD sooner?" Saluni asks. "These girls' mother doesn't want them to record. Perhaps when she hears them sing on a CD she will change her mind. The sooner we get that CD the better."

"It's no big deal to get the CD to you before I go to the next festival . . . soon after the Kalfiefees. After all it is a live recording and I don't have to mix or master anything. All I am saying is that the approach to record companies and the aggressive marketing of your voices can only happen after I've done the rounds of the festivals."

He sets an appointment with Saluni for next week. She is ecstatic, and the Bored Twins—who really don't seem to care much about their impending fame and have no ambition to be anything else but what they already are—are thrilled for her. They walk back home, but silently this time, even though it is a struggle to contain their joy. They do not want the crowd to follow them back to the mansion. A crowd high on euphoria may linger until the parents return from the vineyards, and the mother would know what Saluni had done.

In the evening the Whale Caller is in the bedroom waiting for Saluni to return. He lies supine on the bed fully clothed and sniffs the air hoping to catch even the faintest whiff of the mouldy and sweet smell that often lingers long after Saluni is gone. He catches himself counting the panels on the ceiling. His fears are confirmed: he is beginning to adopt Saluni's compulsive habits. He is determined to stop this before it becomes serious. He would not like to see himself returning to the door up to five times to make sure that it is locked, and then returning to the house again on the sixth trip to make certain that the hot plate has been switched off.

Saluni bursts into the room. She is brimming with ideas now that stardom is nigh. She boasts to the Whale Caller how she is going to travel in her own jet plane, captivating audiences in the capitals of the world. But before that she wants to melodise their lives so that when the time comes they will take to the new life like the southern rights to the southern seas. The Whale Caller does not think the promises of the radio man should be taken seriously, but doesn't want to dampen her spirits. She knows him enough to sense his scepticism.

"You *are* coming with me in my jet plane, are you not?"

"I will fly with you in your jet plane, Saluni, in the same way that I window shop for delicacies with you."

"It's not the same, man. It *is not* the same. We eat only with our eyes when we window shop for food. This time we won't be flying with our eyes. Our whole bodies will be on that jet plane. We will fly out of Hermanus to Johannesburg and then to the rest of the world . . . to Dakar, London, Paris . . . to Hollywood, man. We'll actually take Hollywood by storm. *Saluni and the Bored Twins*. With the radio man as our manager and agent. And you as . . . as what? What do you want to be in this whole set-up?"

"There is no airport in Hermanus, Saluni."

"So what? We'll take a limousine to Cape Town and fly from there. Why do you want to make everything difficult, man? Are you jealous of my fame?"

"What if the mother of the Bored Twins does not allow this to happen?"

"She will, man. When she sees the CD and smells all the money we'll be making she'll let the girls go. You must decide now what you want to be in this set-up."

"I just want to be where you are, Saluni. I want to be in your dreams."

"And you will be, man. I never forget my friends when I am famous. You will warm my bed. When I come back from singing at Carnegie Hall I will find my bed warm. It is a wonderful arrangement. And don't worry about the Bored Twins. I only need them at the beginning. When I hit the real big time I won't need them anymore. I'll dispatch them back to Hermanus. I'll be a solo act. I will bowl them over on my own . . . just me and my backing band."

She breaks into a blues song and acknowledges imaginary applause.

"I am sure you will, Saluni," says the Whale Caller. "I am sure you will."

"In the meantime you must do something about your life too," she says. "While we are waiting for the festivals around South Africa to come to an end we need to find a way to increase our income, so that we can raise our standard of living a bit. When I hit the big time the good life must not come as a total shock to our bodies."

"I have been happy living like this all my life, Saluni."

"Happy? You don't know the meaning of the word."

"Satisfied. I have been satisfied living like this all my life."

"That was before I became famous, man. Now things have changed."

When she is excited like this the sweet and mouldy smell exudes from her in gushes. She leaves the room, promising that when she returns she will have a bombshell of an idea. The sweet and mouldy smell lingers. He remembers his mother.

She does return with an idea, although to the Whale Caller it doesn't seem to be such a bombshell. She suggests that he must catch fish and sell it instead of complaining about the meagreness of his pension. Angling will also add variety to their diet. They will not just depend on the window-shopping ritual to provide some respite from macaroni and cheese. "After all," she adds, "you used to be a fisherman during your wanderings. You must have learnt a thing or two about catching fish."

As far as the Whale Caller is concerned this is not such an original idea. Long before Saluni became part of his life he considered line fishing for a living a few times, but discarded the idea when he realised that it would take him away from his whales for long periods. He was also discouraged by the fact that he would have first to obtain a fishing permit at the post office, which would only allow him ten fish a day. The permit would further prohibit him from exceeding five fish of any particular species. He therefore decided to forget about the idea. He was satisfied with the meagre pension at the time because there was no Saluni to look after. His needs were few and he managed quite well. Now there is Saluni, with her civilised living and all. It is a different life. They do need the extra income even if it is derived from such small quotas. Perhaps he could devote two days of the week to fishing. There is no harm in investing a little money on tackle, bait and forceps for removing hooks from the fish. Yes, he will take Saluni's suggestion.

"You will see," Saluni assures him. "You will get places when you listen to me. Who knows? Maybe one day fame will also find you. Just stick around with me, man, and fame will either find you or you will find it."

The Wendy house becomes busy once more. And not just from breathlessness. Saluni revives civilised living. Since the tulips of the mansion are still on strike the vase on the table now has grasses and fresh wild flowers, including some fynbos from Hoy's Koppie, which is protected by government environmental authorities, and shouldn't be in anyone's vase. Civilised living now includes a change of diet. Cream of mushroom soup as a starter.

Fried cabbage. Fried rice. Very few window-shopping expeditions these days, but more candlelight dinners at the Wendy house. Fish. Although he is really a fried fish man, she introduces other ways of preparing it. Grilled fish. Curried fish. Pickled fish.

It is the fish that the Whale Caller catches in the sea. Fish-catching days are pleasant for Saluni because she does not have to share him with Sharisha. Often they walk on cliff paths to his favourite fishing spot that is thirty minutes east of the Old Harbour at an easy pace. This is a spot that never disappoints in its yield of bottom-feeding fish such as the hottentot and the stump-nose—both red and white. But today they find that it has been invaded by a forest of kelp. Seals and their puppies are playing a game of hide-and-seek in the kelp. The Whale Caller knows immediately that there won't be any fish there. He moves on to another spot, with Saluni in tow, with her running commentary on the beckoning pleasures of fame. He finds just the right spot at the Kwaaiwater near the mouth of the Mossel River. There is cob water here—the sea is muddy brown close to the coast, a sign that the place is teeming with fish of the cob variety. He takes off the top of his overalls and ties its arms around his waist. He sits bare-chested on a cliff and casts his line into the sea. After an hour or so he has caught only fish as small as the chokka, that children hook at night off the quay at the new harbour.

"We'll use this as bait," he says.

"Shame on your tiny pilchards," she says. "I am sure even a child can catch better fish. I tell you every day, man, we can't walk all this distance just to catch fish that are as small as my thumb."

"You leave the fishing to me, Saluni, and I'll leave stardom to you."

"At Castle Rock and Gearing Point near the Old Harbour people catch better fish. And that is on our doorstep."

"It is always crowded there, Saluni, with sea anglers fighting for a small space on piers and harbour walls. Anyway, the fresh air and the walk will do you a lot of good. Now that you are a star you have to maintain your beautiful figure, you know that."

She nearly tells him that the only good thing about this walk is that it takes them far away from Sharisha and her spoilt brat. But she remembers that she has vowed not to mention Sharisha's name to him again. She must pretend that the whale is no bother at all in order to beat it at its own game. That is why she sometimes joins him as he sits on the peninsula for hours drooling over the creatures. She even pretends to drool with him, while inside she is laughing at the foolishness of it all. As usual, when the Whale Caller is not there, she flashes or moons the stupid whale, and this never fails to destabilise it and drive it away to the sheltered bay to join other calving whales.

There is a bite. A fish is hooked, and judging from its struggle, it is not the puny ones that Saluni has been mocking. He plays it for some time until it gets tired. Then he lands it. It is a plump bluish grey fish, about thirty-five centimetres long.

"It is a broad bream," says an excited Saluni. "This one you are not selling, man. It is for our table."

"It is a hottentot, Saluni," he says. "It is easy to confuse them. Yes, this one is yours, Saluni. I caught it for you. See how beautiful it looks in its gleaming colours? It is as beautiful as you."

Saluni is squatting behind him, displaying a big toothless smile.

"At least now you are doing something, man," she says, scratching his hairy back as he guts the hottentot. "You've stopped playing."

"If you think it's easy to catch a fish you should try it."

"If you think it's easy to be a star you should try it."

"I never argue with you about that, Saluni," he says. "I never do."

Fishing is not for people in a hurry. It needs patience. Another hour passes without any luck. Saluni is beginning to feel that the man is not so hot after all. And then he catches a red roman. Her faith in him is revived, and with it the scratching of his back. This one will be sold and will bring in some cash to add to the growing fortune that she, as the treasurer, keeps in a scoff tin under the bed.

But soon their haven is invaded by other anglers. And they all concentrate on the area near the river mouth. The Whale Caller knows immediately that it must be the kabeljou run. During this season shoaling kabeljou is found wherever the water is dirty. The sandy bottoms of river mouths are the favourite haunts of the shoals. They are very elusive though, and are mostly caught by divers in spearfishing expeditions. But anglers always try their luck. Stories are told of anglers who grew old trying to break a record set by one Mr W. R. Selkirk, who landed the biggest fish ever caught with rod and line to date anywhere in the world. And it happened right here in Hermanus on April 28, 1922. No decent angler forgets that date. And the fish? It was a four-metre-long shark that weighed 986 kilograms, drawn from these waters after a five-and-a-half-hour struggle.

Most anglers are realistic enough to know that this record may be broken only in tall tales. In any event harming sharks is regarded as objectionable. South Africa was the first country in the world to outlaw shark fishing. The objective, instead, is to break another Hermanus record set by the Honourable William Philip Schreiner, K.C. C.M.G., who caught a fifty-kilogram kabeljou. The prestige of breaking a fishing record set by none other than that distinguished son of a German missionary who became the prime minister of the Cape in 1898, a Rugby Union official, a constitutional lawyer who was part of a fondly remembered 1909 delegation to London to petition for a franchise for black people, and brother of author Olive Schreiner, is what spurs the men gathering here to return year after year for the kabeljou run. None of them, however, is able to say what year exactly the great man actually caught the kabeljou. Most believe that it is a record even older than the Selkirk one. There is debate about that even as they choose their prime spots and ceremonially cast their nylon lines into the water.

They are not really match anglers in the true sense of the word in that they do not engage in organised competitive fishing. They do not compete to see who will have the biggest catch in total weight. Most are specimen anglers looking only for the kabeljou. There is no official referee or judge, and at the end of the day no trophies or cash prizes will be awarded. Anglers come and go as they wish, without anyone timing them. Some get tired of trying and walk back to town to sample other pleasures. But there is some competitiveness though, since each one is looking for that prized catch, and the ultimate glory will be in breaking the Honourable Schreiner's record.

The Whale Caller is not happy with the invasion. He comes here precisely because it is a quiet spot. But then it is the mouth of a river and therefore it attracts such characters. There is nothing he can do about it except mumble his disapproval when an angler does something unseemly, such as use a piece of lead to sink the hook. Although it is illegal to do so since it pollutes the water, selfish people do it all the time. He mutters even more when an angler has a snag because of the rushing waves. An inexperienced angler loses his whole tackle and another one's line snaps.

"Forget about other people," Saluni tells him, "and focus on your work."

"It is dangerous to the wildlife, Saluni. Hooks and tackle in the sea will kill many innocent fish and other sea creatures."

"We are catching them here, man. They are going to die in any case. And we're going to eat them. What's the difference?"

Oh, this Saluni! She will never understand these things. He chuckles at her logic.

There is a bite. A fish is toying with the bait. He lifts the rod sharply in order to drive the barbed treble hook home. There is a struggle. He stands up and braces his foot against the boulder as he plays the fish, trying to tire it. But the fish is too strong. He slips and is almost dragged down the cliff into the sea. He does not let go of the rod and manages to dig into the ground between two firm rocks. The struggle continues. By now the other anglers have become spectators. They cheer and egg him on. When the fish seems to be getting the upper hand three men instinctively rush to assist him but others stop them. A man needs to savour the glory of catching the big one on his own.

"Come on, man," screeches Saluni. "You can't let it go now."

It takes him more than an hour to land the fish. It is the biggest kabeljou that the spectators have ever seen. It is longer than the Whale Caller's height and certainly bulkier than Saluni's body. It still has some fight left in it. But not for long. Soon it is dead and he is gutting it.

"Get us a weighing basket," says one man. "Who has a weighing basket?"

No one has a weighing basket that can weigh such a big fish.

"He must have broken the record," says another man. "This must be the biggest kabeljou ever caught in the waters of Hermanus. Of the world even."

"Who ever thought big-game fishing can be done so successfully from the cliffs?" yet another asks of no one in particular.

The Whale Caller is exhausted. He lies next to his fish, trying to catch his breath. His arms ache and his knees are bleeding. His overalls are torn at the knees. While Saluni is massaging his sweat-drenched nape and shining pate, assuring him that he will be fine again in no time, a man lifts up the fish and poses with it. His companion takes some photographs.

"He is going to lie about that when he gets home," Saluni whispers to the Whale Caller. "He's going to claim that he caught the fish."

"It doesn't matter, Saluni. The fish knows who caught it."

When a second man and a third want to pose with the fish Saluni puts a stop to it. They must pay, she demands, before they can pose with the fish. The Whale Caller is embarrassed, but he is unable to do anything to stop her. Soon there is a long queue of people who want a picture with the fish. Saluni collects the money while the Whale Caller sits on the ground looking astonished. In an hour she has collected more money than they have ever made in a week of selling fresh line fish.

"This is going to be our business, man," says Saluni as they negotiate the winding cliff paths back to town, with the Whale Caller carrying the heavy fish on his shoulders. "We are going to make a lot of money renting out this fish."

"All I want to know is how much this fish weighs," says the Whale Caller.

When they reach the town they find that people have been alerted to the big catch. There are newspaper photographers, and radio and television reporters waiting to interview the Whale Caller. They take the kabeljou to the fishing club to be weighed on their very accurate Atlas scale. Forty-three kilograms! It does not break the record but it is big enough to celebrate.

"What are you going to do with this fish?" asks a woman in the crowd.

"Taking it home, of course," says Saluni.

"I want to buy it," says a fishmonger. "Name your price."

"I want to buy it too," says the man who runs the restaurant on the stilts.

"We are not selling it," says Saluni.

"We are not?" asks the Whale Caller. "Is that not why we catch fish . . . to sell it?"

"Not this one," says Saluni firmly.

As they walk home with the fish on his shoulders she mildly chastises him for disagreeing with her in public. And she adds:

"And don't think that because you are now going to appear in newspapers and on television you are more famous than me. People who sing are more of celebrities than those who catch fish."

"I never claimed any fame, Saluni. I am sure those photographs they took of me and the fish are just for brochures and videos that advertise Hermanus. Nothing important."

"Just as well because they left me out of the picture. And you said nothing, man. You were happy to keep all the fame yourself. I was there when you caught that fish but they only photographed you. And you didn't complain."

"People photograph what they want to photograph in this new South Africa, Saluni. It is something beyond our control."

"Well, they won't just photograph this fish for nothing next time. They can photograph you for free since you want to be cheap with yourself, but not this fish. They must pay, man. We are going to make a lot of money with this fish. I'll be your manager, man. Just leave everything to me."

She slowly and deliberately explains the economics of this new venture. There are no quotas when you rent out your fish. There is no government to limit you to ten fish. You make money from the same fish over and over again.

The fish is too big to fit in their fridge. So it spends the night on top of it.

The next morning they go out to the beach with a sign: *Rent-a-Fish*. Once more holidaymakers pose with the kabeljou. Even those who don't have any ambition of being anglers pay a few coins to Saluni and she prepares them for a pose. They stand holding the kabeljou with a nylon line that has been tied around its gills and lift it up above their heads so that its length is perpendicular to the ground. They stand in the sea, with the water only up to their shins, holding tackle with their left hands. Other family members click away. By the end of the day they have made more money than they would have earned from selling ten fish.

The next day the fish is starting to stink and the Whale Caller wants to go to Sharisha. But Saluni is undeterred. There is money to be made.

"There is life in this fish yet," she says. "We can make a lot of money still."

"We agreed, Saluni . . . I would fish only two days a week. Three days at most. I need to check out the whales, Saluni."

"I am not asking you to fish, man. Just to help me take this darn fish to the beach. The whales will always be there. You know I'll go with you to watch the whales. Remember this fish won't last forever."

So, once more they take the fish to the beach. By midday it fills the whole area with its stench. People begin to complain. "Why would I want to photograph myself with a stinking kabeljou?" a man asks.

"It won't stink in the photograph," Saluni responds.

But no one wants to come near the fish. The Whale Caller gets rid of it in one of the dumpsters in town.

After he has indulged himself with Sharisha and the young one for a few days, he is persuaded to go back to the mouth of the river to catch another kabeljou before they move upriver to spawn. "Try to remember what you did when you caught that big one the other day," Saluni advises. He does catch a kabeljou or two. They are never as big as the forty-three-kilogram one. But for failed anglers and tourists at a loose end they are good enough to pose with.

The rent-a-fish business thrives.


Saluni. Money is the least of her problems. She is the treasurer and business manager of the rent-a-fish enterprise, although she makes it clear to the Whale Caller that this is only a temporary arrangement. He will have to learn to manage the business himself because as soon as the radio man returns with the demo CDs she will be flying high around the capitals of the world, entertaining heads of state and attending premieres and receiving international awards. He must enjoy her services while he can.

"I suspect you will let the rent-a-fish business die when I am gone," she says.

"I'll do my best, Saluni," he says.

"I am the brains behind this business. Without me you'll let it go bust, man."

"I'd rather sell the fish than rent it out, Saluni. And when you are gone there won't be a need even for that. I'll just become my old self again."

"You see what I mean, man? All my efforts will be wasted."

"They'll be wasted in any case. Didn't you say you'll fly with me?"

"Yes, but not immediately. I need to get settled first. You don't just drag a man to Hollywood before you get settled."

"I will miss you, Saluni, when you are a big star. Do remember us little people when you reach your paradise," he says, and then he chuckles to himself.

"You are not a little person at all. You are big and strong. You are a blue whale, remember? How can I forget you, man? How can I forget a blue whale like you?"

They sit on the bed. They are both overwhelmed by sickness. It has never really left them, this habit of making each other sick. It subsides when there is tension between them and returns when there is harmony. Now the sickness is throbbing in their chests. It throbs like this in the Whale Caller whenever Saluni casts off her iron mask and displays a pleasant and vulnerable face.

But sometimes she forgets that she has decided to be agreeable in order to defeat Sharisha at her own game and relapses into her old self. When it is time to sleep she only opens her side of the bed and slithers into the blankets like a snake, without preparing the bedding for both of them as he does when he happens to come to bed first. He makes a snide comment about stars who do things only for themselves and disregard the needs of other people with whom they live. She pounces.

"Oh, man," she says, "you can be so petty."

"Do you know what the Bible says, Saluni? Do unto others."

"So much for wanting to be my slave."

"Me? A slave?"

"Oh, yes, you offered. That first night."

"That was coitus talking," he says with a new twinkle in his eye.

"I hold men to their promises."

But as soon as she has said this she remembers her resolve to be *nice*.

"Okay then," she says, "I'll open your side of the bed too. I don't know if it makes any difference, man, but I'll do it because that's what you want. See? I can be nice too, man. Don't you forget that."


The sickness worsens with Saluni's increasing tenderness. It makes them want to be together all the time. Saluni hasn't been back to the mansion since the recording. She fears that the mother may have found out that she defied her, and she is not prepared to face the woman without the CD. The CD will surely melt all the anger she may be harbouring against her. She will laugh at her own folly when she listens to the beautiful music on the recording while the girls continue to have their angelic voices intact. She does miss the euphoria, but it is not such a searing longing since it is ameliorated by the sickness. The sickness is all-consuming. It eats their insides and makes the ailing ones sweat and forces them to reach for each other out of the blue in the middle of nowhere and just lose each other in each other's breath. But in the midst of it all Saluni does not forget to uphold the dignity and grace of stardom.

She uses some of the rent-a-fish money to buy herself a fur coat from the flea market. Although the lining is moth-eaten, the otter fur still looks good on the outside. For a long time she wishes winter would come quickly so that she can be seen strutting in her coat on the runways that are the streets of Hermanus. Not only will the winter give her the opportunity to wear the coat, but winter may drive Sharisha to the southern seas so she won't have to put up with her nonsense. She is wary of the fact that Sharisha may decide not to go, as she did last winter. But surely sooner or later she will have to introduce the young one to a life of krill in the southern seas. Nature demands that Sharisha goes to cold climes whether she likes it or not.

Summer days are not in any particular hurry to go anywhere. Saluni grows impatient and decides to wear her coat irrespective of what the weather says. She is wearing it this Sunday morning as she sits on a rock like a basking naiad, her feet playing with seaweed in the water. The Whale Caller sits behind her on another rock. There are no whales in sight, which makes the morning even more pleasant for Saluni. The air from the sea is hot and humid.

"Perhaps you should give it a rest, Saluni," says the Whale Caller. "I can imagine how much you are sweating under that coat."

Saluni can think of a few choice words to hurl in his direction, but in the spirit of the new attitude she decides against it. She just hums softly to herself and continues her game with the seaweed. This emboldens him enough to voice another criticism: "You know, Saluni, some poor animal had to die for you to look beautiful like that?"

"They die every day, man . . . the animals . . . they die so we can eat them or wear them as shoes. So why not wear them as fur coats? Some are killed by you, man. What do you do with the fish that you catch? Fondle and caress and kiss them and then throw them back into the sea?"

"It's all thanks to you, Saluni. I was satisfied with my macaroni and cheese."

"Haven't I heard that somewhere before? You were satisfied with your life full stop. But now you are not just satisfied. You are happy. You were never happy until I came into your life."

He is digesting this, repeating the word "happy" twice or thrice. Saluni walks out of the water and joins him on his rock. She holds his hand.

"Yes, you are happy . . . very happy! You are just not aware of it. We are both very happy."

This scares the Whale Caller, but he tries to be brave about it. If this be happiness, then he will face it like a man. He will face the sickness, for clearly it is happiness's bedfellow. He sees Lunga Tubu hopping about from rock to rock without a care in the world. He feels sorry for him: one day he will grow up into a man and some woman will make him sick with happiness. That's a man's lot. The cross that he has to bear with fortitude. He is coming towards them, Lunga Tubu. The Whale Caller wonders why. The logical thing to do would be to avoid them . . . to give Saluni's mothering tendencies as wide a berth as possible. But here he comes and stands in front of them and greets them, politely calling them "aunt" and "uncle." He looks relieved that Saluni does not make any attempt to mollycoddle him.

"He has returned, Aunt Saluni," says Lunga Tubu. "The radio man is back."

"Has he brought the CDs?" asks Saluni, jumping up, grasping the boy by both shoulders and shaking the information out of him.

"Yes, he has brought some CDs," says Lunga Tubu, "and he wants to see you. He is at the Seacrest Hotel in Seventh Street."

Saluni looks at the Whale Caller triumphantly: "You didn't

believe he would return, did you? You thought he was a scoundrel who had run away with our voices."

"I never said anything like that, Saluni."

"You didn't say it but you thought it. One only had to look at your face to see that you were questioning my credentials as a star. Now what do you say about it, man? A big-time agent wants to see me . . . at a hotel. What do you say about that?"

"I say go for it, Saluni," says the Whale Caller, pretending some enthusiasm.

There may be something in this whole business after all. Otherwise why would the radio man come all the way from Cape Town? But if Saluni does go, what will happen to him? How is he going to live without Saluni? And if she does become a star she will surely forget about him. He can't leave Hermanus. He can't follow Saluni to Hollywood. He will be out of place there without the sea and the whales and the seagulls and the hot smells of rotting kelp and the salt air brushing against his silver grey beard and the southeaster lashing against his body and the Wendy house and Hermanus.

Under his breath he curses the radio man. But he offers: "I will go with you to the hotel, Saluni."

"Me too," says Lunga Tubu.

Saluni lifts her fur coat to her shoulders and runs up the cliff path. She is closely followed by the Whale Caller, who is closely followed by Lunga Tubu. They race along the path until it joins Main Road. They turn right into Main Road, winding with it towards the Mossel River. But before they can cross the bridge she stops, perhaps to catch her breath. They all stop.

"That's better, Saluni," says the Whale Caller. "You don't want to be all sweaty and breathless when you reach the hotel. I think you should take it easy, Saluni."

"Why don't you tell the truth, man," says Saluni. "You just can't keep up."

"You stopped first, Saluni. Not me."

She stopped because she's just had a brilliant idea, she says. She must go to the mansion and get the Bored Twins and their parents to come with her to meet the radio man. When the mother hears the radio man outlining the big plans for their stardom and when she listens to the wonderful CD, she will finally get over her concerns. She will let the girls go off to conquer the world.

"But you said the parents spend all day away from the mansion," says the Whale Caller.

"Why do you always want to come up with some obstacle, man? Don't you want me to be a star?"

"I do, Saluni. I do. It's just that I don't want you to go all the way to the mansion only to find that the parents are not there."

"If you had any good intentions you would have imagined that they are there since it is Sunday morning."

She turns and takes a westerly direction and follows Main Road out of town. She walks very fast, sometimes breaking into a run. The man and the boy do likewise, until they reach the mansion. As good fortune would have it the donkey cart is parked outside. The father appears from around the corner pulling a donkey by the leather strap of its bridle. He is harnessing it to the cart when Saluni and her entourage arrive.

"There is no rest for the hungry," he tells his visitors. "We are going out to collect bones and scrap metal."

Saluni explains their mission. She confesses that during the Kalfiefees she took the girls to town to record. Now the radio man is back with the CD. The father must convince his wife to come and meet the radio man and listen to the CD. She outlines to the man the significance of this great event and the financial rewards that the family will reap. Saluni's description of the beckoning stardom is so vivid that the man can see banknotes floating in front of his eyes. But he knows that when his wife hears that

Saluni defied her and took her daughters to town, she will be so wrathful that no promises of lucre will make her go to the hotel to meet the man she believes is a thief of voices.

"Don't tell her about it yet," says Lunga Tubu. "Let it be a surprise."

"You are a sly one," says the Whale Caller. "It might just work. Just tell her that before you go to collect bones and scrap metal you must meet a man in town who may have an interesting business proposition for you."

"At least now you two are becoming helpful instead of putting obstacles in my way," says Saluni, obviously pleased with the suggestion. "We need the girls too, man. They must hear their CD. Come with the girls."

"And how do I explain that to my wife? No, Saluni, you are asking for too much now," says the father as he walks into the house.

After a few moments he returns with the mother. They all ride on the donkey cart to town. After crossing the Mossel River bridge into the suburb of Voelklip where the hotel is located, Saluni takes out a compact mirror from her sequinned handbag and looks at herself. She rearranges her hair. She applies a little blusher, some lipstick and mascara. She brushes her fur coat with her hands for any speck of dust that may have the temerity to sit on it.

The receptionist phones the radio man and he swaggers down from his room. He is taken aback to see the motley crew. After the introductions and assurances from Saluni that everyone present has a vested interest in the business at hand (which continues to remain nameless for the mother's sake) he invites them to his room.

"Where are the girls?" the radio man asks when everyone is settled on his bed, on the dressing table stool and on the two easy chairs.

"Girls?" asks the mother, becoming suspicious. "What girls?"

"The singing girls, of course," says the radio man. *"Saluni and the Bored Twins!"*

"They can't make it today," says Saluni. "Their parents are representing them. We just want to listen to the CD and hear your plans for making us international stars."

The radio man gets agitated. He screams: "I need those girls here . . . now!"

Everyone is puzzled by this sudden loss of temper.

"Calm down, man," says Saluni. "Just play us the CD."

"It didn't work," says the radio man. "Something I can't understand happened."

He takes out a CD from his bag and plays it on a portable machine on the bedside table. The voices of the Bored Twins are distorted. Saluni's voice comes out clearly in its richness, but the girls' voices are unrecognisable. They sound like mating cats. The mother angrily turns to the father: "And you knew all this?"

"I only knew this morning," says the father. "These people deceived me too. They came this morning with their story."

"I swear I don't know what happened here," says the radio man. "I came back to arrange for a new recording. It was wonderful when I was listening to the three of you. I sound-engineered the recording myself and everything was wonderful. I am just as mystified as you are that the CD came out this way. I want to take *Saluni and the Bored Twins* to a proper state-of-the-art recording studio in Cape Town."

"Not my children!" the mother bursts out. "They are not going to Cape Town. They are not going to record their voices ever again."

"But, please, you can't do this to your children," Saluni appeals.

"I do not want to have anything to do with you, Saluni," cries the mother. "Do not talk to me. I do not want to see you near my children ever."

"If you want to be that spiteful, then you can stay with your children, man. I am going to the recording studios in Cape Town. I am going to be a solo act."

"I can't record you on your own, Saluni," says the radio man. "The girls are the main attraction, not you. If they are not part of this, then there is no deal."

This hurts Saluni deeply. She looks at the Whale Caller to see if he is gloating. He is not. His head is bowed in embarrassment on her behalf.

"I really don't know how this happened," the radio man keeps repeating.

"I told you so," says the mother, glaring at Saluni. "You are fortunate that the machine failed to steal their voices. It tried and failed. That is why the voices on the recording didn't come out right. They sound like the voices of ghosts. You nearly destroyed my kids. They should just be happy that they still have their beautiful voices."

She leaves the room in a huff and her husband follows her. They climb onto their donkey cart and ride away. Saluni tries to plead with the radio man to give her a chance but he is adamant that he would not be able to sell her act. He brutally tells her that there is nothing special about her singing. She has the kind of voice that one can hear in any tavern across the country. The Bored Twins were the act he was really interested in. Sooner or later he would have discarded Saluni for the Bored Twins. They would be a successful international act without her rough voice to mess up their angelic voices.

This is too much for the Whale Caller. He smashes his huge fist into the face of the radio man, who goes crashing to the floor. He lies there seeing multicoloured stars. The Whale Caller grasps

Saluni's and Lunga Tubu's hands and leads them out of the room
and away from the hotel. As they walk along Seventh Street back
to the Old Harbour area the Whale Caller expresses his regret
that he had to resort to violence. He keeps repeating that he
never wanted to hurt anyone.

"Stop whining, man," says Saluni. "That bastard deserved it.
You are *the* man, man. You don't let anyone mess with your
woman."

The whole town is excited about the eclipse of the sun, but not
Saluni. People are buying dark glasses that will enable them to
look at the eclipsed sun. Those who cannot afford the expensive
glasses that have been made especially for looking at the sun make
their own by blackening glass with fire and smoke. Others look for
old negatives of photographs, which are also reputed to be effec-
tive in protecting the eyes from the wrath of a sun that is being
upstaged by an impertinent moon. When the eclipse happens later
in the day they will be ready. Everyone knows that only a fool
would look at the eclipse with naked eyes, for that is a surefire
way of inviting blindness.

Saluni does not participate in the eclipse madness. Her dreams
of Hollywood have been crushed and for days now she has been
nursing her bruised feelings. She sinks into the silence of depression. The Whale Caller tends to her and feeds her. She does not
care about civilised living anymore. She drinks broth from a mug
and survives on that. Then she explodes into a rage, walking up
and down Main Road cursing aloud at all those who have betrayed
her in the past and those who intend to do so in the future. She
counts the whales, particularly Sharisha, among those who will
have their day of reckoning sooner than they realise. Days of silence alternate with days of rage. Days of silence fill the Whale
Caller with sadness because she becomes such a pitiful figure. At

least rage becomes her. Self-pity drains all dignity out of her. The Whale Caller understands that there is nothing personal about these mood swings. He blames it all on the radio man, and this salves his conscience a little for hitting him.

This morning of the eclipse he busies himself with preparing a glass for looking at the sun. At first he hopes the dark brown beer bottles will do the trick. But then he decides it will be much safer to do the tried and tested—he breaks a cold drink bottle and coats it with an even black layer from burning papers just outside the Wendy house. Saluni is standing at the door in her fur coat and red pencil-heel shoes, watching him mournfully.

"I am going to make one for you too, Saluni," he says.

"I don't care about it, man."

"It is a wonder of nature, Saluni. You will see; it will make you feel better. And they say it is going to be a total eclipse this time . . . just after midday. Hermanus will fall into darkness."

"I just can't work myself into an orgasm over darkness, man," she says, and walks into the house. "I am going to bed. Switch on the lights if your damn eclipse comes while I am asleep."

His heart bleeds for her. It does become worse when she doesn't lash out at the world . . . when the storm rages silently inside her. But there is nothing he can do about it. He has tried to comfort her, to tell her that another radio man—one who will be smart enough to recognise her true talent without the Bored Twins—will come one day. But she only stares at him as if she does not really believe him . . . as if it does not matter anymore . . . as if she has resigned herself to a fameless life.

"I am going down to the sea, Saluni," he says through the doorway. "I'll be back before the eclipse."

She does not respond. Maybe she is already napping. All the better if she is because he will feel less guilty about leaving her in this state. But he desperately needs some respite from her sullenness.

He finds Sharisha and the child in the blue depths off the peninsula. She seems to be teaching the young one how to use the baleen to sieve prey from the water. Or perhaps they are just competing in some whale game that the Whale Caller has never seen before. He has not brought his kelp horn this time, so he just sits on a rock and laughs at their antics.

All of a sudden the game stops and Sharisha rallies protectively to the young one. She has fixed her eyes on the crag behind the Whale Caller. He turns to look up and sees Saluni walking gracefully in her stilettos and fur coat down the concrete cliff path. Sharisha starts to sail away but changes her mind and moves in towards the peninsula.

"You should have seen them, Saluni," says the Whale Caller. "They were having so much fun."

"What kind of a man are you? You can see that I am not well and yet you leave me for these stupid whales."

"You said you were going to sleep, Saluni. What went wrong? You were not bothered about them anymore. You promised we would not fight over Sharisha again."

"Obviously you took advantage of that. From now on it's either the fish or me."

She tries to shoo Sharisha away, but the whale holds its own. It bellows deeply. It sounds more like a groan. This worries the Whale Caller. He has never seen Sharisha like this; furiously blowing and sending tremors under the water that reach the rocks of the peninsula. She seems to be gearing for a fight. If only he had brought his kelp horn with him he would have calmed her with the tune she knows so well.

"We must go home now," says Saluni.

"We can't leave Sharisha like this. There is something wrong."

"Every time it is Sharisha this, Sharisha that!"

She races to the edge of the peninsula. The Whale Caller now knows that she came especially to pick a fight with Sharisha. Under the fur coat she wears nothing but her God-given skin, making her intentions very clear: she intends to flash Sharisha to death. She opens the coat, raises her leg and screams: "Take that, you foolish fish!"

But Sharisha has decided to assert herself. She does not budge. She stares Saluni straight in the eye. She does not look scandalised as she usually does when Saluni moons or flashes her. She looks defiant. Instead it is the Whale Caller who looks scandalised.

Saluni tries again. She opens her coat, raising the other leg and shouting: "You take that, stupid fish!" And then moving from one leg to the other in a frenzied dance, all the while opening and closing the front of her coat and screaming: "And that! And that!"

Still Sharisha does not move. Her defiant stare is unflinching. It is clearly a standoff that Saluni cannot win. She is devastated. She runs up the cliff path weeping, back to the Wendy house.

The Whale Caller remains confused for a while. Sharisha continues with her deep bellowing. The Whale Caller becomes frantic. He should have brought his kelp horn. Somehow he needs to calm Sharisha, to comfort her, to assure her that everything is fine. There is kelp all around him. But it is wet and even soggy. It cannot produce any music. He locks the fingers of both his hands together and shapes his hands into a roundish sound box. He blows into the hole created by his thumbs and produces deep bellows similar to Sharisha's. It works! Sharisha seems to calm down. Her anger gradually melts as he continues to bellow. She bellows back. They exchange bellows for a long time. The child finds this game thrilling and joins with its own weak bellows. These feeble attempts leave the Whale Caller chuckling to himself. He is having such a wonderful time that he does not notice that darkness is gradually creeping in.

He had almost forgotten about the eclipse. He blows the final

bellow to say goodbye and runs up the cliff path. When he gets
home he is shocked to find Saluni standing outside looking at the
eclipse with her naked eyes.

"You are in a warlike mood today, Saluni," he says. "First you
pick on Sharisha and now you are challenging the sun."

"You would take her side, wouldn't you?"

"You started the whole fight, Saluni. She was minding her
own business and you came and started the fight," he says as he
reaches for her, trying to save her from her own foolishness.

"Don't touch me."

She opens her eyes even wider and defiantly fixes her glare on
the sun, outbraving it into darkness. The Whale Caller panics.

"You will go blind, Saluni."

She turns and looks in his direction and breaks into laughter.
She laughs for a long time, jumping about in a jig of victory and
joyfully shouting: "I am blind . . . I am already blind!"


Saluni. She lives in a world of darkness. Her eyes are wide open,
yet her world remains black long after the eclipse is gone. The
Whale Caller keeps on asking: "Why did you do it, Saluni, why?"
She calmly responds that she went blind because there was nothing worth seeing in the world anymore. After all, she has lost Hollywood. And she has lost him to Sharisha.

"You have not lost me," he says. "I am here with you."

It does not escape the Whale Caller that she seems to enjoy her
blindness. She has a permanent smile. There is a look of peace
about her. She hopes that for the first time in her life she has banished her fear of the dark. Darkness exists as antinomy to light. If
she can't see any light, she can't see any darkness either. This
thought gives her a sense of freedom. Now she can travel the
world without fear. She keeps repeating as if to convince herself:

"In blindness I see no light, and without light there is no darkness."

Two days after the eclipse she wakes up early in the morning and announces that she is leaving. She wants to get away from the town that has nothing but ugly memories for her—ranging from the insults she has suffered from whales to the pain of being banished from the Bored Twins by a heartless parent. Even the good memories are now mangled by blindness. Hermanus holds nothing for her but ugliness.

She packs her clothes in a paper bag and then dresses in her green corduroy pants, black pencil-heel boots and a red polo-neck shirt. She also wears her trusty fur coat. She sprays perfume on everything she is wearing, covering, but not quite, her sweet and mouldy smell for a while. All this time the Whale Caller thinks she can't be serious. She wouldn't dare go out there alone walking sightlessly and without any destination.

"It is hot, Saluni," he says. "Your taffeta dress will be better."

"It will ultimately get cold. I will be on the road for many seasons. I must be prepared."

She takes her paper bag and leaves. She walks out of the gate. She is serious. The Whale Caller runs after her, calling her back. She stumbles on, almost falling. He reaches her and pleads with her to come back home. But she is adamant that she needs to put great distance between the town and herself. The Whale Caller then offers to walk the road with her, to look after her.

"No, you stay here," she says. "I'll find my way around the world."

"I can't let you go alone, Saluni. You are blind. You will get lost. Just wait here and I'll get a few of my things. I'll join you on the road. After all, I have walked the road before. I know a thing or two about the road."

As he rushes back to the Wendy house she calls after him:

"Don't forget to bring the fish money from the scoff tin under the bed!" and then she mutters to herself: "I will enslave him with my blindness."

They walk down Main Road in the easterly direction until Main Road becomes Seventh Street. They walk past the rows of beautiful houses on both sides of the street, many of them in Cape Dutch style. Some have B&B signs outside. Everyone wants to cash in on the tourism frenzy, observes the Whale Caller to himself. He holds Saluni's hand so as to guide her safely. With the other hand he holds his kelp horn. He carries a rucksack on his back containing canned fish, biscuits, his underwear and other small items. He wears his denim dungarees and hasn't brought any change of clothes. He hopes Saluni's road-madness will wear off and soon they will be walking back to the Wendy house.

On Saluni's instructions they branch off from the tarred road onto a dirt road. There are thick bushes growing on both sides of the road, filling the air with mentholated scents. They walk on for a few hours on the fine gravel until they reach a green-roofed white house on the shoreline. The Whale Caller knocks but there is no response. He looks through the curtainless windows. All the rooms are empty. Saluni wonders why they should be wasting time when they have such a long way to go. He tries the door. It is not locked. He suggests that they should spend the night there. It is only midday and they are just a few kilometres from town. He hopes that common sense will prevail and she will demand to be guided back to the Wendy house. Stopping at this deserted house will buy him time. He leads her to the veranda that juts into the sea on stilts. They sit on a bench and enjoy the breeze from the sea.

"We could stay here for ever," he says. "It is such a beautiful place."

"It must belong to someone," she says.

"Well, there is no one here. No furniture either. Just this bench on the veranda. Perhaps we should stay here for some days whilst we consider our next move."

"We don't need to consider our next move, man. We just walk. We don't need to get to any particular place either. We just walk. That's what we'll do. Walk."

"Poor house," says the Whale Caller resignedly. "What a waste!"

"Think, man, think. Why would a house like this be unoccupied when there is homelessness all over the district? There is something wrong with it, man. We wouldn't stay here even if we didn't need to walk the road."

He must think of another trick. Somehow there must be something back in Hermanus that would tempt her to return. He remembers Mr. Yodd. Saluni and Mr. Yodd have become quite cosy recently, even though he was not amused at his failure to make her bleed with his laughter. The Whale Caller suggests that it is a shame to leave Hermanus without saying goodbye to Mr. Yodd.

"He can look after himself," says Saluni.

"He will miss you though."

"I have nothing to do with him. He's not my problem. He will miss you. He has always missed you. And you are free to go back to him."

"You took him over, Saluni. He is now yours. You bribed him with oblations to the extent that he had no time for me."

"You can have him back for all I care. I don't need him. I have my blindness now."

He curses the blindness under his breath. They sit quietly for a while. He wonders what Sharisha could be doing at that very moment. Perhaps teaching the young one new tricks. Breaching gloriously to the skies, and then splashing down in thunderous abandon. Playing spyhopping tricks in the blue depths. Sooner or later she will miss him. He takes out his kelp horn and blows softly. Not Sharisha's song. Just meaningless notes as if he is testing the horn.

"You had to bring that accursed horn!" screeches Saluni.

"Just to keep myself busy on the road, Saluni."

"You might as well throw it away. It is useless without your big fish."

"I can see it now . . . you planned it all, Saluni . . . the blindness . . . so that you could take me away from Sharisha into the wilderness."

"I didn't invite you, did I? I wanted to be on my own. I didn't ask you to join me on the road. You can go back to your big fish for all I care."

The next morning they are on the road again, trudging along the shoreline. For some reason Saluni wants them to take the most difficult paths: those that meander over rocky ledges and cross bridgeless streams that hide deep in the gorges. It is as if she is bent on punishing him—and herself in the process. On making him fry in his own guilty sweat. He has to hold her hand all the time lest she tumbles down some cliff and breaks her neck. In the village of Gansbaai they take a rest on a limestone cliff. From here Saluni smells the ocean and the Whale Caller sees it down below extending for kilometres into the horizon. Not even a speckle of a whale. Only a small boat of divers close to the shoreline. And the feverish antics of bottlenose dolphins and hovering gannets as they follow shoals. On the first level of limestone cliffs just above the green shallows Cape fur seals are basking in the sun.

From this promontory known as Danger Point the Whale Caller can see the rocky islet that is famous for the shipwrecks of a bygone era. In the silence that exists between him and the blind woman he resuscitates an old habit: that of ambling in the mists of the past. It is 1852 and he is one of the sailors on HMS *Birken-head*. He is a glorious soldier in Her Majesty's conquering army sailing westwards to the navy base of Stellenbosch in the troop-ship. Great storms rise and toss HMS *Birkenhead* against the rocks and wreck it. There are only three lifeboats, which are all sacri-ficed for the civilian passengers. After helping Saluni to a lifeboat, he joins the other brave soldiers of Her Majesty's brave army, and stands to attention with a salute and an anthem that appeals to God to save the glorious queen as the ship sinks. He is one of the four hundred and forty-five people, most of them soldiers, who perish in the shipwreck. He dies a happy man, knowing that Saluni has been saved.

"Where are we here?" Saluni asks, bringing him back to the present.

He is amused at the fact that he—a man who dreads killing the fish he catches for his very survival—has just been a soldier. And of all soldiers a soldier of the colonising British!

"We are in Gansbaai," he says, without betraying the fact that he left her for a while.

"We have been walking for hours and we are still in Her-manus?"

"We are in Gansbaai, not Hermanus."

"Don't be daft, man; Gansbaai was merged with Hermanus and Stanford and Kleinmond in the last municipal elections. How come we are still in Hermanus? We left yesterday, man. Are you trying to trick me or something?"

"We move slowly, Saluni, because of your blindness and your insistence that we stay off the good roads."

After considering the matter for some time she says it does not really matter where they are as long as they keep on walking. In any event they do not have a destination. It should not trouble them at all if they take a hundred years to reach nowhere. The Whale Caller opens a tin of sardines and they eat the fish with biscuits. After the meal she flings the can away, and as he goes to retrieve it he reprimands her for making the shoreline dirty.

"Do we have dustbins here?" she asks.

"We don't. We'll take the can with us and throw it into a dustbin when we find one," says the Whale Caller, picking it up.

"That's going to be your problem," she says. "I am not carrying any smelly tins."

He stumbles across something hidden among the rocks. He moves a boulder and lifts up a sisal sack. From the smell he knows immediately what it is: abalone—or perlemoen, as it is called here. He puts his hand in the sack and it comes out with a purplish brown sea snail whose muscular foot is as broad as his open hand. Never has he seen such big abalone before. The bag is full of perlemoen of varying sizes and colours, ranging from grey to deep purple. He takes the bag to Saluni.

"Look what I found, Saluni," he says.

"I can't look, man. I am blind. But whatever it is it stinks like dead fish."

Before the Whale Caller can tell her what his discovery is a puny man in faded jeans, tattered T-shirt, filthy baseball cap and sneakers that long ago lost their colours, emerges from the fynbos behind them and approaches the Whale Caller cautiously. They size each other up, as if gearing for a fight. Then the man breaks into a smile.

"Give it to me," he says. "It's mine."

"Who is this?" asks Saluni.

"It is a poacher, Saluni," says the Whale Caller. "A perlemoen poacher."

"I am not a poacher. That perlemoen is for the pot. I don't sell it," says the man, moving backwards as if ready to escape.

"It can't be for the pot," says the Whale Caller. "The law allows you only four perlemoens a day for the pot. You are a poacher."

"Are you an undercover cop or what? Are you from the Scorpions?"

"Just give him his damn things, man," says Saluni. "You don't want to mess with poachers."

She knows them from the taverns. Stories are told of how poachers can be deadly when they are cornered. The man gains courage from Saluni's support. He concludes that the two cannot be Scorpions after all. But the Whale Caller is big and the puny man has no intention of tackling him for his bag of stolen goods. He'd better be friendly. He smiles once more and asks the Whale Caller please to give a poor man a break.

"Come on, man," says Saluni sharply. "Give the man his things."

The Whale Caller hands the bag to the puny man, muttering as much to himself as to anyone else: "But this is wrong. It is all wrong. Do you know how long it takes for those perlemoens to mature? Eight years. Eight years, I tell you."

"What do you care if it takes twenty years, man?" asks Saluni. "It is none of your business."

"We have got to eat, sir," says the puny man. "We have got to feed our children. Big companies are making money out of these perlemoens. The government gives them quotas. What about us, sir? Do you think if I apply for quotas I will get them? How are we expected to survive?"

He tells them of the woes of the village where the whole economy depends on poaching. Well-known poachers have become rich, building double-storey houses in dusty townships. Why must he be the only one who remains poor for the rest of his life? He invites them to spend the night at his shack so that they can see what he is talking about. After some persuasion from the Whale Caller Saluni agrees that they accept his invitation—not to see what he is talking about, but because they have to sleep somewhere.

He lives in what he refers to as the coloured township of
Blompark. And indeed double-storey buildings rise above the
shacks and the small state-subsidised houses that dot the township. The puny man still lives in a shack, but he hopes that one
day he too will have a double-storey house. He tells them how he
started harvesting the rocks on the kelp beds for the precious
creatures. It was for the pot. But the temptation was too great.
Soon he was harvesting to sell. Now his ambition is to have direct
access to the white middlemen who in turn sell to the Chinese
syndicate bosses. There are established racial hierarchies in the illegal abalone trade. Coloured folk sell their harvest to white men
who pay about two hundred rands a kilogram. The white men sell
to the Chinese men for about a thousand rands a kilogram. The
Chinese ship the abalone to the Far East where they get about
two thousand five hundred rands a kilogram for it. And these are
the old prices. The puny man has heard that prices have gone up,
although he has not yet benefited from that. He is at the very bottom of the food chain. He sells to better-established coloured
poachers who only pay him fifty rands a kilogram. He now wants
to deal directly with the white men who pay two hundred rands
per kilogram. That would make all the difference to his life. But
the rich coloured poachers are not eager to increase the circle of
people who have direct access.

As the puny man tells them of his woes a brand-new van stops
outside. It is the man who has come to collect the abalone. He
weighs it on a basket fish scale and pays the puny man his money.
He drives away to collect from other puny men. He used to be a
poacher himself. Now he is the middleman between the puny men
and the white men. And he has become so rich that he is now a
law unto himself. He is respected by the Gansbaai community because he is one of those who keeps the economy of the village going. When the Scorpions tighten the screws, the puny man tells his
guests, the whole village suffers. Business in pubs, furniture shops

and even video shops falls to the extent that some have to close down only to reopen when poaching activity resumes with the departure of the police, who are obviously unable to tighten the screws indefinitely.

The puny man regales them with poaching stories as he prepares them a meal of rice and fried abalone. As they eat Saluni says to the Whale Caller: "You must eat more of this perlemoen. God knows you need it. You have not touched me since we left Hermanus."

"I don't have any more, unfortunately," says the puny man. "I sell almost all of it. I leave just a little for the pot."

"Don't worry," says the Whale Caller. "I don't need any more perlemoen."

"Don't tell me you don't know why perlemoen is so popular in the Far East," says Saluni.

"Of course I know; it is an aphrodisiac," says the puny man.

"Everyone knows that," says the Whale Caller, rather embarrassed. "You don't have to sing about it."

"So now you know why you must eat more of the perlemoen as long as we are here surrounded by it," she says.

"It is finished, ma'am," says the puny man apologetically.

The Whale Caller is scandalised. He shifts closer to her on the bench on which they are sitting and whispers in her ear: "You are blind, Saluni. How can you say such things?"

By nine the Whale Caller is bored with poaching stories and Saluni wants to sleep. The puny man prepares a place for them on one side of the shack while he will sleep on the opposite side. The Whale Caller asks if he would allow them to leave the light on all night, but the puny man will have none of that.

"I can't sleep in the dark," says Saluni. "If you think we are going to finish your paraffin in the lamp, I have my own candle in my bag."

It has nothing to do with saving paraffin, the puny man explains. He would not be able to sleep with the light on. It would remind him of prison, where he spent a few months for poaching. The solitary naked bulb was left on for the whole night in his cell, making it impossible for him to sleep. He spent many sleepless nights in that jail and wasted away. That is why he is so thin now. He could steal only a few winks at the work detail. Now that he is king of his own castle he cannot subject himself to that punishment again. The honoured guests must remember that without sleep he can't harvest the sea the next morning. One needs all one's energy to dislodge abalone from the rocks on kelp beds.

"She is afraid of the dark," pleads the Whale Caller.

"She is blind for Christ sake!" the puny man bursts out. "What does she need the light for?"

It is the same question that the Whale Caller had asked her last night when they were preparing to sleep in the deserted house by the sea. She insisted that she could feel the darkness even in her blindness. "I never imagined that darkness would find me even in blindness," she said. So much for the freedom that she declared she had gained soon after losing her sight! They had the candle burning until daybreak.

"You don't talk like that about me," says Saluni.

"We are this man's guests, Saluni," says the Whale Caller. "We can't start fighting him in his own house."

"He must not be selfish, man, even if it is his house. It is just a shack after all. Nothing like our beautiful Wendy house with electricity and everything."

The Whale Caller signals to their host not to worry for he will solve the whole problem. The puny man sits in the corner sulking. Saluni can sense his rebellion, and to pre-empt any stupid action on his part she thinks it wise to let him know who is boss even in his house. "Look at him," she says to the puny man, pointing in the direction of the Whale Caller. "He is going to hit you. See those big strong hands? He's going to hit you so hard you'll wish you'd never been born."

"I don't hit people, Saluni," says an embarrassed Whale Caller.

"You did hit the radio man who was being rude to me."

"And I have regretted it ever since."

Saluni turns to the puny man once more and says: "Don't be deceived by his mild manner. You should see him when he is aroused. He is a tiger."

Saluni strips to her petticoat and gets into the bedding on the floor. In no time she is snoring. The Whale Caller takes the paraffin lamp outside and extinguishes the flame so that the smell of the wick does not alert Saluni to that fact. Back in the room he takes off his overalls and sleeps next to her. But she suddenly sits up and seems to have difficulty breathing.

"He switched the light off, didn't he?" she asks.

"I don't switch things off, ma'am," says the puny man. "Unlike rich folk like you who live in better houses, I don't have electricity here."

"I can feel the darkness in my body."

"It is just your imagination, Saluni," the Whale Caller assures her. "The lamp is still on. I think you are just having a nightmare."

"Are you sure, man? Are you sure there is light?"

In the cracks between corrugated iron and plastic sheets left by shoddy workmanship on the shack he can see the stars winking at him. There must be a moon somewhere out of his line of sight, even if it is a small piece floating in the sky. There is some light . . . out there.

"There is light," he says quite bravely. "Let's sleep now, Saluni. We have a long way to go tomorrow."

His voice has the ring of truth. But Saluni cannot understand why sleep doesn't come, however hard she tries to summon it. She

fidgets and tosses and turns, making it impossible for the Whale
Caller to sleep as well.


She wants them to move further away from the coastal pathways
lest some rude whales appear and distract his attention from the
demands of the road. They almost did early in the morning. He
spotted two Bryde's whales and a group of the smaller triangular-
headed minke whales off Pearly Beach and almost lost his head
with excitement. That's when she decreed that instead of following the coastline—which is in any event too rugged to negotiate safely even for a woman who is determined to punish their
bodies—they should make their way inland.

The Whale Caller has tied a rope—a gift from their gracious
host, who was all too pleased to see them go—around Saluni's
waist and leads her with it. The paths meander back to a well-
maintained gravel road. For a while they are followed by a group
of mischievous baboons who seem bent on teasing them. They ignore the primates and walk on. The baboons scatter into the
bushes when a donkey cart approaches and stops next to the walking couple. A toothless old man under a straw hat gives them a
ride up to the village of Elim, almost twenty kilometres away.

They walk among the expertly thatched cottages, past the
church with a German-made clock that is reputed to have been
ticking since 1764, past the village shopping centre and into the
post office. The Whale Caller insists that he must write to the
widower who lets him the Wendy house, and explain that he had
to leave town unexpectedly and that the kindly landlord should
rest assured that when he returns, whenever that will be, he will
pay every cent of the outstanding rent. He is already gearing
himself for months on the road since he does not know when
Saluni will get tired and demand to be led on her leash back to
peaceful Hermanus.

After writing the letter and mailing it he suggests that they should have a nice meal at one of the cosy restaurants in the village. He reminds her of her yearning for civilised living. But she is not interested in any of that. All she wants is the road. They buy a loaf of bread and fish and chips at a café as provisions. The Whale Caller remembers to purchase a packet of candles as well as a box of matches. Just as they are walking out he sees a display of sunglasses.

"I am buying you sunglasses, Saluni," he says.

"Why?"

"So that people will not have expectations from you that cannot be fulfilled."

"Yeah. So that they can raise their voices when they speak to me."

He buys the glasses and she wears them. Once more they face the challenges of the road. They take a north-easterly direction, choosing a combination of well-paved roads and then looping off to overgrown pathways that are obviously rarely used by humans. They walk through a medley of green pastures and rocky terrain and apple orchards and deep gorges. They are like stars that have lost their way in the sky. Sometimes only echoes accompany their footsteps, and at other times flocks of sheep and a solitary shepherd break the rhythm. It is, in fact, in the hovel of a toothless young shepherd in brown South African Railways and Harbours overalls—the whole region abounds with toothless men and women—that they find refuge for the night, a few kilometres past the small town of Bredasdorp.

The shepherd proves to be, according to Saluni's declamations the following day, a man of boundless wisdom and home-grown philosophies. He, for instance, admires them for the courage of embarking on a journey without destination. If everyone in the world engaged in such journeys the world would know peace. He commends Saluni for opting for blindness in a world that would be better off with everyone in it walking in perpetual blindness. All the problems of the world emanate from the arrogance of sight. In blindness one is able to reach into a dimension buried in the very depths of one's soul and recover the beautiful things that one has known in previous existences. Now that he has met Saluni he is considering blindness for himself because he believes that will give him two or three other parallel consciousnesses. He may not only stop with his own blindness. He may blind his sheep and goats as well. They have become his companions and he cannot leave them behind on his way to nirvana. He crowns his wisdom by allowing his guests to light their candle throughout the night.

He takes advantage of the candlelight to read them passages from the Song of Solomon until Saluni is lulled into the deep sleep of content babies. It becomes obvious to the Whale Caller that these passages are directed at Saluni, and all of a sudden he finds the shepherd's voice quite irritating. The shepherd is not aware that Saluni is fast asleep and continues reading: *Behold, you are fair, my love! Behold you are fair! You have dove's eyes behind your veil. Your hair is like a flock of goats, going down from Mount Gilead. Your teeth are like a flock of shorn sheep which have come up from the washing, every one of which bears twins, and none is barren among them.*

"You are wasting your breath," says the Whale Caller. "She is asleep."

"She can hear my voice in her dreams," says the shepherd, putting his tattered Bible next to his pillow. Soon he is competing with Saluni in snoring. The Whale Caller notes a self-satisfied smile on the shepherd's face. He spends the whole night nursing an anger he never knew existed in him. What a brazen young upstart: making advances to his Saluni in his presence and not even hiding it!

The Whale Caller wakes Saluni at the crack of dawn and says that they must leave right away. She protests that it is still early for the road, but he threatens to leave without her.

"If he leaves you here I will take care of you," says the yawning shepherd.

"I take care of her all right," says the Whale Caller.

"And so you should. We don't commend the eagle for flying."

Saluni wakes up and puts on her clothes.

"You say you take care of her but you want her to go without even washing herself . . . without even brushing her teeth," says the shepherd.

Saluni does not comment. She is pleased to let the men fight it out.

"What business is it of this young man whether you are clean or not?" the Whale Caller asks, tying the rope around Saluni's waist. "We must leave at once. Imagine, comparing you to his sheep and goats!"

"It is the Bible that compares her, not me," says the shepherd proudly. "The Bible knows the beauty of her soul that lies behind the veil of blindness, and it knows the beauty of sheep and goats."

"Let us go, Saluni," insists the Whale Caller. "We have a long distance to walk."

"I can walk the extra distance for her," declares the shepherd. "I am willing to go blind for her. Me and my sheep and my goats will all go blind for her."

The Whale Caller picks up his rucksack and her paper bag and tugs her out of the hovel. The shepherd blocks his way and pleads: "At least let me read her one more passage from the Song of Songs."

"Get out of my way," shouts the Whale Caller.

"Let the man read, man," says Saluni. "It is the Bible after all. How much harm can it do?"

"Don't you encourage him now, Saluni," says the Whale Caller.

The shepherd reads in the thin light of the morning: *O my love, you are as beautiful as Tirzah, lovely as Jerusalem, awesome as an army with banners! Turn your eyes away from me, for they have overcome me. Your hair is like a flock of goats going down from Gilead.*

The Whale Caller breaks out into what he imagines is mocking laughter.

"She is blind, man," he says in unconvincing guffaws, "and her hair is black. Well, it has traces of red now, but it is black in its natural state."

"It doesn't matter," says Saluni. "You are just jealous that the man sees my beauty to which you are blind. How many times have you told me how lovely I am?"

"You know already that you are beautiful, Saluni," says the Whale Caller defensively. "We all know that."

"I can sing songs of your loveliness every day if you stay with me," says the shepherd. "I can read you the Song of Songs every dawn before I go to tend my flock."

"You will do no such thing," says the Whale Caller, pushing the man very hard. He lands on the ground on his buttocks.

"That's not a nice thing to do to a man who reads such wonderful verses from the Bible," says Saluni, feeling around with her feet until they find the shepherd where he is sitting on the ground, still holding his Bible. She says to the shepherd: "You are a very sweet man. But don't anger him now. I have seen him hit a man with that huge fist and he was out cold for the whole day. We left before he came to his senses. Perhaps he is still unconscious even now."

"I don't hit people, Saluni," protests the Whale Caller.

"He is obviously a violent type," says the shepherd. "But he can't keep you by force, Saluni. You must stay with me. You must stay for my Song of Songs."

"He is the only man who should read me the Song of Songs," says Saluni sweetly. "The best you can do is to give us your Bible, and then he'll read me the Song of Songs."

The shepherd reluctantly parts with his tattered Bible. He is still sitting on the ground as he waves her goodbye: "Go well, celestial lady!" The new information that she is celestial leaves her with a broad smile that lasts for hours.

On the road the Whale Caller begins to get irritated by the smug smile.

"I could see you were enjoying the attention," he accuses her. "Don't deny it now; you were leading him on."

"I don't deny anything. I don't know what you are talking about."

He never thought he could nag, but now he does. He goes on about how disappointed he is in her that she should betray him at the sight of the first shepherd they come across, just like Judas Iscariot betrayed Jesus. He goes on about honour and honesty and trust, until she bursts out: "Don't talk to me like that, man, I am a love child." And then, as usual when she has declared the fact that she is a love child, she goes into narrating the story of her conception: "It was a cloudy day as it is today."

"No, it is not cloudy, Saluni," he says quite spitefully.

"You were not there when I was conceived. It was cloudy."

"Today it is not. The sun will soon come up and it will be shining and hot. Not a single cloud in the sky."

"You like to contradict me for no reason, don't you?"

Today he must stand his ground: "It is bright, Saluni; it is bright!"

"In my mind it is cloudy. I can make it cloudy if I want to," she declares with finality, and then adds, breaking into that irritating smile again: "You are just jealous because the shepherd saw what you could not see in me."

She is still smiling, and he is still sulking when, at midday, they stop on the banks of the Breede River. The sulks and the smile continue as he washes their underwear and spreads it on the rocks to dry. She feels sorry for him and assures him that she will never leave him, even for a man as wonderful as the shepherd. She reminds him that the shepherd was offering a life of romance and fulfilment, yet she is prepared to sacrifice all that for her handsome Whale Caller. The handsome Whale Caller must also try to be romantic. He must tell her how much he loves her and how celestial she is. He must read her such wonderful love poetry as is found in the Bible. He must dream about her.

He concedes to himself that it may be possible to meet her demands, however embarrassing they may be. But dreaming about her . . .

"You must dream about me, man, willy-nilly!" she orders.

Late in the afternoon they are still at the Breede River. Harmony has returned between them. With it the sickness. They are bathing in the water and are splashing it around. Their clothes are spread on the rocks to dry. She teaches him tavern songs—the censored version that she used to sing with the Bored Twins—and they create a ruckus that brings the fish to the surface of the water.

After this refreshing bath he brushes her hair and braids it into two long ropes.

They have been walking for many days. From the Breede River they went northwards until they reached Swellendam. There Saluni insisted that they buy a bottle of wine and a packet of cigarettes. Now she occasionally takes a sacramental drop from the bottle and a puff from her long cigarette holder, diffusing her incense in the morning air of the N2 Highway. They have changed direction and are now walking westwards along the highway. He is not bothered by the smoke because he can only catch a whiff of it. They are separated by the two-metre rope with which he leads her.

"I love you, Saluni," he says, seemingly out of the blue. It is not easy to utter these words. He has agonised over them for a long time. He remembered the shepherd and then agonised one more time. But there, he has said it! And his nose has not fallen off. Saluni purrs like a pampered kitten. He likes the effect these words have on her. He utters them over and over again, jumping up and down in front of her and dancing with the rope that is tied around her waist. She cannot see the dance, but she can feel it and can also hear the rhythm of his feet as they hit the ground. She displays a wide toothless grin.

She expects to hear the magic words every day. Sometimes he forgets to utter them, and she reminds him: "You haven't told me that you love me today."

"I was going to."

"When? After I have reminded you?"

The Whale Caller merely chuckles. Although he finds it a little stifling or even a chore when she turns it into a duty, he does not allow it to destroy their present fulfilment. He only hopes that it will not become another ritual, like her obsessing about small meaningless things such as counting the panels on the ceiling of their Wendy house. He remembers how she tried to initiate him into the rituals of her neurosis.

When they sit in idleness under rest-stop trees he composes a song on the kelp horn for her. He blows his horn and Saluni giggles like a schoolgirl. She seeks him with her hands and feels his face with her fingers. Her unseeing eyes are glassy with unshed tears. Oh, this Saluni! She becomes so lovable and desirable when she is vulnerable. Breathless days return. On the side of the roads. In the bushes where they spend the nights. In the culverts and under highway bridges. Every time she hears Saluni's song on the horn she becomes thirsty for him. Their sickness has taken another form. It is not searing as before. It is a mild thumping of the heart that is nevertheless as debilitating as the previous bouts that were violent on the body. It continues unabated, keeping a steady rhythm. Until they do something about it. Under the bridges breathlessness prevails.

Along the highway the walking becomes routine. To relieve the monotony that is biting on her she decides to walk backwards. For a long distance she walks facing where she has come from, with him facing ahead and tugging her with the rope that he has now tied around his own waist as well. He is struck by a brilliant idea: read the Song of Songs for her. If the presumptuous shepherd thinks he is the only one who can captivate her with biblical poems written in the voices of a maiden and her lover, he is mistaken. He too can sing about the biblical delights of physical love: *How beautiful are your feet in sandals, O prince's daughter! The curves of your thighs are like jewels, the work of the hands of a skilful workman. Your navel is a rounded goblet; it lacks no blended beverage. Your waist is a heap of wheat set about with lilies. Your two breasts are like two fawns, twins of a gazelle. Your neck is like an ivory tower, your eyes like the pools in . . .*

His voice is swallowed by thundering motorcycles. A big group of very fat men with greying beards and faded jeans and leather jackets sitting on proud Honda and Harley-Davidson monsters. Most have girlfriends or wives on the pillions. They stop to witness the strange sight and start laughing, calling them names and throwing empty cans of beer at them. He rallies around Saluni, protecting her with his body from the raining cans. And then the bikers happily ride away, leaving them wounded and mystified. Although the N2 is generally busy, motorists have up to now ignored them. They do not understand what they did to the drunken bikers to deserve this. The Whale Caller suggests that as soon as they get to Riviersonderend they should branch off from the highway and head north over the Hottentot Holland Mountains to escape such insults from those who have been rendered arrogant by wealth.

"It is the arrogance that has taken them to where they are to-day," he says, consoling a badly shaken Saluni. "It does that, arrogance. It propels you to great heights and then leaves you crashing down. I am not sure whether these louts are on an upward whirl or a downward spiral. It does not matter. Arrogance will be their demise."

They resume their interrupted walk. He turns once more to the Song of Songs: *How fair and how pleasant you are, O love, with your delights! This stature of yours is like a palm tree, and your breasts like its clusters. I said, "I will go up to the palm tree, I will take hold of its branches." Let now your breasts be like clusters of the vine, the fragrance of your breasts like apples, and the roof of your mouth like the best wine. The wine goes down smoothly for my beloved, moving gently the lips of sleepers. I am my beloved's, and his desire is toward me. Come, my beloved, let us go forth to the field; let us lodge in the villages.*

With this they repair to the field on the side of the road. This becomes his favourite passage and he reads it whenever he feels the need to repair to the vineyards, and to the apple orchards and to the dongas and to the bushes.

The Hottentot Holland Mountains are arduous. There is some respite in breathlessness. What the Whale Caller used to refer to as the cleansing rituals back at the Wendy house. Soon breathlessness becomes routine. And boring. Even the Bible fails to arouse them to new fervour. But Saluni knows exactly how they can add excitement to what is fast becoming an obligation. She suggests that the Whale Caller should talk dirty in the middle of the cleansing ritual. At the first experiment he utters a few mild sentences that are not dirty at all: something about the laundry that must be done at the next stream. She is not pleased, and demands: "How can you expect to send me floating in the stars if you can't talk dirty?" She asks him to repeat after her as she recites crude and pet names of male and female genitalia in all the eleven official languages of South Africa and their slang and dialects, most of which he has never even heard spoken by anyone. Although this sends her into a frenzy, the names sound so strange and funny that he breaks out laughing, losing his concentration and his precious erection. After the botched ritual she promises that at the next town she will buy him a book that will teach him how to talk dirty. He just laughs the whole thing off, for he knows he'll never be able to talk dirty even if he were to go to the university for a degree in it.

On the mountain bridle-paths the Whale Caller is fearful that their nighttime candles will invite wild animals. He snuffs the candle out and pretends that it is still burning. When she begins to feel the darkness he assures her that it is just her imagination. The flame is still flickering. She fidgets her way to sleep under the fur coat that they both use as a blanket. Invariably when there is no light she has nightmares. The Whale Caller is bound to strike the match and light the candle once more. When he is sure that she has gone into a restful sleep he quickly smothers the life out of the flame with his fingers, lest he be betrayed by the smell of the smouldering wick. This becomes his on-and-off game for the whole night. The fear of legendary mountain lions!

When the moon is full Saluni is in her element. She sings and dances on the mountain cliffs. The Whale Caller is always fearful that she will fall. But the energy of the moon gives sight to her feet. He blows his horn and plays Saluni's song. And they both dance until they are absolutely exhausted. Then they picnic on red prickly pears to which they have helped themselves on the mountainside prickly pear farms. In the valleys between high mountains they play on the skeletons of tractors and harvesters that died on the dirt roads many years ago. They plough vast tracts of the lands of their minds and harvest a stack of golden wheat that reaches to the clouds.

# FIVE

IT WAS A FREAK WAVE that hit Hermanus. It had all started on Friday morning with heavy winter rain and storms that lasted for the whole day. Gale-force winds rampaging at one hundred and fifty kilometres an hour lashed the town, leaving a trail of dejected debris. The next morning the seventeen-metre-high wave smashed down on the town. Houses were waterlogged; chairs, books and tables were seen floating out of broken windows. Fifteen minutes later a second wave vomited more jetsam from the first onslaught back into the streets of the town that prided itself on its orderliness. The water hurled massive rocks through the houses, bringing down their walls.

On the Sunday morning the Whale Caller walks among the ruins. Almost all the houses closest to the sea are damaged. He is dragging his rope along the Main Road, which is strewn with seaweed and sand. The rope is no longer tied around Saluni's waist. She follows a few metres behind, now and then stopping to prod with her toes piles of bits of shattered trees and refuse that lie scattered on the gardens, road and pavement. Sometimes she stops to talk to the municipal workers who have started cleaning up the mess. They tell her that the storms attacked their

Zwelihle Township on the outskirts of Hermanus as well. The Whale Caller does not stop. He wades on through the sodden sand until he reaches his house.

The Wendy house is no longer where it used to be at the far corner of the back garden. It now nestles lopsidedly against the gaping hole to one side of the front door of widower's house, but none of its wooden panels is broken. The widower has sought refuge here because his house is uninhabitable. The Whale Caller can see the fridge, the television, the stove, the washing machine and other household gadgets scattered all over the backyard where the Wendy house used to be. The widower tells him that things were so bad that even he himself was floating in the kitchen and had calmly resigned himself to certain death. It proved not to be so certain after all, thanks to the fact that as soon as he was thrown out of the door he grabbed hold of a floating tree. He had then seen the Wendy house bobbing about, now and then seeming to be engulfed by the raging wave. He was amazed that it escaped serious damage when even brick and concrete walls had tumbled down.

He vacates the Wendy house for the Whale Caller. He is going to book into a bed-and-breakfast place in the less damaged inner suburbs of the town until his house has been rebuilt. He is confident that he'll be able to get a place since there are very few tourists in town because it is not the whale-watching season. The gales have at least chosen the right time to destroy the town. The reconstruction of Hermanus starts tomorrow. The insurance companies are pissing their pants. Assessors and investigators are already sniffing around, trying very hard to find any excuse not to pay.

When Saluni finally arrives he is busy sweeping out the sea lice that are crawling all over the place. It was the town's main problem today, the widower had said. The houses of Hermanus are infested with sea lice.

Saluni and the Whale Caller do not exchange a single word. She just stands there with a mournful look. Then she sits on the bed on the new blankets that have been left there by the widower.

They have not exchanged a word for a week, since their big quarrel where he declared that she was ugly.


They were on their way down the Hottentot Holland Mountains where they had spent several months of idyllic picnicking and dancing. They had been driven down by winter rains and flurries of snow. They were trudging along the road between the towns of Genadendal and Grabouw when night caught up with them. They decided to camp on the roadside near a clump of bushes. He constructed a shelter for them with branches and leaves. He lit the candle and snuffed the flame out as soon as he thought Saluni was fast asleep. As usual she fidgeted, her body quailing in the darkness it had recognised, but she tried to convince herself that it was all in her imagination since he kept assuring her that the candle was still burning.

It was a pitch-black night because of dark clouds that hid the stars. Saluni was more twitchy than usual and had nightmares. She could see the shepherd reading her verses from the Songs of Solomon. He was quite different from the way she had imagined him when they were at his hovel so many months ago. He was very handsome, but seemed to be made of transparent wax. He was naked, except for a woollen cap on his head. The Whale Caller took out a cigarette lighter from his rucksack and set the cap on fire. The flame transformed it into a wick and it burned slowly as the shepherd began to melt like a candle. Yet he just sat there like a confounded Buddha and continued to read the wonderful passages. Molten wax covered the floor until it drowned the wick and his voice. Darkness fell. With it a hollow silence. The Whale Caller then broke into rude laughter which made her sit up. She reached out for the Whale Caller, felt him there beside her. He was not laughing.

He knew she had woken up from a nightmare and wanted to light the candle quickly, pretending that it had gone out accidentally, but decided against it. He hoped she would soon fall asleep again.

There is light on the horizon; the headlights of an approaching car. "There is a car coming," whispered Saluni. The Whale Caller wondered how she knew because the sound of the engine had not reached them yet. Vibrations. Blind people are said to be sensitive to the slightest vibrations. But Saluni's eyes seemed to follow the movement of the light as it kept on flashing across the horizon and then disappeared only to paint the skies again as the road followed by the vehicle twisted and turned.

"Do you see something, Saluni?" he asked.

"I can see the light," she said, trying very hard to be calm. "But the sky is dark. Where have the stars gone?"

After some time they could hear the sound of the engine. An old truck drove by and soon the light and the sound were lost on the winding mountain roads. There was silence for some time, as both were taking in what had just happened. The Whale Caller jumped up and danced in celebration: "You can see, Saluni. Your sight is back."

"It is no cause for celebration," said Saluni. "If it is true that my sight has returned, then I should mourn."

It had indeed returned. She could see his vague outline in the dark. She could see the darkness too, so she was shaking and breathing with difficulty.

"You should be happy, Saluni. You are free from the bondage of blindness. You can walk without being guided by the rope. You can walk without your goggles."

"You lied to me," she said.

He remembered the candle and struck a match. He explained that he had been fearful that wild animals would be attracted by the light, but she did not believe his story. For the first time after many months of peace and harmony and sickness she raised her voice at him: "I trusted you and you lied to me. How do you think I feel to discover that the man I trusted with my life is a liar?"

"It was for our safety, Saluni," he protested.

"What else have you lied to me about?"

"Nothing, Saluni, nothing."

Saluni insisted that there must be many other things he had lied about. Obviously, she charged, he must have been lying when he vowed on those mountains that he loved her more than any whale that ever lived and that he dreamt about her.

"Did you or did you not dream about me?" she asked.

When he jibbed she demanded an answer at once. He was unable to lie about it and confessed that he did not dream about her. That was the end of that discussion. Of any discussion.

From there on they walked the road silently. No more Saluni's song on the kelp horn. No more declarations of love. No more dancing or picnicking on so much prickly pear that it clogged their bowels. No more biblical verses on the delights of physical love. No more breathless days and nights. Just the rhythm of their feet as they pounded the road. He walked in front with the rope tied around his waist snaking its way behind him on the ground. She walked a few metres behind him, determined not to utter a word to him. When a rabbit crossed her path she addressed it with all the terms of endearment that would otherwise have been lavished on him.

Rain failed to break their silence. It pelted them with fat drops as they walked towards the coastal village of Kleinmond. They did not stop to take cover anywhere. They were completely drenched by the time they passed the village, taking the easterly direction along the coast. In her tattered fur coat she looked like a malnourished half-drowned mouse in dark glasses. He was not a better sight in his threadbare dungarees.

They had caught the tail end of the storm, but the winds were still strong enough to sweep them off their feet from time to time, only to drop them on the muddy earth again where, after struggling to find their balance, they resumed the long walk. People everywhere were talking of the gale-force winds that had hit Hermanus.

It dawned on Saluni that they were walking back to Hermanus. They had gone full circle without realising it. Or at least without Saluni realising it. She suspected that the Whale Caller knew all along that he was leading her back to Hermanus. A man who had spent half his life walking from one coastal town and village to another right up to Windhoek could not claim to have lost all sense of direction all of a sudden.

She broke the silence: "You did it on purpose, didn't you?"

He did not respond. She ran to catch up with him and stood in front of him.

"It is because you hate happiness," she accused him. "You did it to destroy the happiness we had on the road."

"If this be happiness, then I am glad I know nothing about it," he said, edging around her and resuming the journey.

The villages of Onrus and Vermont had suffered terribly from the winds. The streets were clogged with sand and kelp. The Whale Caller stopped to lend a hand to a family whose car was stuck in the mud. Saluni walked on, hoping that he would plead with her to wait for him. When he did not she stopped and waited, tapping her foot impatiently while he pushed the car. After a long struggle the car was out and the family on its way.

Saluni was fuming: "You care for strangers more than you care for me."

It was better when there was silence between them, thought

the Whale Caller. Perhaps if he did not respond they would revert to the silence.

"You are good to strangers. You don't lie to them. Only to me. You lied about the candle and you lied about your dreams and you lied about returning to Hermanus. Liar! Liar! Liar!"

Still he did not react. He hoped that she would soon give up and silence would reign once more.

"Damn it, man, why are you always so good? It's boring, man. I hate it when you are always so good. What are you trying to do, man; show me up?"

"I am good to you too, Saluni," he responded at last. "Or at least I try to be. It's just that you don't see it."

Here he was going to make his final stand. He no longer cared what happened after that. He had had it up to here with her, he told her. He took this walk for her. He was always doing things for her but got no appreciation in the end. Hers was only to take. He got nothing in return.

"Nothing?" asked Saluni in bewilderment. "You call washing your little thing inside me nothing?"

Life was not only a series of cleansing ceremonies, he said. He wished for a woman who would take care of him the way his mother used to take care of his father.

"What do you know about women?" she asked. "You don't look to me like someone who has any experience of women."

"I have known women in my life . . . when I used to walk the coast. I have known unkind and uncaring women like you. But I have also known women who made their men feel special . . . who took care of them and coddled them. When foolish men are pampered like that they behave like arrogant kings . . . as if it is their God-given right as men to be treated that way. But wise men recognise it as a privilege and an honour. They relish the pampering and pamper their women back. Each pampering the other the best way he or she knows. They will do anything to make such women happy. If she feels like chocolate in the middle of the night the man will happily wake up to buy her chocolate, even as the woman protests that she was only joking and that the chocolate can still be bought tomorrow morning. I have known women, Saluni, and I have known women."

This diatribe left Saluni stunned for a while. Then she burst into tears: "I gave up my shepherd . . . and for what? For you to talk to me like this . . . to call me names? Don't you ever talk to me again for the rest of your life."

"Suits me," he said.

"It suits you because you don't care. You never cared."

"I care, Saluni. I have always cared."

"If you care, when did you last tell me you love me? When did you last say I am beautiful?"

"How can I say you are beautiful when you are so ugly . . ."

"I am what?" she screeched, drowning his ". . . to me." This was all a huge shock to her because she had never known him to say such horrible things to her. So he did have a cruel streak in him after all. No man had ever told her that she was ugly. Even when she was a baby people used to touch her cheeks in supermarket aisles and comment on her cuteness. As she was growing up in the inland provinces neighbours never forgot to mention that she had inherited her mother's beauty and boys never forgot to fight over her. In the taverns of Hermanus men who had sailed all the seas of the world praised her beauty and her voice. And here was a mere whale caller calling her ugly. Her hurt was very deep.

Once more the silent walk. In the rain. Sometimes there was a little snivelling from her. Then back to the silence. Until they reached Hermanus.

After sweeping the lice out of the Wendy house the Whale Caller takes out his tuxedo from the trunk under the bed. It is soggy and muddy from the very fine sand that has found its way through the cracks at the edges of the trunk. He dons it nonetheless, takes his kelp horn and walks out of the house and through the gate. Saluni remains sitting on the bed, not knowing what to do next. He looks like a man of light brown mud and he endures the pain of the grains of sand rubbing against his body as he walks on the streets that are still choked with the sea's leavings despite the attempts of the municipal workers to clear them. It is an unseasonably warm winter day and soon the mud on his suit is dry and caked. He goes straight to the peninsula, yearning for Sharisha. She who never calls him names or yells at him. Who never demeans or humiliates him. No, not Sharisha. She celebrates his presence and never takes it for granted.

The sea is still black in its rage, although the winds have simmered down. The whole peninsula is covered with mud and seaweed and other flotsam coughed up by the water when it finally receded. He sits on a mud-covered boulder and blows his horn. Sharisha may have gone back to the southern seas for winter. It does not matter. He will blow the kelp horn until it saps the life out of him. Whenever she returns she will feel the vibrations that have been left by his sounds even if he no longer exists. He will just blow and blow until he collapses on the mud. By sheer force of his imagination he will bring Sharisha into being right in front of him and they will dance. Until he can't dance anymore. Until he collapses on the mud. He must collapse. It is the one thing that remains for him to look forward to. Collapse. He will play until he collapses on the mud and becomes one with it. Future generations will tread on him and no one will remember that he ever lived. No one should remember. Except Sharisha. She will know. She will mourn.

His eyes are tightly closed as he blows Sharisha's song that he has now adapted into jeremiads. For some time he is not aware that Sharisha herself has come to save him from the death he is hankering after. As he blows the horn furiously and uncontrollably she comes swimming just as furiously. She has been longing for the horn. She has not heard it for a long time. All she wants is to bathe herself in its sounds. To let the horn penetrate every aperture of her body until she climaxes. To lose herself in the dances of the past. She is too mesmerised to realise that she has recklessly crossed the line that separates the blue depths from the green shallows. All the sea is black and not even a whale can distinguish the blue depths from the green shallows. When he opens his eyes from the reverie of syncopation she is parked in front of his eyes, so close that he thinks he can almost touch her if he stretches out his hand. She is not quite that close though. But certainly she is less than a hundred metres from the shoreline. Perhaps less than fifty. Her stomach lies on the sand. He stops playing.

At first he thinks he has conjured her up in his imagination. But when he hears the deep bellows that send tremors to the muddy peninsula he knows she is all too real. And all too close. He has never seen her this close. The black waves recede and she is left lying on the rocky sand. She has beached herself.

"Help!" he screams, running to her. "The whale is stranded!"

He touches Sharisha for the first time, running his hand over and over her smooth skin. She looks scared. "You will be all right," he says. "I'll make darn sure that you are all right."

Straggling whale watchers have seen what has happened. Soon a crowd has gathered around Sharisha. They try to push her back into the water. The Whale Caller is fearful that they will hurt her. He helps to push while admonishing those he thinks are being rough. Among those who are watching from the shoreline he can see Saluni. She must be rejoicing, he thinks. Is this not what she has always prayed for?

"We need more hands," shouts a man. "The whale is too heavy."

"You'll all be in trouble," responds another from the shore. "The law forbids you to touch a whale."

An official, obviously from some environmental agency, takes pains to explain that it is indeed unlawful to touch, disturb, kill or harass whales, or come closer than three hundred metres to them. But this does not include bona fide efforts to render assistance to a stranded or beached whale.

By late afternoon they still have not been able to move the whale. The place is now teeming with police officers and bureaucrats from various government departments that deal with fisheries and nature conservation. Emergency rescue teams have been flown in from Cape Town. They spray Sharisha with water to keep her skin moist. An official suggests that a shelter be erected to provide her with shade. The rescuers decide against it. Although it is still quite hot, the sun will soon set. The whale will have some respite. In the meantime they try to keep her flippers and tail flukes cool with more water.

Sharisha is not helping much with her own struggling. She almost rolls onto her side. The rescuers have to push her and then prop her up so that the blowhole is facing upwards. The blowhole must always face upwards if the whale is to be saved from certain death. The onlookers have become too noisy and the rescuers try to keep them at a distance. Even the men who have initially helped are told to move as far back as possible and not to make any noise, for that will only agitate the stranded whale and make things worse. The Whale Caller is offended that he too is told to move away. He tries to resist. An official pushes him away. He pretends to walk away but sneaks back to a different part of the whale. This infuriates the emergency workers. One loses patience with him and tells him to get the hell out of here or they are going to arrest him for interfering with the rescue effort. He reluctantly moves away, silently lamenting the fact that people who know nothing about Sharisha have taken over and her life is in their hands.

He goes back to where he had been sitting when he played the horn and lured Sharisha to such danger. She will be rescued though. These arrogant people seem to know what they are doing. They will rescue her. He finds his kelp horn lying between two rocks. He wonders how it escaped being trampled to pieces by the gawpers.

The emergency workers use spades and shovels to build a sandbank near Sharisha. It collects water to keep her wet. And it also prevents her from further rolling towards the shoreline. Already there are patches of blood on her fins as a result of rolling that one time when the workers had to prop her up so that the blowhole would face upwards.

The voyeurs have thinned. Night has fallen and they gradually drift off to their homes and hotels until only a small team of emergency workers and scientists from the aquarium and whale museum is left. And the Whale Caller. He vows that he will not budge from that place until Sharisha is rescued. He watches the emergency workers as they place sisal sacks on her and then occasionally splash buckets of water on them. They are very careful not to cover the blowhole with the sacks or with anything else. More water is splashed on the flippers and flukes.

He is tempted to blow his horn but thinks better of it. He does not want to annoy the rescuers, who claim that any noise will make things worse for the whale. He just sits in silent vigil. He looks like a raw clay statue.

Under his breath he tries to sing her away from the beach. Away from the shallows to freedom. To the southern seas. If only she had migrated to the southern seas she would not be lying here helpless, stripped of all dignity. If he fails to sing her away he will try to sing giant waves into coming and sweeping her into the depths of the ocean. He remembers the Dreaming that he heard from the same sailor who told him about the shark callers of New Ireland and about Starfish Man and Whale Man. Way way back in

the Dreamtime of Australian Aborigines the stranding of whales
and dolphins attracted people to binges of feasting, as it did with
the Khoikhoi of old in what later became the Western Cape.
Their Strong Men used to attract whales to the shore with songs
and rattles and medicines. However, in the Ramindjeri clan,
whose totem was the whale, Kondoli nga:tji, there was one Strong
Man who could sing to make a female whale and her calf escape
the shallow waters. The Ramindjeri, who produced canoes and
nets and fished at a place called Yilki before the eons and dimen-
sions of Dreamtime came to pass and Yilki became Encounter Bay,
loved and respected the Strong Man for his power to save the female of the species and the future generations that would replenish the seas. He will become the Strong Man of Hermanus.

The Whale Caller prays for the powers of the Ramindjeri
Strong Man and tries to sing Sharisha away from the danger. His
voice cannot be heard for the plea for her life is uttered only inside him. He focuses his mind on Sharisha, looking her in the eye,
hoping to send his messages of salvation to her mind. He beams
them out in vain. He can't reach her. He can never acquire the
powers of those whose totem is Kondoli nga:tji. Perhaps he should
just leave everything to the experts from Cape Town. They will
save Sharisha. They will surely save her.

His night is haunted by the sweet and mouldy smell.

Saluni. She is squatting behind a mud-covered bush watching him
grieve. She watches over him the whole night. Like a guardian angel. Behind the bush. He sits motionless for the whole night, and
does not even stand up to relieve himself. She wonders how he
managed that because usually he goes out to pass water up to
three times a night. It is strange how grief can shut down the

body's pumps of life. Sometimes it shuts down even the ultimate pump, and the griever lives only in obituaries. It will not happen to him though. He is a strong man. He will get over it. It is just a fish after all. How she wishes she could go to him, and hold him in her arms, and keep him warm now that the temperature has plummeted overnight, and tell him that everything will be fine. On many occasions throughout the night she is tempted to go to him, to tell him that they still have a chance to start on a new page. She is willing to forgive and forget if he is. But she does not have the courage to walk the few steps down the cliff path. She suspects he will not hear her because his mind is with the beached whale. Once more that whale is coming between them.

Now the sun is up and the busybodies are streaming back. She regrets that she failed to take the opportunity presented by the silence of the night. Perhaps there will be another night. Once more everyone will leave and she will have her chance. Provided they have not saved the whale by then. Otherwise she will meet him at the Wendy house and she will tell him the words she wanted to tell him last night. Reconciliation won't quite be the same at the Wendy house. At this place of grief her overtures would acquire sincerity. They would show that she is not the uncaring woman he thinks she is.

She watches him watching the rescuers, who are trying once more to keep Sharisha cool as the winter sun returns with a repeat performance of yesterday's heat. They tie a rope to her tail and all pull in unison, attempting to drag her out of the shallow water to freedom. "A boat," a man suggests. "Its engine will cause a racket but it will save the whale." People remember how a humpback that had beached itself near Van Staden's River Mouth in the Eastern Cape was saved that way. In no time the engine of a pilot boat is revving about sixty metres offshore. The rope tied to the whale's tail is connected to the boat by swimmers. The boat then tries to drag the whale away from the shore into the surf. But this southern right is too heavy. And the rough sea has no intention of cooperating with the pilot boat. The rescuers have to stop the attempt when they realise that the only thing they will achieve is to inflict further injury on the whale. Already they can see blood oozing out where the rope has dug deep into the flesh.

A young southern right is wistfully watching all this activity from what would be the blue depths if the sea was not so black. No one knows where it came from or why it is watching a beached whale. It is just curiosity, a scientist explains. Southern rights are known for their curiosity. But Saluni can see the callosities that the Whale Caller has always been so proud of. The little Three Sisters Hills just like the mother's. It is Sharisha's calf.

Politicians arrive: city fathers and mothers; mayors and members of Parliament from rival political parties; hacks and hangers-on. They all want a photo opportunity with the whale. Cameras click away. Television crews interview the politicians instead of the emergency workers and scientists who have spent the night trying to rescue the whale. Politicians make better sound bites and will not mess up the news programmes with facts. The rescuers are irritated by the flurry of activity that contributes nothing to saving the whale. Unfortunately politicians like to think that they were created for some useful purpose on earth. They hog the spotlight and make sure that the newspaper reporters are noting down their views on how the whale can be saved. One even brings a box of tubes of suntan lotion that he suggests should be spread on Sharisha's back.

"That is the worst thing you can do to a beached whale," says a scientist.

An onlooker wonders aloud why politicians are such a dumb lot, as if they have all come from the same dysfunctional womb. Another spectator thinks she has the answer: "Any moron can be a politician. You only have to declare yourself one to be one. But to be a scientist you need some measure of intelligence." This generates guffaws from those who are within earshot. Saluni observes that the Whale Caller does not join in the laughter. He is looking fixedly at Sharisha. And then after some time he turns his eyes to the calf. And then back to Sharisha. Each gets about five minutes of his gaze at a time.

New waves come and break on the rocks near Sharisha and on her body. There are cheers all around. There is hope yet for Sharisha. But the water recedes again and she is more naked than ever. There has been no change in her position.

A member of the provincial legislature wants to know how the stranding happened. It is as if he expects somebody to be held responsible and that heads should roll, in the parlance of his trade.

"There are many reasons for stranding," explains a scientist from the whale museum. "Sometimes whales just become disorientated and end up on the beach. It is likely that this is what happened in this case. Poor navigation because she was disorientated by the storm. Who knows? Loss of orientation can even be due to parasites and diseases and interference by ships."

Although the Whale Caller betrays no emotion, Saluni is well aware that he can hear all this, and that he must be feeling terribly guilty. Scientists are not as intelligent as the onlooker thought they were after all.

The scientists and emergency workers confer in a huddle. Saluni cannot hear what they are saying. The discussion is very animated. She notes that the politicians don't seem too pleased to be left out of the conference. They wait expectantly and surge forwards when one of the scientists leaves his group to make an announcement. Even the onlookers are attentive. "We have decided to kill the whale," he says.

The Whale Caller breaks the silence: "She is still alive, surely she can be saved. You people can't be that cruel."

All eyes turn to the muddy vagrant. No one recognises him as the man who used to play a kelp horn for the whales.

"It is an act of kindness and not cruelty," says the scientist. "The whale is still alive but weak and barely breathing. Its lungs are partially collapsed. We must end its suffering once and for all. We are going to use explosives . . . probably trigger an internal implosion."

"What about an injection?" asks a mayor of a neighbouring town. "It would be humane to use an injection."

The local politicians glare at him angrily as if to say: *Go strand your own whale. This one belongs to Hermanus. You can't partake in our glory.*

The scientist patiently explains to him, obviously for the benefit of everyone else, that the whale is too big to be killed by a lethal injection or shooting. Explosives will save the whale from further agony and will ensure a quick death. The politicians from the national legislature are more concerned about South Africa's image in the international community. "They will accuse us of savagery and barbarism," says a member of Parliament. "The markets will react negatively. The rand will go down."

"The rand will go down if we stand here and do nothing," says the scientist, beginning to lose patience.

"The rand will go down in any case," says a sceptic. "Someone farts in Bolivia and the rand comes tumbling down."

This brings about another round of guffaws, which the member of Parliament interprets to be at his expense. He leaves in a huff, his entourage in tow.

Saluni watches as they rig Sharisha with dynamite. The insolent fish was bound to come to a sticky end. At last there will be peace in the world. And in the Wendy house. She can see the Whale Caller's pain as the emergency workers place more than five hundred kilograms of dynamite in all the strategic places, especially close to Sharisha's head. He will get over it. When he realises the folly of his infatuation with the fish he is sure to get over it.

The spectators are ordered to move as far back as possible, and to lie flat on the ground. The Whale Caller does not move. He just sits there as if in a daze. Saluni feels like jumping out of her hiding place, grabbing him by the hand and dragging him away to sanity. But she decides against it. He is likely not to take kindly to that. It would probably only make things worse. She retreats with the rest of the onlookers to a much safer distance above the cliffs.

Like a high priest in a ritual sacrifice, a man stands over a contraption that is connected to the whale with a long red cable. With all due solemnity he triggers the explosives. Sharisha goes up in a gigantic ball of smoke and flame. Saluni is not lying down. She is watching the Whale Caller, who has steadfastly remained dangerously close to the explosion down below. He is not lying down either. He is looking intently at the red, yellow and white flames as Sharisha rises in the sky. It is like Guy Fawkes fireworks. The glorious death brightens the sky like the pyrotechnics that are used by rock bands in cities like Cape Town and Johannesburg. The sounds are like those of a thousand heavy-metal bands that are particularly heavy on spandex and playing all at once, deafening as one stick of dynamite ignites another in rapid succession. The onlookers cheer and applaud like the carnival crowd they have become. Saluni throws up.

The Whale Caller sits silent and still as blubber rains on him. Until he is completely larded with it. Seagulls are attracted by the strong stench of death. They brave the black smoke and descend to scavenge on the tiny pieces that are strewn on the sand and on the rocks. The sea has become very calm.

Saluni. She is filled with remorse. She believes that somehow she has brought about Sharisha's death. She does not know how it is her fault, but it has to be. She wished it. She willed it. She did it.

Now she regrets it. She wants to obliterate the picture from her mind. The big ball of fire. The black smoke. The seagulls. Wine will do it. The Bored Twins will do it. Yes, wine and the Bored Twins will do it. She turns her back on that place of death and walks away, leaving the man sitting in the middle of the stench, streams of muddy oil running down his unmoving body.

After buying three bottles of wine she flees to the mansion.

The tulips are in full bloom and the girls fill the air with peals of joy when they see Saluni. Euphoria surges once again in her chest. How did she survive for so long without these girls? They hug and kiss and cry and giggle and laugh and hold hands and skip among the tulips. The girls' neglected state dilutes her joy with sadness. They are smudged with mud and their once white dresses are brown. She must do something about it immediately. She herds them into the house and gives them a thorough bath. They monkey around, splashing the water all over the place. In their wetness they now and then get the urge to hug her and kiss her and climb on her back, riding her like a horse. She is gratified because in her life she has never seen anyone showing so much excitement at the mere sight of her. All the months with an unappreciative man on the road are blotted out and she decides that from now on she will bask in the aura of the Bored Twins till the end of time. That man can sit there and mourn his whale until he becomes nothing but bones, for all she cares.

After thoroughly scrubbing their bodies she applies baby oil and uses Johnson's baby powder on all their little nooks and crannies so that they don't smell like earthworms anymore. In the built-in wardrobe in their room she finds special dresses that are reserved for special days. It is a special day because they are celebrating their reunion. She dresses them in the sparkling white dresses. She brushes their hair, and once more they look like they are going to sprout wings and fly to the sky.

They sit outside on the kitchen stoep and sing. She takes regular sips from a bottle of wine as she boisterously belts out censored versions of tavern songs. The girls back her in their angelic voices. They beat pots and pans with spoons and forks. Luckily there are no neighbours for miles around, otherwise they would have complained of the din. Or possibly they would have ignored the rackety backing instruments and bathed their battered souls in the angelic voices of the twins.

In no time Saluni has finished the first bottle and is caressing the second one, holding it to her breasts and lulling it to sleep like a baby. And then ripping off its cap and gulping down the contents like water. Her songs are now slurred and erratic. The Bored Twins soldier on and bring harmony to songs that have gone so wild that they would otherwise be classified as senseless noise. The second bottle is empty and she goes for the third one. But one of the twins snatches it from her hands and runs away. Saluni stands up and staggers after her.

The girls lure Saluni to their secret room—the basement wine cellar—and try to play a game of hide-and-seek with her. But she is too drunk. She just lies on the floor babbling. She is no fun when she is like this. They soon get bored with her and leave her there as she lies, banging the door after them. She jumps up and staggers to the door. She tries to open it. The girls have bolted it from the outside. She shouts at them, calling them names and insulting their mother's private parts. But they can't hear her. They have left to play in the swamps, forgetting all about her. She is too drunk to keep up the rumpus and goes to sleep on the floor.

She wakes up after many hours to find herself floating in darkness. She screams. She can't breathe in such overwhelming darkness. Darkness seeps into her body. It runs wild in her veins, threatening to burst them open. It clogs her nostrils. She gropes around until she finds the heavy wooden door. She hits it with both her fists, shouting: "You can't do this to me, man. I am a love child! Get me out of here!"

In between the unheeded screams she thinks of the Whale Caller. She longs for the Whale Caller. She needs another chance with him—another journey of blindness. It is not too late for her to learn the art of loving and being loved unconditionally. When she gets out of here she will go straight to the Whale Caller and smother him with so much love he won't know what hit him. More than anything else she wants to share his grief and to comfort him. And to take care of him.

She screams again and again. She fears that her voice will become hoarse and she won't be able to call the parents' attention to her fate. That is her only hope now—the arrival of the parents. She must save her voice for them. She is willing to risk the mother's anger at her returning to the mansion. But she has no idea what time it is. She fears that she will not survive the night in such darkness. She'd better scream again and again. She takes a break to imagine the wonderful things she will do for the Whale Caller once she attains her freedom. And then resumes the screaming.

The twins are returning from the swamps when they hear her hoarsening shrieks. They are unusually spotless for people who have been playing in the mud. They were very careful even as they fished out frogs from the ponds because their Aunt Saluni had taken so much trouble to make them look so beautiful. Her screeching now sends fear through their angelic bodies. Their parents will be returning soon and the mother won't be too pleased with them to find Saluni here. Why is she making all this noise? Does she want to betray them to their mother? It must be the wine. They'd better go down to the cellar and calm her down and assure her that they will hide her there and their mother will never find out. It will be their secret, just the three of them.

As soon as they open the door a sweat-drenched Saluni bolts out. She runs blindly up the steps and along the passage. Her only thought is the Whale Caller. She must find the Whale Caller. She must get outside where the stars and perhaps the moon will bring relief to her bursting veins. She must run with all her strength until she gets to the streetlights of Hermanus. She must reach the safety of the Wendy house. If he is not there he is sure to be at the place of death. She will find him and save him from further grief. The twins are chasing her, for they fear that in her inebriated state she will do harm to herself. As she bolts out of the kitchen door to the freedom of the outside world one of the twins appeals to her: "Don't run away, Aunt Saluni. You will trip and fall and hurt yourself."

The bigger twin picks up a rock and hurls it at Saluni, hoping to make her stop. It hits her on the head and she staggers and falls to the ground. The smaller twin takes another rock and hits her on the head. This becomes a game. They are giggling in their angelic voices and pelting her with stones, as the Old Testament sinless used to do to female sinners of the flesh. Or as literal interpreters of some of the great scriptures of the world do to women they deem adulteresses. The twins' ritual comes to an end when they realise that there is no longer any movement in her. She has stopped breathing. They kneel beside her, shaking her, trying to revive her and crying: "Sorry, auntie . . . sorry, auntie."

The smaller twin brings water from the kitchen and pours it on her face. They keep on repeating in their angelic voices: "Sorry, auntie . . . sorry, auntie." Tears are streaming down their cheeks.

She does not wake up. Her swollen and blood-soaked sleep is permanent. They drag her petite body into the garden. It lies in state near one of the rockeries. The twins leave it there and go into the house to await their parents, who will be bringing supper with them. But they are not happy that their Aunt Saluni is exposed to the elements like that. They go back to the garden and cover her body with the petals of tulips.


The Whale Caller returns to the place where the ritual murder was committed yesterday. He grieves but takes solace in the beauty of the death. She could have lived to be fifty years old. Southern rights live that long. If he had not selfishly called her with his horn to heal wounds inflicted on him by Saluni she would not have come to such a terrible end.

Saluni. He needs her more than ever. He will forgive anything when it comes to Saluni. He is the one who needs her forgiveness actually. He was too rash. He should have been more patient with her. He shouldn't have used such harsh words to her.

He sits down and blows Saluni's song on the kelp horn. The song that he composed during the journey of blindness. He blows and blows but Saluni does not come. Instead, out there in the sea he can see Sharisha's young one sailing slowly towards him, making ripples to the rhythm of his horn. He stops playing. He must not enslave the young one with his kelp horn. Softly he says: "Go, little one. You do not want to know me." The wind will carry his words to Sharisha's child.

He walks down the crag, past the brittle boats on the slipway, to Mr. Yodd's grotto. He needs flagellation. He is taking his kelp horn as an expiatory offering. He has no need for it anymore. All he needs is mortification. Surely Mr. Yodd will be happy to see him. He must have missed him. Saluni was never a good substitute for him because she never let herself be mortified. Mortification becomes him.

The grotto is blocked by sand and seaweed and bits of debris.

HOY, MR. YODD! Mr. Yodd? Mr. Yodd?

HE IS THE HERMANUS PENITENT and he comes to wave goodbye to the sea. He can hear Lunga Tubu's voice coming from the waves, singing a Pavarotti song. Maybe one day Pavarotti will adopt him. He can also hear the restaurant owner cursing the boy and chasing him away. He turns his back on Walker Bay for the last time. Even the tremendous energy of the rocks and the waves and the moon will not draw him back. He will walk from town to town flogging himself with shame and wearing a sandwich board that announces to everyone: *I am the Hermanus Penitent.*